THOMAS LOCKE has resided in numerous countries over the past twenty years, with assignments in Europe, Africa and the Middle East. He pursued a highly successful business career, including a period as marketing manager of an international pharmaceutical company, before becoming a full-time writer in 1991.

Drawing on this rich experience, as well as extensive travels and research, Thomas Locke has developed a remarkable range of characters and settings. His other novels for Lion include *The Delta Factor*, *The Omega Network* and *To the Ends of the Earth*, which appears in 1996. He and his wife currently live in Henley-on-Thames, Oxfordshire.

Praise for
The Delta Factor and
The Omega Network:

'A compulsive read'
Tony Hall,
MD, BBC News and Current Affairs

'A winner...
whicl
and diff

GW00646394

'Adrenali
...shing News

The
AQABA
EXCHANGE

Thomas Locke

A LION BOOK

First published by
Bethany House Publishers
under the title *Riders of the Pale Horse*
First UK edition published by
Lion Publishing plc
Sandy Lane West, Oxford, England
ISBN 0 7459 3180 4
Albatross Books Pty Ltd
PO Box 320, Sutherland, NSW 2232, Australia
ISBN 0 7324 0893 8

This edition 1996
10 9 8 7 6 5 4 3 2 1 0

A catalogue record for this book is available
from the British Library

Maps reproduced by kind permission
of Bethany House Publishers

Printed and bound in Great Britain
by Cox & Wyman Ltd, Reading

This book is dedicated to
Cyril Price
with heartfelt thanks
for the wisdom and humor
which helped me learn and survive
in the Arab world.
And to his wife, Nancy,
for the splendid gatherings
through which we keep these memories alive.

Prologue

It was the quietest argument in the history of Russian nuclear science.

They were quarreling softly not for fear that people in the other labs might hear them. There was no chance of that. Despite the exterior walls being over two feet thick, the wind had such force that the entire central lab building rumbled like a huge bass drum. No, they were quiet because they did not want to wake their sleeping child. The wind did not bother her, for she was a true child of the Russian steppes. But she always cried when her parents argued. Their impending departure was hard enough without her wails.

They crouched behind the particle analyzer, which like most of the other lab machinery did not work. Their cramped alcove was carpeted with litter and dust. The cleaners had not ventured back there since the downfall of the Soviet Empire. Why should they, when their pay had slipped to twelve dollars a month and their families were slowly starving? At least the scientists were still fairly well fed.

"I am not leaving without you," the woman quietly declared.

The scientist still wore his lab coat and cloth-soled shoes. His lank blond hair framed a face that looked perpetually hungry. Months of fear and worry had turned his cheeks cavernous and drawn his eyes back in their dark-ringed sockets. He hugged the sleeping child closer to his chest and softly replied, "If they find me, they shoot me. Is that what you want?"

"I want our daughter to have a father," the woman replied, her voice a faint wail. "I want a future together with my husband."

"This also do I want," the scientist replied. "It is for this and only this that we risk all."

"But together, Alexis," she pleaded, the words so often spoken they had long since become a litany.

"We shall be together," he replied, all force drained from his voice. He droned the words, his attention as much on the slumbering girl as on what he said. His daughter was three days from her fourth birthday and shared her mother's dark coloring and almost Oriental features. Her blood carried the heritage of ten generations of Mongol raiders. "It is all planned," Alexis told his wife. "You know this as well as I."

"Yes? So you force us to travel four thousand kilometers alone, hoping against hope that you will send for us?"

Alexis searched his wife's face. Despite the harsh demands of the past two years, her dark features still sparked with youth and passion and beauty. He eased his finger from the child's clutches, reached over and stroked her cheek. "You have been my life's only love, Alena."

Angrily she shook her head, casting his hand away. "And down south? They do not shoot escaped scientists in the south?"

The lab's outer door squeaked on rusting hinges, and they froze into terrified stillness. Footsteps scrunched across the grimy floor, and when the guard's battered cap came into view they heaved vast sighs of relief. "You are ready?"

"We are."

"Loading has commenced. I will come for you in five minutes. You must move swiftly."

"Thank you, Ivan Ivanovichu. You are a good friend."

"I am a man with four starving children, and for ten rubles more would flee with you." He inspected them nervously, then withdrew, saying, "Be on guard. They are a strange lot, these gypsies of the road."

When the door had creaked closed, Alena grasped his arm. "Answer me," she hissed. "You will answer me or I will return to our quarters."

"And do what?" he replied calmly. He could not return her anger. Not now. His entire world began and ended with these two precious ones. "Wait for our daughter to starve?"

"Things might improve."

11

"We have been living on that myth for over two years now. It is time to face facts. The life here is meaningless. The situation here is beyond hopeless. To stay is to accept death."

"Then come with us," she pleaded, her fingers digging into the flesh of his arm. "Without you I am nothing, have nothing. I beg you, come!"

"What can I tell you that I have not already said?" He brushed a feather of dark hair from his daughter's sleeping face and felt his heart squeezed by the impossible beauty of her. "To the south there is war. War upon war. There are no controls on the southern borders."

"Then take us with you!"

"I cannot," he replied softly, yet as unbending as the Siberian soil locked in winter. "I will not. It is too dangerous."

"Too dangerous for us and not for you?"

"Too dangerous for you and our daughter. From Grozny I travel with Ilya and Yuri. This you know. The guides have instructed us to travel without our families. It is not a route for children. This you also know. Each additional person adds to the risk." He looked up, willing her to see the love in his gaze. "I must go alone, Alena. For us."

The door creaked open once more. The guard called quietly over the wind's deep drone, "It is time."

"We come," Alexis called back.

"Tell me again," she pleaded desperately, rising with him. "Let me know your hope since I have none of my own."

"Tbilisi," he repeated, the words a soothing chant. "We escape over the Caucasus into Georgia. From the capital Tbilisi we fly to Jordan. Amman, Aqaba, then a boat to Iraq. Then work and money, Alena. Enough money for a life. Enough money for hope."

She searched his face with a feverish gaze, her defiance slipping away to the agony he knew it covered. A tear escaped from the side of her eye and trickled down the face he had come to know and love so well, so very well. She whispered shakily, "And us?"

"Graz," he soothed, saying the word as he would an intimacy. "You travel to the detention camp in Austria. Processing takes six weeks. This is well known. By then I will send for you." With both arms now supporting his daughter, he leaned forward and stroked Alena's cheek with his own. He drank in the scent of her, willing himself to etch the memory deep. "Go. Await my word. I will contact you. I *will*."

"Come now or they go without you," hissed the guard.

"Take the satchels," Alexis said, and slipped out from behind the machine, giving silent thanks that his daughter still slept. "We are ready."

As with all personnel in these days of want and misery, the guard's uniform was little more than rags. His cap was battered and sweat-stained, his coat lacked buttons, his trousers were so worn they had been washed of their color. His shoes flip-flapped as he walked out and scanned the corridor, then returned to wave them forward. "All clear."

The three of them hustled down the long central hall. Mildew and ancient spider webs clustered in the ceiling corners. Their footsteps rang overloud as they hurried past what once had been the centerpiece of Soviet scientific achievement, now as desolate as a forgotten mausoleum.

They turned the final corner, and the wind grew so loud that it covered the sounds of Alena's weeping. They pushed through the inner doors, and instantly the noise became a ferocious howl.

His daughter stirred sleepily in his arms. "Papa?"

"Shh, little one, all is well. We must go outside." He turned to his wife's tear-streaked face. "The towel, Alena."

His daughter was indeed a child of the steppes. At four years she knew enough to remain still as the dampened towel was tucked in around her eyes and nose and mouth and ears. Alexis gripped her more firmly, then nodded to the guard. "Let us go."

As soon as they opened the outer doors, the wind sought to rip them apart.

Russians called their steppes the earthen sea. There in the Siberian borderlands it lay flat and featureless from the Arctic forests to the southern mountains, three thousand kilometers of aching emptiness. In such autumn days as these, Arctic winds came shrieking down from the north, with nothing to slow their fierce blasts until they struck the Caucasus mountains another thousand kilometers farther south. The soil was dry and bare of snow to hold it in place. The wind plucked up giant fistfuls and flung it with such ferocity that paint could be stripped from a car in a matter of hours. It was a maddening wind, a blinding force that could lift entire trees and send them whipping unseen onto houses and trucks and people.

Arms interlocked for added strength, together they fought their way across the laboratory compound to the outer loading platforms. There was no way for them to check their progress visually. Around them swirled impenetrable clouds of yellow-black dust. They walked by memory alone.

Suddenly above the wind's blast came the roar of great diesel engines, and Alena wailed in her husband's ear. He forced her forward until the first great dark beast appeared in front of them. The guard shouted words that were lost in the wind, but his signals were clear—this was Alena's truck.

Alexis felt the child in his arms stiffen with fear from the strange roaring shape in front of them. He bent over and buried his face in the towel that protected his daughter, then straightened and allowed his sobbing wife to clasp his neck. He placed his lips upon her ear and shouted as loud as he was able, "I am ever with you, Alena!"

Together with the guard he forced his wife up into the truck's open door, then lifted his daughter up to her. The satchels came next. He climbed up the step, and in the cabin's relative calm he embraced them once again. Then he stepped back and slammed the door, searching through the yellow storm for a final glimpse of his world beyond the grimy window.

His daughter pulled the towel free and instantly realized that she was on the inside and her father on the outside. She flung herself at the closed window and screamed at the top of her voice, *"Papa!"*

He stepped down from the truck and watched his daughter claw at the glass, shrieking the single word over and over. *"Papa!"*

The truck roared its defiance of the storm and pulled away. Alexis stood and faced the tumult until his daughter's screams had faded to meld with the wind's shrill blast.

The guard gripped Alexis' arm and pulled him to the next truck. They embraced in the way of friends in the Orient, a swift hug to either shoulder, and Alexis was surprised to find tears streaking the guard's seamed features. In order to keep the moment untainted, Alexis did not place the final payment into his hand, but rather shoved it deep into the man's pocket, then gripped him by the neck. He shouted, "You are indeed a friend, Ivan Ivanovichu."

"My world collapses and sweeps away all of value, even friends," the guard replied, then shoved him brusquely toward the truck. "Go while the portal is open. And when your way is clear, remember me."

Alexis climbed aboard, slammed the cabin door, and looked down at his friend. The man stood defiantly against a wind so fierce it threatened to blast him from the earth's surface, and shouted up a single word of farewell.

Remember.

The new United States Embassy in Amman was a cross between an Arabian Nights palace and a functional American office building. The exterior was covered in desert stone, with rose-tinted borders around numerous windows. The structure dominated an entire hilltop in a newer suburb of town, and afforded a wonderful view over Amman's old quarter.

Judith Armstead had held her current position for almost four years, and still had not tired of the panorama.

There was no such view from the room they now occupied, however. The windowless conference room had the deadened feel of a bomb shelter. Which was not surprising, given that the chamber was located in the embassy's sub-basement and surrounded by two feet of steel-reinforced concrete. The Americans had learned from the Moscow embassy debacle, where the structure had been so riddled with listening devices that they had been forced to tear it down and start again. When the Jordanians had insisted upon the Americans using local labor, the Americans had worked out a fitting compromise; vetted construction workers had been flown in to lay the basements and foundation, where all the sensitive operations were housed. The Jordanians were then allowed to construct the public rooms on top of this, but never permitted to enter what lay beneath. Although Judith Armstead had spent as much time here as her office, she had never grown accustomed to the sub-basement's tomblike spaces.

This room still made her skin crawl.

Judith Armstead pushed the file across the conference table. "I've received Washington's permission to share this with you."

Cyril Price, liason between Her Majesty's Government and local operations, looked at the closed file before him, but made no move to open it. "And about time as well."

"Don't be so snide. It's not like your side has had the welcome mat out." Judith Armstead was a stern, no-nonsense woman with clear gray eyes and a very direct gaze. She wore a navy-blue skirt and jacket of severe lines, no jewelry, and little makeup. Her gray hair was cut short and worn straight. Her expression was as determined as her tone. Her title of cultural attaché meant as little as the stated purpose behind Cyril's current visit. "Aren't you going to read it?"

"Afraid I don't need to."

She smirked. "You're not going to try and tell me you've got a mole."

"Nothing of the sort. I simply think that our meeting here, in your embassy's most secure chamber, is sufficient to confirm what our side has recently suspected."

Judith leaned back and crossed her arms. "Which is?"

"That Aqaba has become a major staging area," Cyril replied. "For both goods and scientists."

She studied him a moment before admitting, "All right. I'm impressed."

Cyril Price accepted the accolade with a slight nod. He was a tall, slender man whose glossy silver mane and tailored suit granted him a sleek elegance. He carried his polish with that astonishing ability of the English upper class to be courtly without the slightest hint of effeminacy. His reputation had awed Judith from the outset, and only recently had she found herself able to speak with him as an equal. Cyril went on, "I think it is time for a bit more openness on both sides. We intercepted yet another consignment in Munich two nights ago."

"Using the overland bus route?"

"The very same." His expression turned bleak as he took a folded sheet from his pocket and passed it over. "Ten kilos of highly enriched uranium. The real thing this time. And headed for here."

"The borders with Belorussia and Ukraine have turned leaky as a sieve," she said, reading rapidly. "Not to mention security around the Russian missile placements."

"Nor is it any better around their laboratories, I take it."

"Like watching lemmings take to the sea," she agreed. "We picked up a smuggling group operating across the Caucasus just last week."

"Boxes?"

She shook her head. "Bodies. Claimed to be the only one in the area working with scientists. But even if they were, which I doubt, others will be only too happy to step into their shoes. It's become a smugglers' paradise up there."

"And all fingers," Cyril finished for her, "point to Aqaba."

Judith Armstead leaned across the table. "We need to identify the shipping point and close it down. The Jordanians are absolutely no help whatsoever. They're so determined to smooth out relations with the West that any new problem is simply ignored." She stopped, then asked, "We were wondering if you had any people in place."

It came as no surprise to either that the Americans would request such help. Fiascos on the ground, such as the most recent scandal in France over economic espionage, continued to tie the CIA's hands. The British operated under no such restrictions. Since they had never possessed the cash required for spy satellites, they continued to focus their attention on live agents, as they had ever since the days of the Great Game.

Regretfully, Cyril shook his head. "I am afraid not. The extremist cells have proven almost impossible to infiltrate."

"That's what I told Washington to expect," Judith said, leaning back, and failing to fully mask her disappointment. Placing an agent into a sensitive field position was extremely difficult. The Americans had spent twenty years trying to place an agent within the Chinese Communist hierarchy, and in the end they still failed. Establishing an agent is normally considered to be a ten-year project. In a region dominated by unstable regimes and fledgling terrorist movements, setting up agents was deadly work.

"Then we're stuck."

"Not necessarily." Cyril covered his momentary hesitation by smoothing a nonexistent crease to his trousers. He then raised his eyes, and continued, "I might have an ally to our cause. An American, actually. An old friend."

A spark of renewed interest brightened Judith's gaze. "In Aqaba?"

"Operates all over southern Jordan, actually. Runs a clinic for the poorest of the poor. He would never agree to become an active participant, of course. But he did allow us to use his infirmary as a base of operations. We set an agent there, one of our local operatives. Awful choice."

Judith was glad for a genuine reason to smile. "Not Smathers."

"You've met him, I see." Cyril sighed. "Almost ruined us before we had a chance to start. Ben Shannon, that's my friend, has reluctantly agreed to speak with me. Don't know what I'm going to suggest, to be perfectly frank. Starting from scratch with a new operative and simply searching for clues would be hopeless at this point."

"Time is beyond critical," Judith Armstead agreed.

"Mmmm. We must draw them out. Force their hand, as it were." He rose to his feet. "I must be off."

"Where to?"

"First to Aqaba, then to London." He hesitated at the door, turned back, and remarked, "You know, what we really require is a lure."

1

He stepped onto the runway of the Chechen-Ingush airport and paused to sniff the steamy September air. A swarthy soldier in a decrepit uniform watched him with eyes as dark as his moustache. The new arrival smiled blandly, took in the well-oiled machine gun, and announced to no one in particular, "There's money in the air and riches in the wind."

The soldier barked a guttural command and swung his weapon toward the arrivals hall. Robards replied with a full-fledged grin, shouldered his battered satchel, and sauntered off.

In his thirty-seven years, Barton Jameson Robards had won and lost more fortunes than many small countries. In a bar-room confession to a buddy too drunk to remember, he had once said, "Finding it isn't near as much trouble as making it mine. Losing it isn't any trouble at all."

Robards stood a hair over six-foot-six and sported a jaw like the front fender of a Mack truck. His hair was black, his eyes steel-gray, his way with women indifferent or demanding, depending on his mood of the moment. His friends, and they were almost as numerous as his enemies, called him Rogue, after the bull elephant who preferred his own company unless the heat was on him, and who reigned supreme over whatever turf he decided to claim as his own.

Rogue Robards didn't consider himself a particularly greedy man. All he wanted was his own yacht, his own tropical island, his own Rolls, his own Swiss bank account sporting some number followed by at least nine zeros, and a string of nubile secretaries to smile adoringly as he dictated his autobiography. He had long since decided on the title—*Laws Are for Little People*.

The arrivals building, a converted airplane hangar of World War II vintage, was as cheerful as an empty morgue. Voices splashed like a heavy rain off distant metal walls and roofs and concrete floors.

Robards clumped his leather satchel down on the steel customs table and opened it without being asked. Experience had taught him that anybody as big as he was, dressed in flight jacket and laced-up boots and pressed cords while everybody else wore either the local garb or grimy business suits, was going to get searched. Opening his luggage unasked usually saved a few minutes and disarmed the worst of the questions.

"Anything to declare?" the officer asked, his accent mangling the English words into insensibility.

"Merely sixteen smidgens of ground worm food and a can of green guppies," Robards replied, certain the man had memorized the question and knew no other English at all. He shook his head and lifted out his shaving kit; holding the bag toward the soldier, he said in a casual drawl, "I left my pet catfish on board with the baby alligator. I hope they get along."

The customs guard released him with a curt wave and turned to the next passenger. A bald-headed businessman raised his multilayered chin to give Robards a thoroughly confused look. Robards replied with a buccaneer's grin, hefted his satchel, and sauntered toward the exit.

There was a good deal of the pirate in Rogue Robards. Once a solid deal had taken him to New York—a solid deal being one that allowed him to walk away with his money and his life. His lady of the hour had used a costume ball to dress him up in pirate garb; fold-down boots, baggy black trousers, drawstring shirt, sword, and ostrich-plume hat. Standing on a chair to tie his eye patch into place, she had examined his reflection in the full-length mirror and declared, "You were born four hundred years too late."

"I've always had a soft spot for hidden treasure," Robards had agreed.

"Now the question is whether I'm going to risk letting you loose in a roomful of New York women," the lady had added, getting as much of his shoulders and neck as she could manage in a full nelson. "After a steady diet of Wall Street yuppies, they might just eat you alive."

Rogue Robards described himself as a product of the Florida property boom. His daddy had been a swamp creature lured from the Everglades by Gulf Coast developers, who feared rolling out their blueprints on a log that suddenly grew fangs and a tail and showed a marked desire to eat them, Ray-Ban specs and all. His momma had been a washed-out woman decked in shades of gray, whose days had been filled with the drudgery of hard work and the happy sounds of a drunk husband beating the living daylights out of their only boy. Thankfully, the boy had grown up fast enough to keep his pappy from inflicting permanent damage, and left home at the ripe old age of fourteen, after landing a punch that drove his father through the front wall of their two-ply home.

Next had come three years of roaming the drier reaches of Texas and marking time in a variety of oil fields and other places too remote to feel the nosy influence of social workers and child-labor investigators. Then Rogue Robards had come into town one evening with a paycheck burning a hole in his Levi's, and the next morning he had sought refuge from a monumental hangover in a Marine recruiting office. The spit-and-polish NCOs had taken one look at his strapping physique, ignored his somewhat off-center list and the way he shaded his eyes from the glare of their fluorescent overheads, and practically begged him to sign on the dotted line.

Vietnam had swallowed up Robards, chewed him up, and spat him out. He was left scarred down deep, pitted with wounds that stubbornly refused to heal. He had then taken the only step he saw as both open and sensible, given the circumstances.

Rogue Robards had become a mercenary.

Sunlight hit him like metal striking an anvil as Robards emerged from the hangar and sauntered toward the rank of taxis. Rank was definitely the right word here—the newest car in the lineup was a DeSoto of late fifties vintage with more rust than paint. But Robards liked the look of that vehicle and its driver, who had parked his car beneath the lot's single sheltering palm. The man leaned silently against his car and watched while his compatriots started a raunchy chorus of pleas for Robards' business. The man's only reaction to Robards' approach was a slight stiffening of his spine.

Robards dropped his satchel at the man's feet. "Hot day."

"I await a fare," the man replied in oddly formal English.

"Your fare's just arrived," Robards said.

The man inspected him frankly. "You are representing the Siemens Company?"

"If that's what it takes to get a ride."

"Why me? You can see, twenty other cars are here, and they are all eager to take you anywhere you want to go."

27

Robards stayed put. "Where did you learn your English?"

The driver inspected him for a long moment, then replied, "I worked for an American base on the Turkish side of the border. A sergeant at the post, he had a multitude of books. I read them all."

"Impressive. Might have been that we knew the same man."

The driver was clearly skeptical. "And yours— he had a love affair with his bunk?"

"And a crew cut gone gray, and eyes filled with unlived passions. He lived for his books and cultivated a belly more like a cauldron than a pot." Robards wiped at sweat. "Shakespeare and Tolstoy in battered paperbacks. Wooden packing crates filled with everything from Dickens to Harold Robbins."

"It might have been the same man," the driver conceded.

"Or maybe just a kindred spirit. The Marines breed a lot of strange characters in the seasons between wars."

The driver smirked. "So you were one of those few good men."

"At least until I enlisted. Afterward they called me something else." Robards reached down and tossed his satchel into the car's backseat. "What is your name?"

"Anatoly. And you?"

"Barton Robards. My friends call me Rogue."

"You can afford to pay a driver?"

"Pay him well now and promise more later."

"Later does not often arrive in this country, in this time."

"If it doesn't for me, you'll hear about it soon enough," Robards assured him. "My generosity increases in pace with my wealth. It is my greatest failing."

"Not to me." Anatoly gave Robards' face a closer examination. "A hotel, you need?"

"With more charm than glitz," Robards agreed. "I have no need of newness, and too much air conditioning gives me the hives."

"A taste of the old world, perhaps."

"Clean would be a plus. And fresh sheets."

"Food without gristle," Anatoly said, walking around the car and climbing in. "I comprehend."

"Also a minimum of flies and other winged creatures," Robards said, joining him in the front seat. "I have grown attached to my own blood."

The ancient auto groaned and creaked but ambled forward in a rocking good humor. The slender driver handled the vast steering wheel and its chrome-plated horn with ease. "What brings you to our formerly fair land?"

"I heard rumors of several small wars."

"No war is small for the ones involved."

"True. But so long as foreign powers are not involved, it cannot be called large."

"Also true. You seek small wars? It sounds like a risky life."

"No. It is not the war I seek but the opportunity. And yes, it's a risky life."

29

"And you call such wars an opportunity. Interesting."

"A war often makes holes. Or windows. Or cracks in the woodwork, whatever you like to call them. Places for an agile man to slip through."

"I prefer to join with surer things these days. Life alone has more risks than I care to take."

"The war has not been kind to you?"

"War and kindness are words that mingle like oil and water." Anatoly drove with as much pressure on the horn as the gas pedal. He swerved deftly around an overloaded ox cart.

"I have heard that these wars have left certain people in great need of certain items."

"That too I have heard."

"Put out the word," Robards insisted. "Speak of a man you have known for ages—"

"Minutes, even," Anatoly corrected.

"—long enough to trust," Robards continued smoothly, "who has interest in helping resolve the problem."

"Which one?"

"Whichever has been left undone. Whichever pays. Delivering the odd container. Finding the lost. Rescuing the captured. Healing the rift. Righting the wrong, or if not, wreaking havoc upon the wrongdoers."

Anatoly was silent for a long moment, then mused aloud, "There is something."

"There usually is."

"It is, of course, quite dangerous."

"Of course."

"And not entirely legal," Anatoly continued.

Robards merely shrugged.

Anatoly slowed at an intersection manned by troops stationed by an armored personnel carrier. Once safely through, he asked, "Would you consider working for a church?"

Robards tried to mask his shock. "It would make for a certain change."

Anatoly pulled up in front of a decidedly third-rate hotel, honked his horn, and said to Robards, "Then see to your bath and meal and rest while I return for my sweating passenger. I shall then speak with the church people and see if perhaps they are ready to meet with the likes of you."

Rogue Robards lay drifting in and out of sleep in standard jet-lag dozes. Through his window drifted the cacophony of a third-world city—revving motors and blaring horns and diesel fumes and shouting voices and strange music played through speakers shattered by the constant load. To Robards the din played itself out like a familiar lullaby.

The tentative knock came as a welcome relief. He rolled from the bed, crossed the room, and opened his door. The young man who faced him looked so much like a fish out of water that Rogue could not help but grin.

"Mister Robards?"

"The one and only. What can I do for you?"

The young man seemed uncomfortable with his own skin. "Your taxi driver? Anatoly? He said you might be able to help us with a problem we have?"

Robards crossed bulky arms across his chest. "Do you make a habit out of turning every sentence into a question?"

"Only when I'm nervous." The young man scratched his cheek, caught his hand, and brought it back down under control.

"Which must be most of the time around here."

"It's not much different here than any other place," the young man replied.

"Watch it, now," Robards said. "Keep that up and I might decide underneath that mild-mannered exterior lurks what'd pass for a sense of humor."

Brown eyes drifted up long enough to inspect Robards' face for derision. Finding none, they settled back on the floor. "My name is Wade Waters."

A grin stretched the leathery skin of his face. "Yeah, I'd say you had a pretty good reason for skipping town. You from the States?"

"Illinois. But now I work at the clinic of a local mission."

"Mission as in religious?"

"Is there a problem with that?"

"Not from my end," Robards said evenly. "But not many of you people want to have much to do with the likes of me."

Wade Waters started to say something, then stopped and asked, "Would you mind coming and having a talk with our director?"

Robards reached to the bedside table for shades, keys, money clip, and knife and pocketed it all in practiced motions. "Lead on, Sanchez."

"Who?"

Robards showed genuine surprise. "Don't tell me you've never heard of Don Quixote."

"Oh. Sure." The young man rattled down two flights of rickety stairs, crossed the scuffed lobby floor, and entered the bright afternoon sunlight. "I might even prefer it to Wade."

"Watch it there," Robards said, slipping on mirror shades. "You gotta learn to trap that humor, keep it outta sight."

In the lowlands around Grozny, the capital of Russia's Chechen-Ingush region, autumn held on long and surrendered only after a hard and dusty struggle. The Caucasus foothills were a world unto themselves; even nature seemed to accept that no normal rules applied here. When winter finally did arrive, it landed with a ferocity so sudden that every year a few people were caught unawares and left frozen to an iron-hard ground. But this year autumn had fought a more valiant battle than usual, with temperatures remaining in the eighties for long after the first snow normally would have fallen. The locals responded with customary pessimism and predicted that the snows when they came would be heavy enough to bury houses.

The town's Russian sector was busy, but no busier than usual for that time of day. Buses from all the nearby villages made their disgruntled way across desolate roads soon to be lost beneath the ice, and deposited their hot and stinking and tired passengers at the market gates. Robards stepped lightly alongside Wade. He moved easily through the tightly packed throngs, granted room by his obvious foreignness and his imposing size.

The mission stood at the far end of the market from the mosque. Despite the cool shade visible through its wide-open doors, the church was an island of empty calm. The mission was surrounded by a chest-high, lime-daubed wall with a portal of rough-hewn timber. The gate was manned by beggars who won coveted holy spaces by right of age and infirmity. Robards dropped a few pennies into a clawlike hand emerging from a filthy burlap cloak. He was rewarded with a twitch of life and the traditional groaned blessing.

At that moment a nearby rag heap erupted into life. The crone's eyes spit a brilliant light as she pointed one shaking finger directly at Wade Waters and began screaming words Robards could not understand.

With the swiftness of a world whose only entertainment is the public spectacle, people gathered. Faces examined the pair with chattering curiosity. The crowd clustered close, leaving sufficient space for the old woman to dance. The two Westerners were trapped within a vacuum of heat and dust and isolation. What amazed Robards as much as the woman's screaming was Wade's reaction. He positively cringed, as though embarrassed by some act he himself had committed.

"Are you the man they call Robards?" Another white face emerged from behind the nearby wall and shouted to Robards over the crowd and the old woman's continual din. "I am Reverend Phillips. I say, wouldn't you be more comfortable in here?"

"Friend, that's one invitation I don't need to hear twice." Robards grabbed the wall and leapt over it, landing with a thud in the dusty yard, then turned and helped Wade.

The crone danced in through the open gate. She stopped and leveled her scrawny finger within inches of Wade's chest. The crowd pressed in around the wall and watched with joyful curiosity.

"Let's go inside, shall we?" The frocked little man motioned toward the church. His accent was thoroughly British, his manner delicate and offended by all the furor. "They won't follow us any farther than here. The mullahs don't allow it. This is a sort of no-man's-land. Not that we aren't constantly being harassed by the pestilent mullahs."

Once inside the mission portals, Robards found himself surrounded by relative peace. Outside the crone continued her screeching invective. "That old lady was making my skin crawl."

"Yes, they do tend to have an unsettling effect," the parson agreed. "When they're like that it's hard to tell when they will go from happy and gay to nasty and dangerous."

"Could you tell what she was saying?"

"Step up here where they can't see us." The parson led him up to the front of the church, where a narrow doorway led to a closet-sized vestry. He paid absolutely no mind whatsoever to the sweating Wade. "Oh, she was saying what they always do."

"They? Who is they?"

"I'm sure I don't know." Reverend Phillips was clearly distressed by the whole line of discussion. "Some group of troublemakers the local mullahs sent over, no doubt."

"They are Christian," Wade protested in his ever-soft voice. "This side of the market borders the Russian section."

"Christian in name only," the parson countered crossly. "And this close to the border, they pay more attention to the mullah's orders than they do any priest or parson. Besides, with these beggars you can't make any such generalizations. They know no borders."

"But what did the woman say?" Robards pressed.

"Oh," Reverend Phillips waved distractedly in Wade's general direction. "They call him a healer of nations."

Robards cast an astonished glance toward Wade. "This happens every time you come around?"

Wade nodded, trapped in painful shame. "I gave her some medicine for a sore on her foot."

"Yes," the parson replied testily. "And look what happened. Just as I warned. You should never have started all that nonsense."

Robards looked from one to the other, asked, "What nonsense?"

"He insisted on going out and treating beggars where they lay on the street," the parson said, positively incensed by the idea. "As if we didn't have enough trouble already with those insufferable mullahs and all their idiotic restrictions. I ask you, why on earth would anyone bother to go against their orders and enter our mission if this, this *boy* is going to turn around and treat everyone he can find out in the gutters?"

Wade made no attempt to defend himself. He stared silently at the floor by his feet.

"Oh, my goodness, where on earth are my manners." Reverend Phillips waved a delicately veined hand at one of his rickety chairs. "Have a seat, won't you. As big as you are, when you're standing in these confines it doesn't leave room for us to breathe."

Robards did as he was told. "Aren't there any local doctors?"

"Not any more," Wade replied.

"All the professionals were Russians," the parson explained. "Long before this uprising began, the Chechen made the local Russian population extremely nervous. They threatened them on the streets, in the markets, wherever. Those who had the opportunity to make a life for themselves elsewhere have long since departed."

"They said it was because they wished to make the Chechen state truly Chechen," Wade added.

"But really it was just a way of robbing people. They forced the Russians to leave in a panic, then stole everything left behind, and sold rights to the empty apartments on the black market."

Robards nodded. It was a story as old as war. "I hear you have a problem."

"Quite a large one, actually. You see, there is this rather irritating little war just to the south of us."

"Several of them, if I've heard correctly."

"Yes, well, for some reason known only to God and unnamed officials in London, we have been selected as a drop-off point for medicines intended for a Red Cross center that serves stranded villages."

"Where?"

He waved a vague hand toward distant blue-clad mountains beyond his window. "Somewhere in the Caucasus. I'm sure I don't know where, exactly."

"In the highlands, near Carcash," Wade said quietly. "In the tribal borderlands between Georgia, Ossetia, and Russia."

"Not a healthy place to be raising a family just now," Robards offered.

"As you can see," the parson interjected, "that leaves us with quite a problem. There were supposed to be some people coming down from the center to collect these medicines. They are five weeks overdue—"

"Nine," Wade corrected mildly.

The parson shot him an irritated glance. "What

it all boils down to, Mister Robards, is we have a large portion of our mission space going to medicines that are not ours in the first place."

"I'm afraid they're in trouble," Wade said, his eyes on his shoes.

"Nonsense," the parson snapped. "No doubt they are simply too busy to come down and see to things. Either that or they already have everything they require."

"I've sent three messages up by local transport," Wade persisted softly. "I haven't heard anything back."

The little parson looked ready to boil over. Robards interrupted with, "Just how much medicine are we talking about?"

It was Wade who answered. "Three tons. About two truckloads. Mostly medicine, but there's a spare generator and equipment for a portable surgery."

"Be that as it may," Reverend Phillips snapped, "what is important is that I simply cannot permit this massive pile of goods intended for someone else to continue to clutter my establishment. You cannot imagine the problems this amount of goods has caused. I have had to spend simply staggering sums for twenty-four-hour guards."

"Speaking of which," Robards interrupted smoothly. "You gentlemen might work out of the goodness of your hearts, but I operate from baser means."

A gleam of hope appeared in the parson's eyes. "Then you will deliver it?"

"If we can work out a suitable arrangement," Robards replied, "I don't see why not."

"We were also left a certain sum intended for the Red Cross center," Reverend Phillips said. "If we continue to wait for these miscreants to arrive, the guards will use it up in a matter of days."

"Months," Wade corrected. "It was a pretty large sum of money."

The parson stifled a rebuke and instead ordered, "Go find the manifest. I am sure our Mister Robards would like to see what we wish for him to carry."

As soon as the door closed behind Wade, Reverend Phillips leaned closer and said, "I want you to take that young man with you."

"Insurance, sure."

The parson showed confusion. "I beg your pardon?"

"As insurance that the goods arrive where they're supposed to," Robards said. "No problem."

"Oh yes. Of course. Of course." The parson gathered himself. "I absolutely must have some peace and quiet around here. You saw the disorder he causes. It is the same, day in and day out. I simply cannot carry out my work under such conditions. Things cannot be allowed to continue as they are."

Wade Waters would never have described himself as a missionary. He was where he was not by design, not even by chance, but rather by sheer mistake.

Wade's mother had spent his early years convincing everyone within reach that she was a legend in her own time. Dinner parties were a chance to place Wade on a pedestal and proclaim, see what I raised, the missionary-to-be, no doubt he'll go off somewhere and give his life to the unwashed heathens. She had made monumental scenes at family gatherings over her baby boy's upcoming demise in darkest wherever. Wade had endured it all with quiet resignation and the feeling that he had learned to hold his breath for hours.

His father was a lab technician, a nearsighted, quiet little man who felt distinctly ill at ease with anything that could not be studied at the safe distance of a microscope. He had watched his son grow from embryo to teenager with rising confusion, never interfering with his wife's ideas of child rearing.

At university, Wade studied public health and minored in French and Spanish. Having nothing better to do, he signed up for optional courses at the local college of nursing. To his surprise, Wade showed a strong aptitude for the work. He loaded up his last two years, and earned dual degrees in public health and nursing. His mother survived the embarrassment of her son becoming a male nurse by declaring that he was doing vital research in the medical field.

Wade proved to have a true gift for working with sick people. He was incredibly patient and

41

infinitely gentle. He took time for the old and the lonely and the frightened. He accepted the most menial of duties without objection and carried them out professionally. When a local hospital gave him a six-month-trial contract, Wade spent more time on the wards than any other nurse and many of the doctors.

But Wade's mother stayed after him constantly to fulfill his destiny, as she put it. Wade remained silent and did nothing. Exasperated beyond speech, she finally mailed off for missionary application papers herself. During one Sunday afternoon visit, she slammed them down in front of him and demanded he complete the forms then and there.

Wade did not mind. He knew the whole thing was an exercise in futility. He had absolutely no aptitude for missionary work. Anybody but his mother would see that immediately, and send him packing. So Wade filled in the papers for peace's sake, and when it came time to select his destination, he checked the most exotic name on the list: Grozny, capital of The Autonomous Republic of Chechenya, The Russian Federation.

The review board, however, decided to pay more attention to the nursing director at Wade's hospital than to their own impressions of the young man. The nursing director wrote and then followed the letter up with an unsolicited telephone call. She said that the young man had the power of a true healer. He held hands and people simply felt better. He did the work of ten and did so without complaint. She actually had been forced to send the young man home on several occasions. He would be missed at the hospital, but the nursing director was a Christian and would never stand in the way of someone called to service.

It was only at the airport, on the day of his departure for Europe and final mission training, that his mother-the-soap-opera-star had become just a mom. By then it was too late. The fact that Wade was actually leaving hit her with the force of John Henry's hammer, and she had fallen apart. She had sent him down the departures tunnel with her wails echoing in his ears.

Wade had never in his life run across anybody like Rogue Robards. Not even close.

Robards was as solid as he was big—a rock-hard man with skin the color of a well-worn saddle. Though he was in his late thirties, the sheer power of the man made the number of his years unimportant. He exuded an unquestionable confidence, a complete reliance in his own ability to overcome whatever rose up before him. His smile came as easy as the sunrise, but contained neither warmth nor friendliness. It was as cold and confident as the gleam that lit the depths of his grey eyes.

"What do you make of all that fuss raised over you back there?" Rogue demanded.

Wade shrugged. "I guess it's like Reverend Phillips says, they know I tried to help them."

"You a doctor or something?"

"A nurse."

"Why didn't you get qualified as a doctor if you knew you were gonna come over?"

"Maybe I should have."

"Well, there hasn't been a man born who's learned how to backtrack," Robards said easily. "Might as well bury past mistakes and get on with life, right?"

"I guess so," Wade said, marveling at the idea that it could really be as easy as that for somebody. Not for him, of course. Just for anybody.

Wade directed their course along the winding, crumbling streets that skirted the central market. The city was largely destroyed, almost every building pitted with shell holes and blackened by old fires. Few windows were intact. Tall Stalinist towers rose like grim tombstones to an era which was no longer.

Here in the lowland capital, Russian soldiers massed at street corners and held the city to a grim semblance of order. Armored personnel carriers, their flat metal roofs sprouting machine-gun turrets, guarded major intersections. The key thoroughfares leading to and from the central city were defended by tanks, always in pairs, always with soldiers camped on neighboring verges so that the guns were manned round the clock.

With this show of force, and with more soldiers pouring into the city every day, peace reigned in the lowlands with the deceptive calm of a caged tiger. But at night, startling flashes of orange and yellow and red lit the outlying hills, and man-made thunder rolled down from cloudless, star-flecked skies.

"Hold it a second," Robards said. He halted before a rickety street stall. The trader, a bearded hill tribesman, wore the traditional black-knit cap with a little top button. The tribesman did not need girth to look imposing. A knife scar slashed down from a mutilated ear to his dark and scraggly beard. An empty bandolier crossed over his shoulder and fell to his waist, hanging with the ease of one long accustomed to its presence.

Robards asked, "You speak the lingo?"

"Some," Wade admitted. "Russian mostly. I only know a few words of the hill dialects."

Robards eyed him anew. "How long did you say you'd been here?"

"A little over a year."

"You study Russian before you came?"

Wade shook his head. "I've been taking lessons here, though. Every day."

The big man nodded his approval. Once. "Well, ask the fellow here if he understands the tongue of his oppressors—or whatever's the right way to go about it."

"He probably speaks it fairly well. Most city traders do."

"Good stuff. Okay, then ask what his tribe is."

"Chechen," Wade answered instantly.

Robards looked down on him. "You gonna let me talk to the man or not?"

"I can tell the tribe from his clothing," Wade explained. "If you ask questions that you should already know the answer to, he'll assume you won't know the proper price of anything and charge you more. He will anyway, since we're foreigners, but this would raise them even higher."

"You know something?" Robards said. "I'm beginning to think that parson of yours is a purebred fool. How do you know all these things?"

Wade covered his embarrassed confusion with a glance at the stall's wares. The splintered boards were covered with a vast array of tools. "I listen."

"Chechen is Muslim, right?"

"Sunni," Wade agreed. "And one of the most militant tribes."

Robards turned his attention to the stallkeeper. The bearded man had followed the incomprehensible conversation with glittering black eyes. He was accustomed to long and bickering arguments over prices before money exchanged hands, and had the patience of one with nowhere better to go and nothing else to do.

Robards said, "Go ahead and give the gentleman the proper salute."

Wade turned and bobbed his head. "Peace be upon thee and thy family."

"And upon thee, stranger to our lands," the man replied, clearly taken aback by the words coming from the mouth of one so alien. "This is indeed a day of miracles."

"I apologize that I do not speak thy own tongue," Wade continued in Russian, but using the formal tone of the Muslim tribes.

"It is nonetheless an honor to deal with one who has the gift of proper speech," the tribesman replied. "And makes a change from the pestilent soldiers who surround us on all sides."

Robards watched carefully, noted the man's surprise, and knew he had gained an advantage. "Ask him if he's got other goods for sale."

"My friend wishes to know if all thou carest to share with us this day is here on display."

The gleam sparked. "That would depend both upon what is sought and who does the seeking."

"He says, maybe," Wade translated, not understanding the parley at all. "It depends on whether he trusts us or not. What is it you're after?"

"Tell him I'm looking to keep my skin in one piece when we travel into the hills."

"My friend wishes to know if he might acquire safe passage through thy homelands."

The tribesman again showed surprise. "Thou goest into the highlands?"

"If thou and thy peoples might permit us, we would wish it."

"Then make thy peace with Allah," the tribesman replied with no malice to his voice, "for all who enter have great chance of seeing his face. Especially strangers."

"He says we don't have much hope of surviving," Wade said, his pulse racing with fear and something more. There was the scent of adventure here. The touch of the unknown. The drug called danger.

Robards gave an easy shrug, as though expecting nothing more. He reached across the counter, plucked up a dark metal object from among the litter of tools. It was only when he held it up that Wade recognized it as a rifle clip, about fifteen inches long, curved like a saber blade, black and deadly.

"Tell the man that in that case, maybe we ought to buy ourselves a couple of passports."

Wade could not help but glance up at Robards. The man's face had undergone a sudden transformation, as though a mask had been set aside to reveal a brief glimpse of what lay beneath. The confidence of the man was no longer a calm and resting strength. The power was laid bare.

He found himself slightly breathless as he said, "My friend wishes to ask thee if perhaps articles such as this might assist us with our passage."

The tribesman had also noted the change in Robards. Yet instead of alarm, there was only respect in his eyes. A recognition of something shared, something Wade could not fathom. "A wise man always trusts in Allah and then ties his camels carefully," the tribesman replied.

"Kalashnikov AK-47," Robards said, not waiting for the translation. "Probably the updated AKM version. Extensive usage of plastics and metal stampings to reduce weight. Nice to see you guys are using the latest in weaponry. Fires forty rounds per minute in semiautomatic mode, accurate to four hundred meters. Cyclic rate reducer and compensator, can be fitted with an NSP-2 infrared sight. One of the finest automatic rifles ever made."

The tribesman nodded slightly as Wade translated loosely. "Truly your friend knows quality wares."

"And this," Robards continued, fishing through the tools and coming up with a second, stubbier clip. "Druganov SVD sniper's rifle. Best in the world. Ten-round magazine, fires long 7.62 millimeter rimmed bullets. Muzzle has flash suppressor and recoil compensator for a level second shot. Uses a PSO-1 sight with times-four power. Accurate to twelve hundred yards, in the right pair of hands."

"It is indeed as he says," the tribesman said, nodding to the words Wade was able to remember. "Of course, such items are outlawed in these quarters. The pestilent Russian invaders have orders to shoot an armed man on sight unless he is a licensed private guard and on private grounds."

"Tell him we'd be happy to take delivery after dark."

"The veil of night covers many transactions," the tribesman agreed when Wade was finished. "Would it be possible to ask what takes thee along such an uncertain course?"

"We seek to deliver medicines to a clinic in the hills," Wade explained.

The dark eyes turned blank. "One whose flag has a cross of blood upon a white surface?"

"Red Cross, yes," Wade said, his pulse surging. "Thou hast seen them?"

"I have heard only," the tribesman replied, his tone flat.

"We are concerned for their safety," Wade pressed. "It has been too long since we had word from them."

"Of such things I know nothing," the tribesman replied. "I am a simple trader only."

Wade turned to Robards and said disconsolately, "I think something's happened at the clinic."

"He tell you that?"

Wade shook his head. "He just refused to talk about it, like he knows something but doesn't want to say."

"Well, maybe you're right," Robards answered, not concerned by the prospect. "But worrying about it now won't solve a thing. That news just makes it more important to get started." He focused once more on the tribesman. "Tell him we'll be back in touch about the goods."

The tribesman saw them off with the three-pointed hand signal of the devout—first to heart, then lips, then forehead. When they had rejoined the crowds jostling good-naturedly down the rutted way, Wade asked Robards, "How can you trust him?"

"Only way you can trust anybody once you've left civilization behind," Robards replied, moving forward with deceptive speed. "By sleeping with one eye open and not ever trusting anybody completely. Come on, let's go take a look at those trucks."

2

The storm raged so hard the night of her meeting with the infamous Colonel Mendez that Allison could feel the entire United States Consulate building shake on its foundations. But she had no time to worry about her own safety. Papers representing a dozen different crises were spread across her desk, all screaming a silent warning of the coup that was about to happen.

Lightning blasted outside her window, illuminating the stark and frightened features of her two assistants. They stood helplessly, waiting for her to make her decisions and order them into action. But she could not focus. There was too much going on.

The phone rang. She picked it up. It was her boss.

"There's been a cable from Washington," he reported. "Your budget has just been cut by fifty percent. And your mother wants to know why you haven't called her in almost a month."

Allison struggled to keep her voice calm. She

knew that it was important to remain calm in such circumstances. The examiners were always watching for the applicants who broke under pressure. "But I have a government to prop up here."

"You'll think of something," her boss replied. "And call your mother."

As she hung up the receiver, another lightning blast split the night, illuminating scores of dark-clad men scurrying under the trees beyond the consulate compound. They were all headed her way. They carried weapons.

"What do you want us to do?" her number one assistant whispered, fighting back panic.

"I want us to all stay calm," Allison replied. Stay calm above all else, they had told her.

With a horrendous groan, a corner of the roof was lifted by the wind. A massive tree limb crashed through the window. Wind and rain whirled a maelstrom of paper around what before had been her office.

"It's too late for that," her assistant wailed. "Too late! Too late! Too late!"

Allison was just going to tell him that it couldn't be right, it wasn't too late, she still had another twenty minutes before the exam ended, when she realized that the assistant's chant had changed to, "Raggedy Ann, can't keep a man..."

Then the intercom suddenly announced, "Ladies and gentlemen, we have now begun our descent into London's Heathrow Airport. We ask that you now return to your seats, extinguish all cigarettes..."

Allison opened her eyes and grimaced away the last of her dream. Four years since she had passed the Foreign Service Exam and entered the Commerce Department, and still she had nightmares over the high-pressure crisis control test.

She watched as the plane swept through the cloud covering and London appeared beneath them. It could have been worse, she reflected; at least the dream ended before she realized she wore no clothes.

To her everlasting delight, there was a uniformed chauffeur holding up a sign for her as she exited the Customs hall. Allison walked toward him, very glad she had stopped long enough to repair her makeup. She felt as though every eye in the building was upon her.

"I am Allison Taylor," she said.

One gray-gloved hand rose to touch the bill of his cap. "Good morning, ma'am. I am Jules, Mister Price's driver. May I help you with your luggage?"

"Thank you." She let the chauffeur lead her around clusters of foggy-eyed tour groups who whispered among themselves as they tried to figure out if they recognized her. They walked down the passage toward the parking garage, then detoured by a guarded barrier and entered a signposted VIP lot. This is just too cool, Allison decided silently.

"Mister Price has made a reservation for you at rather a pleasant establishment on the outskirts of Oxford," Jules reported, once they were under way in a royal blue Daimler. "But I suppose you have already been informed of these arrangements."

"I wasn't told anything," Allison replied. "Everything was so rushed." There had been a mere forty-eight hours between notification and departure. Not that she was complaining. The offer of a three-month assignment in Europe had come at the perfect moment, as both her personal and her professional lives were in a major slump. "I just hoped somebody would see to things on this end."

"Indeed he has, miss. Mister Price has given his personal attention to your needs."

Allison tried to recall what she could of her father's old friend. Cyril Price held some important post with the British government, but exactly what she did not know. When she was younger, he had been a top-ranking official at the British Embassy in Washington, D.C. Since his departure, his visits had been infrequent and consisted mostly of being closeted away with her father for long and serious discussions. Still, whenever his attention turned her way, Cyril Price had always displayed great charm.

An hour later, the car scrunched down a graveled path and halted before a vast ivy-covered manor house. Allison rubbed the sleep from her eyes, took in the diamond-shaped lead-paned windows, the dual turrets, and the liveried doorman hurrying toward them.

Once Allison had been bowed through the

registration process and shown upstairs, the chauffeur busied himself at the telephone while Allison admired her two-room suite. "Miss Taylor?" The chauffeur offered a telephone. "Mister Price is on the line."

Allison accepted the receiver. "Cyril?"

"Hello, my dear Allison." The familiar upper-crust voice brought back a flood of memories. "I am terribly sorry not to have been able to greet you myself, but something rather unexpected came up this morning."

"Your driver has taken the very best care of me."

"Splendid. I do hope the accommodation is up to your standards."

Allison glanced around the palatial suite, and replied, "It's almost enough for me to forgive you for forcing me to come."

"Not force. Please. Nothing so drastic as that."

"I don't know what else to call it, when I'm ordered to drop everything and fly to England for a conference with you."

"Call it the application of appropriate pressure," he replied smoothly. "Unfortunately I could not spare the time for lengthy and roundabout requests."

"So what is this all about?" Allison gave a little wave as the driver tipped his hat and bowed himself from the room.

"Perhaps it would be advisable for you to enjoy a rest just now," he countered. "I have been unavoidably detained in London until tomorrow evening. Allow me to place Jules at your disposal.

Take in Oxford and perhaps a tour of the Cotswolds. I shall then join you tomorrow evening, and we shall discuss all matters great and small over dinner. Is that acceptable? Splendid. Until then, my dear."

Loading the trucks proved to be a dangerous affair, especially after Rogue ignored the guards' warning.

They had taken their purchases back to the mission compound later that morning, with Robards driving one canvas-topped truck and Wade the other. The trucks were a pair of discarded army-issue troop carriers, noisy and cantankerous as old camels and much less comfortable. Wade's seat was covered with a thin strip of padding that had long since been mashed into something resembling plastic-covered concrete. The steering wheel was a giant affair that bucked and trembled and demanded a steel grip. The gears were spaced three feet apart and ground out a wailing protest at each change. Both trucks stood high and top-heavy on bald tires and bad shocks. The windshields were cracked, the paint blistered, the bodies badly rusted. The trucks shook and rocked and creaked and chugged noisily, even when standing still.

Wade could hardly wait to start their journey.

The seven men guarding the compound were from the town's Ossetian population. They were slightly fairer in complexion and lighter of eye than the Chechen, yet displayed the suspicious squint of the southern folk, and the same hostility toward all but those fully accepted by the clan.

The pair on gate duty barred the way with rifles raised until they spotted Wade, then opened the portals and allowed them through. As Wade stepped from the cab, there was a moment of solemn greetings, a series of nods and respectful words that raised Robards' eyebrows. Wade answered with his customary embarrassed hesitation.

Yet as soon as Wade and Robards made preparations to load the wares, the atmosphere turned ugly. Murmurs became angry protests as Robards slid down the loading ramp and fastened the hinges into place. When he helped Wade do the same for the second truck, the volume rose to dangerous levels.

"What on earth is going on here?" the parson demanded. He scuttled over from the parish office, his cassock raising fitful dust clouds. "Oh, it's you. Back already?"

"No reason not to go ahead and get the job done," Robards said easily, dusting his hands on the sides of his trousers and paying the angry guards no mind. "Who's got the warehouse keys?"

"It's the schoolhouse, actually," Reverend Phillips said, distracted by all the angry shouts and arm waving. "Wade has the keys. What on earth are those guards saying? I can't make it out when they talk among themselves."

Wade selected his words with delicacy. "They don't like to see the medicines moved."

"Stands to reason," Robards said, giving the sky overhead a careful inspection. "They're not going to be overjoyed to hear their jobs just took a hike."

"But I explicitly told them when they were hired that the work was temporary," the parson said petulantly.

"Hearing is one thing and letting go another," Robards said, and pointed at the northern horizon. "I'm not too pleased with the look of those."

Reverend Phillips squinted, searched the heavens, said, "I'm sure I don't know what you're speaking of."

Robards dropped his gaze and inspected the guards who were quieting somewhat under his studied calm. Then he pointed toward a gray-bearded elder who stood by the back wall and watched the proceedings with lively eyes. "That the head honcho over there?"

"Sort of," Wade replied. "At least the others seem to listen when he speaks. His name is Mikhail."

"Ask him what those clouds mean."

Wade did so. The elder neither looked upward nor turned away. He replied with one croaked word, which Wade translated as, "Snow."

"How long?" Robards demanded.

There was another exchange, then, "Four, maybe five days."

Robards nodded his thanks toward the old man, then asked, "When were they last paid?"

The parson protested, "I really don't see—"

"End of last week," Wade replied.

"Tell them anybody who gets in the way won't be paid for this week," Robards commanded. "But if they'll help us load the trucks, each will receive a two-week bonus, cash, when we pull out of here. Tell them our destination is the highlands and we're racing the clouds."

The news of a bonus satisfied all but one burly man with bad teeth and a wandering eye. He gestured threateningly with his rifle, stationing himself between the trucks and the schoolhouse.

Reverend Phillips said worriedly, "Perhaps it would be best if we went inside and discussed this a bit longer."

"That's a great idea," Robards agreed, his eyes on the man blocking his way. "You go right ahead, Reverend. We'll be along directly."

The parson took a step, realized no one was following his lead, and stopped.

The courtyard grew very still. Robards stared at the truculent man, and for a second time Wade saw the casual veneer stripped away. So did the man, and for a moment his resolve weakened. He cursed the other guards for leaving him isolated. Then he swung his rifle around to the ready.

Robards held out a hand toward Wade without taking his eyes off the resistant guard. "Give me the warehouse keys," he said quietly.

The keys danced slightly in Wade's trembling hand, sounding like little bells in the suddenly still air.

The guard's gaze slid away from Robards at the sound, a glance lasting less than half a heartbeat, but it was all Robards needed. He moved so fast that his actions melted into one continuous flow. Suddenly he was standing with the rifle in his hands, and the guard was lying unconscious at his feet.

The elder laughed a creaking bark and clapped his hands at the feat. Robards tossed him the rifle, which he caught one-handed, as though expecting it all along. Robards said, "Tell the old man he's welcome to join us if a guide's pay would interest him."

"Truly I could find the passes in fog or blinding snow," the tribesman replied smoothly, and swept a hand out to include all his clansmen. "Alas, I must see to the well-being of those who rely upon me for bread and hearth."

"He's just upping the price," Robards said when Wade had translated. "Tell him we've got to get these trucks loaded. Then we'll get down to brass tacks." He pointed to the clouds gathering among the high peaks and said, "His first duty is to make all these guys understand that we're racing the wind."

Once the loading had begun, Robards had settled himself on one of the trucks and directed traffic, sending his chosen band out on a score of errands and in the process firmly establishing himself as leader. Mikhail had been persuaded to join them as guide. The other guards had been paid off and sent packing, with Mikhail standing next to Robards to back him up. The taxi driver, Anatoly, was summoned and then dispatched again—first to collect Robards' belongings from the hotel and then to purchase food—before receiving final payment. Wade was sent to set up a rendezvous with the Chechen trader, then to buy maps, and finally to purchase a money belt for all the remaining dollars.

The parson was loathe to see the Red Cross funds drive off into the hazy distance with a total unknown, but Robards was insistent. If there was trouble, he explained, either for themselves or the ones they were being sent to supply, their only hope of escape might well be a ready fund of *valuta*, or hard currency. Wade ended the hand-wringing argument by simply walking away from it, the cash strapped to his waist in a well-worn money-belt.

The caravan passed the blockhouse apartments ringing Grozny just as the sun touched the horizon. As promised, the Chechen trader was waiting for them in an outcrop of trees beyond the only petrol station on that side of the city. They topped up one truck from the fuel cans strapped above the rear wheels. Mikhail took the other truck and all the cans, and waited in line for fuel. Wade acted as translator for Robards and the trader.

They were still at it when the truck returned with both tank and canisters brimming. The Chechen trader watched with narrowed eyes as the Ossetian elder appeared through the gathering gloom.

"Ask our Chechen friend if he's willing to come along as one of our guides," Robards instructed as he stacked the purchased weapons and clips and waxed bullets.

His eyes still on the new arrival, the Chechen replied, "Alas, I am unable to depart from my responsibilities, much as I regret the need to decline such an invitation."

Robards accepted the news with the barest of nods. His voice purposefully casual, he asked Wade, "You think this is a ploy to up the price?"

"He sounds pretty definite," Wade replied. "And he doesn't appear to like the looks of our companion. The Ossetians are seen as usurpers on ancient Chechen homeland."

"Then ask him which in his opinion is the best road for us to take from here to the passes," Rogue said, motioning for Mikhail to carry the purchased arms back to the trucks.

"The Georgian Military Highway begins in Vladikavkaz, the Ossetian capital to the southwest," the trader replied, waving casually toward the night. "The Russian soldiers and the Ingush are fighting there, and the city is no longer a haven of safety for strangers. However, this very road skirts the city and joins with the highway farther south, before the mountains begin."

When Wade had finished translating, Robards gave the trader a friendly nod. "Tell him we're really grateful for the advice, which we'd be foolish not to take. Ask him if we were to drive all night, how far we could get."

"Truly," the Chechen replied, his dark eyes gleaming in the trucks' headlights. "All such undertakings are in the hands of Allah, especially in such troubled times. But if thy way remains safe, then thou shouldst arrive upon the highway with its guards of Russian soldiers before the sun rises yet again."

"Then we'd better get started," Robards said with great cheer, shaking hands and waving the Chechen off with jolly fanfare before climbing into the truck beside Mikhail. Wade walked back and started the second truck beside the elder. As they started down the road, Robards hooted his horn and waved and shouted another round of thanks to the silent Chechen.

Once around the second bend, however, Robards pulled off and stopped. Wade walked up to the lead truck, climbed onto the running board and grabbed hold of the mirror mounting. Through the open window Robards said, "Ask Mikhail here if we can trust the Chechen's advice."

"We can trust him to greet us a second time just as soon as we are far enough removed from Grozny to escape the Russians' surveillance," the old man replied, his voice creaking with vehemence. "We can trust him to bring along a vast number of his Chechen thieves, for they are cowards and lower than the dust beneath our feet and will do nothing unless they outnumber honest men by a hundred to one. Then we can trust them to steal everything we carry, and cut our throats and leave our offspring to mourn us in poverty."

"Sounds about right to me," Robards declared. "Ask him if there is a pass to the east of here."

"There are only a few other passes below the level of the eternal snows in all of the great Caucasus range," he replied firmly, "and they are very distant. There you will find wars as well, and without Russian soldiers to grant a shred of order."

"Then we'll just have to circle around and hope the weather holds," Robards replied. "Ask him what lies directly east of here."

"The territory of the Ingush," the Ossetian elder replied, "who are as treacherous and cowardly as the cursed Chechen, if not more so. Truly the steppes are a haven for wolves who walk on two legs. But at least the Ingush will not be expecting our passage."

"Hope he's right," Robards replied. "Nothing on my map but a great big blank. Reminds me of those ocean charts from a couple hundred years ago. Get away from civilization, and they start drawing in dragons and sea monsters."

Wade asked, "How far will you have to take us out of our way?"

Robards restarted his engine, let it roar long and hard, then replied, "Far enough to keep us alive."

3

Dawn found Wade already up and moving.

They had overnighted at the edge of a small village, where an enterprising Ingush had built a roadside cafe in the hulk of a burned-out bus. They had shared camp with seven other trucks, all laden with farm produce and gathered into a separate enclave. Upon their arrival Mikhail had exchanged formal greetings, to let the others know they were no threat. Since then the two trucks of medical supplies had been left alone.

Rogue squatted next to the road with Mikhail, a greasy map unfolded on the ground in front of them. While Wade broke camp, the pair shared one of Robards' slender cheroots and a tin mug of steaming coffee. They spoke in hand signs and nods as the old man described the rutted road that led toward the hills.

The Caucasus Mountains dominated the distance. Their bases were lost in mists that drifted in the still air. The dawn light tinted their looming, snow-capped peaks with hues of rose and gold. They rested on earthbound clouds and stretched from horizon to horizon, a serrated nine-hundred-mile wall that divided two worlds. To the north lay the endless steppes, the Arctic, the brutal Siberian winds. To the south opened the balmier Mediterranean realms.

Rogue waved Wade over. When he hunkered down beside the pair, Rogue said, "Tell me about the conflict up ahead."

"There are wars up and down the Caucasus range," Wade replied. "But the one which concerns us most is between the Chechen and the Russians. Other than that, there are constant skirmishes between the Chechen, the Ingush, and the Ossetians."

"Ossetia is the state next door, right?"

"Right," Wade agreed. "Well, technically, it's North Ossetia, or Severnaja Osetija. They're another autonomous republic, part of the Russian Federation just like here. Then there's South Ossetia, below the mountain range, which is a part of Georgia."

"And these three tribes don't get along."

"Not for centuries," Wade agreed. "Chechen and Ingush are Muslim; Ossetians are Christians. They hate each other. Then there is the local Russian population, brought in by Stalin to dilute the tribes during his policy of Russification. They made up almost forty percent of the population before the Chechens started fighting to secede. The Chechen warlord recently vowed death to all Russians who attempted to remain in his homeland."

"Chechen warlord," Rogue mused aloud. "This place is getting more interesting by the minute."

Wade took a moment to translate for Mikhail. When he was finished, the old man waved a veined hand toward the mountains. "The Chechen are traders and sheep farmers and cleverer than the Ingush," Mikhail began. "The Ingush tend to hug the land. They put down deeper roots. They raise cattle. They and the Chechen were neighbors and only sometimes enemies until Stalin, may his name be erased from the earth, stole their lands and brought in the Russians. Then more Russians lived on Chechen land than the Chechen themselves. More Chechen died in Siberia than survived to tell the tale. Ingush as well. Now they taste the wind of liberation and seek to steal both what was theirs and what their neighbors have managed to settle— neighbors such as my own Ossetians."

The old man ran a knotted hand around the back of his neck. "The winds of change are not always kind. I myself have lost sons and grandsons to a war that means nothing except misery for everyone."

"Which war was that?" Robards demanded, nodding to Wade for the translation.

"The war beyond the count of man's days. The war that has continued since before the birth of my father's father."

Mikhail stooped, picked up a stick, and drew a crude map in the dust at their feet. "This long line is the Caucasus range, separating Russia from Georgia for all of time. Here to the west of us lies the Black Sea, where the mountains begin their eternal march. The lands bordering sea and western hills belong to the Abkhazi, those whom Stalin left alive. Next to them, south of the mountains still, are the Svaneti, then the Ushguls, then the Ossetians. The Ossetians are the first tribe both north and south of the mountains, because here lies the first great Caucasus pass. We are also the only Christian hill tribe left alive. You as a warrior will understand what this means. Here in the heart of the mountain tribes stands the Ossetian stake, which the Muslim tribes are sworn to tear from the earth and burn on the fires of their hatred."

"What is there to the east of us?" Robards demanded, focused upon the map at his feet.

"North of the mountains, the Chechen and Ingush, as I have said," Mikhail replied, almost chanting the words. "In the southern highlands, some Chechen and Ingush still, but not many. Mostly Tusheti tribes. Some Karachai also, but most Stalin deported to Siberia. They have not returned."

"Is there trouble in that area?"

"For the modern man, there is trouble everywhere," Mikhail replied, "but more here than elsewhere. Farther east the mountains curve down southward and fall into the Dagestani lowlands, which in turn slide into the Caspian Sea."

Robards pointed with the toe of his boot to the region where the mountains begin their curve. "What about to the west here?"

"The Kasheti region of Georgia," Mikhail answered once Wade had translated. "Though they are more a name than a tribe in these days. Stalin had a special hatred for them. Why, no one knows. But almost the entire tribe was scattered. On the other side of the Georgian border, here to the southeast, lies Azerbaijan. Further south, Armenia. To the southwest, Turkey. There again one finds the battle between Muslim and Christian, especially in the Christian enclave inside Azerbaijan."

Robards nodded approvingly. "Your knowledge is great, old man."

"In my youth I journeyed far and wide," the elder replied proudly. "I was a trader, and a good one. Dagestani carpets were my specialty."

"Are there passes down through the Caucasus range to the southern lands?"

"None that are not fiercely guarded by tribesmen." Mikhail squinted. "Was not our objective the highland hospital?"

"Always best to know where the back door's located," Robards replied. "Ask the gent how old he is."

"I am about to see my seventieth year." He cupped his arm close to his chest, and made as though holding an invisible gun. "Yet remain strong enough to hold a Skorpion with one hand and shoot a level line."

"Skorpion's a machine pistol with the kick of a mule," Robards explained to Wade. "Says a lot about the world we're in when an old guy uses that as the symbol of his health. Tell him I hope

I'm in such shape at his age, if I make it that far."

"Your friend carries the scent of good fortune with him," Mikhail replied. "That is why I agreed to come. He should choose to remain and make his home here. There is much work for one such as him, and the hillsmen are known for their long lives. My father still tends his sheep, and my great-uncle swears he will see his two hundredth year."

"We oughta talk once this little jaunt's over," Robards replied. "First I need to see how much chance there is of me walking into somebody else's bullet." He stared at the crude map drawn in the dust and said, "Tell me about the pass we'll be taking."

"We shall join the Georgia Military Highway south of Vladikavkaz, North Ossetia's capital city," the old man replied. "This follows the central and clearest pass through these jutting peaks. It winds through gorges and hairpin turns and drops and ravines before descending into Georgia. The road is the single paved Caucasus artery, not often either washed out or bombed. Too many trucks carrying far too many goods have ground the road's surface to a trail of cracks and bumps and gravel and dust. But at least we should be safe. Russian military convoys travel its length, followed by civilians who bribe the transport officers for the right..."

A swiftly moving cloud brought them all around. Wade searched the windless horizon and realized with a start that the approaching cloud was alive. A sound of honking strengthened as the cloud became hundreds of thousands of migrating waterbirds.

Robards looked an astonished question at Mikhail, who replied through Wade, "North of our campsite is the Volga Delta, a remnant of the wilderness that once held all of Russia in its grasp. Where the great river joins the Caspian Sea, there lies a maze of marshes and streams. Three hundred species of birds live there. Plus the Saigar antelope. Wolves. Wild boar. Steppe eagles."

The cloud of birds arrived overhead, throwing their campsite into fleeting shadows. The bird cries became so loud that the old man had to shout to be heard. "In my father's time, the birds formed flying walls that went on for hours and days on end. Now the flocks pass only in the morning and in the evening, and only for a week at most."

Robards listened, nodded, and watched the sky. There was nothing to see save the cloud of birds. He called the question, "Same time every year?"

When Wade had translated the old man shook his head emphatically. "There is no set time to their pattern, no date upon which the giant gatherings begin. Yet the birds know, as do the Saigar antelope. On a certain day each autumn, as early as the first week in September or as late as November, the herds join and begin to move. And then, a few days later, the first Siberian wind arrives."

As quickly as it began, it ended. The last of the birds passed overhead, and within a few seconds their raucous cries blended with the gathering wind.

"In the autumn," Mikhail continued in a quieter tone, "the steppe's silver featherwood stands burnished by the sun like ripening wheat. It shivers in these gathering winds as though knowing what the birds and the animals know—that soon the wind will turn and howl in icy fury from the north. Here in the south we have only the slightest taste of Russian winter. But I have traveled. I know. Not so far to the north, the land will soon turn to iron, its coat of ice so hard and jagged that tires can be cut to shreds. Then the land is empty as only a Russian steppe can be, lost to the vacuum of unconquered winter, its isolation accented by a lone wolf's howl."

"A good time to be somewhere else." Robards raised his boot and deliberately erased the map scratched into the earth. "Let's move out."

The Caucasus mountains, one of the world's youngest ranges, were not yet worn down and softened by nature. They did not rise gradually from plains to foothills to high reaches. Instead, they *leapt* into being. The world was flat, an endless steppe, and then came the walls of rock crowned by ice and snow. Waterfalls thundered down from all sides. Among the silent giants loomed a dozen peaks higher than Mont Blanc, Europe's tallest mountain. Two thousand glaciers locked the highlands beneath frozen seas a mile and more in depth.

The southern Kalmyk Steppe was a sweeping earthen sea, bound on the south by the Caucasus

Mountains, rimmed to the east and west by the Caspian and Black Seas. To the north there was no boundary, no ending, no rise nor fall nor physical landmark. The name changed with distance, from southern to central to northern, yet in truth the steppe continued in one flat empty stretch from the Caucasus to the Arctic wastelands, a distance of over three thousand kilometers. Winter winds generated in the depths of Siberia howled unchecked down its length until they crashed in frustrated fury against the unyielding Caucasus range.

Today, however, the weather was with them. Warm sunlight marked their traverse along the steppe's southern edge. They kept to byroads which were little more than rutted tracks, circling around several Chechen enclaves, heading ever closer to the mountains that dominated the horizon.

Their journey was noisy and dirty and slow. As the day progressed, the wind became their constant companion. Several miles after they joined the highway, they passed another petrol station. Robards insisted they stop and top up their tanks. They sat in sweltering heat, trying to breathe through the diesel fumes and dust clouds as inch by inch the mammoth line crawled forward.

"Take a look at those," Robards said, when Wade climbed upon his running board during the wait. He jutted his chin toward the meadow flanking the station where a flock of shaggy beasts cropped meager grass.

"They're called yakaws," Wade explained. "A cross between yak and cattle. You see their milk a lot in the markets."

Robards pointed to where shepherds watched the animals, ignoring the station's noisy cacophony. "What tribe are they?"

"I'd guess Ingush," Wade said after a moment's hesitation. "The Chechen generally have sharper features. They are said to be a Persian tribe. The Ingush are probably of Turkish descent. Some say Afghan, though. They are swarthier, a lot have the hawk noses and full features of the Himalayan tribesmen. They're considered the more easygoing of the two, but that's only a matter of degree. As Mikhail said, the Ingush farm and tend cattle. A lot of them wear expensive sable hats or fedoras."

Within a half hour of leaving the station, they began a steady climb. Their speed slowed even more, seldom creeping above twenty miles an hour. The old man rode in the first truck with Robards. Wade found himself not minding the solitude at all. The scenery was vast and ever changing, the road an invitation to explore the interior as well as exterior landscape.

Streams and rivers crisscrossed the highway every mile or so. A dozen waterfalls glistened in the distance. As the two trucks crossed one makeshift wooden bridge, Wade spotted the metal girders of a more modern construction. It was upended and embedded in a monstrous pile of debris, testimony to the spring floods that roared down from above.

The mountains' lower reaches were dreamlands of mist and silver birches. As the trucks ground relentlessly higher, the mists gave way to aching blue-black skies, the birch to ancient firs and then to silver-green meadows.

They rounded yet another curve and a broad, rushing river came into view. At the top of the rise they pulled into a lay-by crowded with trucks and buses and people taking a break from the heat. With his first step into the icy torrent, Wade lost all feeling in his feet. He continued out until the rushing current threatened to pluck him away. The mist hanging above the river dropped the air's temperature by fifty degrees. Wade stood and reveled in the coolness until he saw Rogue wave for him to return.

When he arrived back at the trucks, the old man said with pride, "That is the River Terek. We follow its path all the way to the Krestovy Pass. Pushkin called it the laughing waters. Tolstoy called it the river of smoke."

Mikhail then pointed off to his right to where a rutted track broke off and meandered into a heavily wooded glen. "The entrance to the Fiagdon Valley. There lie the remnants of the Ossetian city called Tsimitar. Beyond that stands the City of the Dead, where until the Middle Ages my people came and buried their kin in family towers built over a thousand years ago. Now there is nothing. Stalin, the killer who was half-Ossetian himself, succeeded where even Tamerlane had failed. Today our valley is empty of life."

Rogue grinned at the news. "Tribes who love to carry steel, fight, sneak across borders with contraband, pass down grudges for centuries, and wear fancy headgear. Tamerlane and the Mongols and a battleground for over two thousand years. Makes me wish I could strap a sword to my side and go riding off on a great white charger."

"It doesn't bother you," Wade countered, "hearing about all the tragedy this land has known?"

Robards gave his easy shrug. "They lived, they died. Same as you and me, sport. Life's only a tragedy for those on the receiving end, a place I avoid." He tossed an empty Pepsi bottle toward a colossal pile of trash. "Come on, time to head for the hills."

As the road rose to meet the mountains, the curves became more extreme, the climb steeper. Ahead of Wade, Robards slowed his truck to a crawl. A protruding rock outcrop crumbled as Rogue's truck hugged the wall for safety. While Wade waited for Rogue to manage the turn, he swiveled in his seat and looked back. To his left, the road dropped away to nothingness. A mountain eagle drifted on an unseen current, its four-foot wingspan unfurled and stable as it screamed at these human interlopers.

Beyond and two thousand feet below, a valley expanded as it left the mountain fastness. The earth was mirrored silver in the harsh afternoon light. Richer bands of green ran alongside delta rivulets which tracked over the burnished autumn steppe. Here and there the utter flatness was broken by solitary foothills, rising and falling like tiny waves upon a silver sea. Winds whistled and moaned, the constant voice of this alien land.

The roar of Rogue's engine signaled Wade that the way was clear. He ground the gears and started forward, inching his way around the bend. Halfway around the curve, he turned back once again.

At that moment, before his vision was blocked by the cliff wall, Wade knew a moment of utter clarity. He felt his own life yawing forth in an instant of realization, a glimpse of choices soon to be forced upon him.

On the one side was the terror of open space with no visible support whatsoever. On the other the strength and power of visible and solid cliffs.

Yet for some reason, it was the cliffs which frightened him most of all.

The dining chambers were straight from the tales of King Arthur—forty-foot ceilings, Cotswold stone walls, medieval tapestries, paintings of grim-faced royals, vast chandeliers, candles everywhere. Allison felt like a little girl playing grown-up as she sat across from Cyril and listened to him discuss their orders with three hovering waiters.

"I think a claret would be best with the duck," Cyril had decided. "Would that be acceptable, my dear?"

"Perfect." Allison glanced about the room, immensely glad she had decided to bring her only formal dress.

Once the serving entourage had departed, he said, "Tell me what you've been doing with yourself all these years."

"Nothing could be more boring. I assume you've heard that I work with the Office of Export Administration. Talk about a snooze."

"On the contrary, I am positively riveted."

She smiled at a sudden memory. "Pop always did say you could charm the pants off the Prime Minister."

"What a horrid thought. I'm quite sure he said no such thing."

"I was actually supposed to be somewhere else, but the export people were tremendously understaffed. Commerce assigned me there 'temporarily.' "

"I see. And that was..."

"Three and a half extremely long years ago."

"Once they realized just how good you were at your job," Cyril interpreted, "they insisted on keeping you."

"Until now. But with all the budget cut-backs, the entire staff is suddenly looking for new jobs." Allison met him with a steady eye. "But you know all this."

Cyril's cool aplomb was momentarily shaken. "I beg your pardon?"

"You wouldn't have brought me over without first having checked me out."

"I must remind myself not to allow your attractiveness to blind me again. You are more like your father than I first thought."

She gave him a look developed during years of sorting through Washington baloney. "And just what special ability am I supposed to have that no one else does?"

He collected himself. "An ability to adapt to the unforeseen. The very same ability which, within six months of your arrival in this horrid dead-end position, caused you to devise a computerized interagency tracking system—"

"How did you hear about that?"

"—A system which proved so successful that you were then seconded to three other agencies to adapt the same system to their needs. All the while you were still held on to tightly by the Export Administration, who by this time had awakened to the fact that they had stumbled upon a real prize."

Allison did not contradict him. "So how did you pry me loose?"

"By appealing to a higher authority," he replied. "Much higher, as a matter of fact. One which had the clout to order this agency to finally relinquish their most beautiful charge."

Her host paused as the wine waiter arrived, and presented the bottle to Cyril. While the wine was being opened, tasted, and poured, Allison caught a glimpse of herself in a mirror hanging upon the opposite wall. She was tall and slender and crowned with abundant red curls. In her younger days, tall and slim had meant skinny and gawky. She had learned not to smile. She had learned to bend her legs and crouch slightly when standing in line, so she would not be taller than everybody else, including the boys. She had learned not to lie out in the summer, since fifteen minutes even with sunblock was enough to turn her lobster-red. She had learned not to pay her hair any attention at all. She had learned to retreat into her books, staying at the top of every class. She had learned to keep her loneliness hidden deep.

Allison smiled nowadays with ease, a beautiful even-toothed smile. Fair skin was suddenly fashionable. Women singed their hair with chemicals in a vain attempt to copy her curls. Lean and rangy figures were in. Her friends spoke of Allison's ideal beauty. Still, Allison had numerous ways to divert the attention, laugh it off. For when Allison Taylor looked into the mirror, her heart still told her she was seeing Raggedy Ann. She was precocious, intelligent, able, eloquent. But on the social side, Allison Taylor walked with two left feet.

"My dear," Cyril said, raising his glass and drawing her attention back to the table. "Thank you so much for joining me."

She clinked glasses, smiled, watched as their duck arrived. Each plate was carried by a different waiter—two for the duck, two for the side plates of steamed vegetables. The main ones were set into place and the silver covers raised in unison to reveal thinly sliced fowl in a rich Madeira sauce. "If this is the way I'm going to be treated for the next three months, I may never go home."

Their talk turned light and reminiscent until the meals were completed. Allison allowed Cyril to steer the conversation through numerous lighthearted veins until she set down her utensils and declared, "All right, I've finished. Time to tell me what's going on."

"Very well." Clearly he had been waiting for that moment. Cyril signaled for the waiter to clear the table. "The situation, as you Americans would say, is beyond critical."

He fiddled with his glass until the waiters had departed, then leaned across the table and said quietly, "At present, there are only nine countries who publicly acknowledge having nuclear weapons: they are Great Britain, France, Russia, Ukraine, Belarus, Kazakhstan, Uzbekistan, China, and the United States. South Africa recently claimed to have developed four nuclear bombs, then dismantled all of them. Three other nations are widely believed to possess such bombs—Israel, India, and Pakistan."

His words struck hard. "Nuclear weapons?"

"Now there are another eight countries actively seeking to acquire nuclear weapons through the new international black market," Cyril continued unabated. "They are Brazil, Argentina, North Korea, Iraq, Iran, Egypt, Syria, and Libya. One great concern is that the rising tide of Islamic fundamentalism may fasten upon these weapons as the ultimate terrorist weapon."

"What on earth do I have to do with nuclear weapons?"

"Bear with me," he replied crisply. "I will get to that soon enough. Three bombs the size of Hiroshima's would be sufficient to destroy two-thirds of Israel's entire population. Or imagine a holiday launch boating up the Thames, docking just opposite Westminster, and igniting a small warhead. Think of what such a bomb and the resulting fallout would do to Manhattan, or Washington, or San Francisco. Terrorists would be able to threaten any of our coastal cities with annihilation. For some time we have had unconfirmed evidence." Cyril then permitted himself a small smile. "As you are new to the game, my dear, I shall interpret that for you."

"Some game," Allison said softly.

"Yes, well, better than other names I might use. In any case, what we call unconfirmed evidence normally resides somewhere between bizarre gossip and a bald-faced lie. But this time we have been able to substantiate at least some of the rumors. There is now evidence that a second route has opened. Perhaps not for fissionable materials, but rather for engineers. You see, just as worrisome to us as the transport of material is the transport of people."

"Know-how," she interpreted. "Transfer of brain power."

"Quite so. In 1994 the West received its first confirmed reports that Iran and Iraq were granting jobs to Soviet nuclear scientists." Cyril studied the depths of his glass. "It is all so unprecedented, you see. The Soviet Union's dismantling itself in the space of just a few years. The largest spy network on earth becoming such a laughingstock they couldn't manage to find their own toes with their shoes off. Terrorists the world over presented with offers to buy fissionable material and hire nuclear scientists as though ordering from Harrods."

"I still don't see where I—"

"Permit me to come to that in a moment." With one finger Cyril began tracing a map-line down along the tablecloth. "On the opposite side of the Caspian Sea from Turkmenistan lies an extremely volatile region shared by the Ukraine, Georgia, Azerbaijan, and Armenia. It appears that the Chechen-Ingush region of southern Russia is now being used as a jumping-off place for this modern-day traffic in people. The product is taken overland through the high passes of the Caucasus Mountains and down into Tbilisi, which is the capital of Georgia."

"Product," she repeated. "It sounds inhuman."

"Not so inhuman, I would imagine, as calling them the creators of atom bombs. Or the perpetrators of mass destruction."

"Where are they headed?"

"Again we have only rumors to go on," Cyril replied. "But an increasing amount of evidence suggests that an international smuggling ring, dealing in both fissionable material and nuclear engineers, is operating in Jordan. Jordan is an ally of Iraq, yet at the same time it remains a friend to the West. Quite a feat of political juggling, as you can imagine. Iraq is prohibited by UN sanctions from using its aircraft or from letting foreign flights in or out of the country. Yet Jordan, which borders Iraq, remains open to the outside world. Once the product is there, then, further overland transport would be quite feasible."

Cyril watched Allison carefully and added, "This group is purported to be located in Aqaba, to be precise."

Allison straightened as yet another flood of memories surfaced. "Aqaba! Isn't that where—"

"Exactly," Cyril interjected. "Ben Shannon has kindly agreed to allow us to place someone within his compound. Unfortunately, we made the error of initially assigning him an agent from our embassy in Amman. Let us simply say that they did not get along. He has now taken the liberty of telling us whom he will work with." The stare intensified. "He is willing to work with us only if you will go in as our agent in the field."

4

On the evening of the second day, Wade's truck
crested a rise to find several hundred campfires
flickering in the distance.

Within another hour the trucks had wound
their way into an encampment filled with roaring
engines, shouting men, diesel fumes, dust, the
smoke of cooking meat, and the bleating of
animals. Wade wrestled the oversized steering
wheel with numbed hands and followed Robards
to an empty space. He backed his vehicle so that
the rear was close to the escarpment, facing out
toward the myriad of flickering shadows.

Robards pulled in beside Wade, drawing so
close the side fenders groaned as they meshed
together. Then he cut his motor and said through
his open window, "This way we'll notice if
somebody decides to pay us a visit."

Wade translated for the old man seated beside
Rogue.

"Tell the warrior that Chechen traders will
come by with food and drink and eyes hunting the

unwary. It would be best if I spoke for us."

"Time to either fish or cut bait," Robards said when Wade had translated. "You want to trust him with our lives?"

"Why are you asking me?"

"Because it's your show, sport. You're what they call the payer. But if you want the advice of your payee, I'd say let the old man handle this."

Wade called through the open window to where the old man sat beside Robards, "We would be grateful for your assistance, uncle."

Without further speech, Mikhail pulled the gun from behind his seat and slid from the truck. He walked out in front, cradled the gun across his chest, and settled into the position of one accustomed to waiting for hours. Light from neighboring fires turned the old man's weapon the color of burnished copper.

"Come on, sport," Rogue called, sidling from his truck. "Let's see to the grub."

Following Robards' lead, Wade set up camp in a small hollow behind the two trucks. From his kneeling position he watched under the high-riding wheels as three pairs of scruffy legs approached the old man. One of the newcomers led a bleating sheep by a rope bridle. "Visitors," he whispered.

"I hear," Rogue replied softly from inside the back end of his truck. "Can you catch what they're saying?"

"No."

The men squatted down by Mikhail, and their

86

faces came into view beneath the truck. All of the strangers were of a type—black hair and unkempt beards and vests with bullet pockets and the knit skullcaps of the mountain Chechen. Their guns fit their hands with the ease of a lifetime's practice. As glittering black eyes searched him out, Wade dropped his gaze to the flickering cooker. "They see me."

"Good," Rogue said for his ears alone. "Here, take this."

Wade accepted their three bedrolls, set them down, then took the extras Rogue had insisted they pack in case the others became wet. "What are you doing?"

"No need for them to know how few we are," Rogue said. "Spread the beddings out. I'll just stay up here out of sight for a while."

Wade did as he was told, saw that his motions were followed by the men up front. He pretended a calm he did not feel and did his best not to look their way. He poured water from one of the drinking canisters into a pot and set it on to boil. The hollow where he worked was formed by a very large tree stump. The knee-high table was a full four feet across, and made an excellent work surface as he went about preparing their dinner.

Eventually the old man returned, a ghost of a smile on his features. "That was very wise, setting out the extra beddings."

"It was Robards' idea," Wade confessed.

"Of course."

At the sound of the old man's voice, Robards sprang lightly from the truck. Wade handed him a plate of canned stew and a fork. He blew on the steaming food and demanded, "Ask the old man if there was any trouble."

"There is trouble everywhere," Mikhail replied, accepting his food with a nod. "Life itself is trouble. But they did not appear overly interested."

"What did he say we were carrying?"

"Parts for these cursed Russian trucks," the old man replied. "Items too heavy to be stolen with ease and not valuable enough to fight over unless the takings were easy."

"One of us will be on duty all night," Robards announced. "Two hours on, four off. I'll take the first watch. One will sleep in the front cab, one in back, one on top."

"I'll take the top position," Wade said quickly.

Robards showed the glimmer of a smile. "Like to do a little stargazing?"

"I'd just like a little fresh air. I feel as if I've been eating dust all day."

"Well, take a couple of extra blankets. The night will get cold up there."

It did. But Wade found he did not mind at all. Robards woke him for his watch with a steaming mug of oversweetened tea and the words, "Be sure and sit up the whole time. Otherwise you might fall back asleep."

Wade sipped and sighed sweet steam and wrapped the blankets up close around his neck. The camp spread out in front of him for a half mile or more in three directions. Silent, still forms huddled around many smoldering fires. Shadow figures walked in quiet vigilance around trucks, tall guns jutting like spears from their shoulders or hanging down alongside their legs. Drunken laughter drifted up from points unseen. Overhead the stars stretched out like a glittering silver blanket, bright enough to paint the entire scene with ghostly luminosity. The peaks surrounding their escarpment sliced sharp edges from the sky, silent sentinels overlooking the madness of man.

Morning was little more than a smudge across the eastern sky when Robards had them break camp and get underway. As usual, the old man rode in the front truck with Robards, while Wade followed close behind and ate the front truck's dust. The morning was cold; Wade's fingers were numbed by the steering wheel in the unheated cabin. His breath frosted the inside of the windshield, each dip in the road jarred his spine, the engine roared so loudly Wade could scarcely hear himself think. But he did not mind.

Every turn in the road brought new vistas. The mountains had the raw, untamed look of a new creation. The sun crested distant peaks and flashed fiery illumination into the morning, transforming the road into a molten river of gold and the dust into figures that coalesced and beckoned and vanished and reformed. Wade shouted a laugh as the next curve revealed a flickering stream from which a flock of sheep drank, oblivious to the thundering motors. He waved to the bearded shepherd with his trio of dogs and ancient rifle and pair of crossed bandoliers. Wade had never felt so alive.

By the time they approached the outskirts of Carcash, however, the thrill of adventure had long since faded beneath a blanket of fatigue and dust and heat. The sun poised mercilessly in a cloudless sky. In his cracked rearview mirror Wade inspected a face caked with white dust and a pair of red-rimmed eyes. His mouth tasted of grit and diesel fumes and the road. He was glad their mission was almost completed.

He followed Robards toward the truck compound that dominated one side of the village. Their passage garnered only a few disinterested glances from passers-by. They were simply two of an unending stream of vehicles.

At Robards' insistence, they paid a premium for spaces against a windowless warehouse wall forming the compound's southern perimeter. Robards backed his truck in at an exaggerated angle, blocking out space for both vehicles. Then they had a quick cold meal and left the old man on guard duty as they set off once more in the second truck.

The village of Carcash filled a shallow, bowl-shaped valley with tumbledown shanties, warehouses, bars, stores charging vastly inflated prices, more bars, restaurants, still more bars, and hotels that were little more than bunkhouses. The buildings that fronted the main highway made a feeble attempt at respectability, with walkways raised to escape both mud and snow. There were only two other passages large enough to be granted the names of streets, and away from the highway they were soon reduced to rutted tracks. Most buildings were reached via unnamed, unlit alleys that wandered in haphazard fashion around dusty garden patches, lines of laundry, corrals for seedy-looking horses, scampering children, and outdoor privies. Few women were visible on the streets, and none walked alone. Many of the men were falling down drunk.

Everyone carried weapons of some sort, from antique blunderbusses with stocks sporting hammered silver plates to sniper rifles with scopes as long as Wade's forearm. The Kalash-nikov with its sickle-shaped clip was clearly the weapon of choice. Knives, some as long as short swords, sprouted from belts, from thighs, from boots, from backpacks. Bandoliers were worn like badges of honor.

Following vague instructions Wade had brought with him, they tried to find the track that led to the nearest Ingush mountain fastness. They had to ask repeatedly for directions; the first several times their requests were answered with hostile stares and indifferent shrugs. Finally Robards halted the truck, grabbed his gun, and climbed down. The next passerby was stopped by Rogue, looming large and stone-faced directly in his path. That time, when Wade asked, the man answered. But when Wade asked if all was well with the Red Cross camp, the man pretended total ignorance. After having the directions confirmed twice more, they set off.

"It doesn't look good," Wade shouted above the engine.

Robards shrugged his unconcern. "No use worrying," he replied. "We'll find out soon enough."

Their way took them along the valley's western side. The rocky promontory clung to a steep cliff and sidled around a series of hair-raising drops. The roadway was mild in grade, designed so that it could be managed in snowy conditions. Around the curves the track was barely wide enough to keep all four tires on the surface. To one side was an unyielding rock wall. To the other was nothing but a swooping drop. Wade found it best not to look out his window at all.

At one level passage Robards braked. He pointed back to tracks curving off the main path and scrunching along an indentation in the wall. Wade followed the pointed finger but did not understand. "What am I supposed to be seeing?"

"That hollow was made so trucks or carts coming from opposite directions can pass each other."

Wade imagined having to back up along that incline. "I'm glad we haven't had to do that."

"That's not what I meant," Robards answered, searching behind them. "Nobody's used that passage in quite a while, by the looks of those tracks."

"So?"

Robards swung back around. "So maybe nothing. Let's go see."

An hour passed before the road broadened and began a sharp descent. As the sun touched the distant western peaks, they rounded a corner and saw what once had been a large pastoral community. Now it was nothing but a blackened shell.

Crumbling rock-walled houses were surrounded by sooty shadows of corrals and hay barns. Nothing moved except large mountain crows riding the high currents. The place was utterly still. Lifeless. Robards halted beyond the village outskirts and slid from the truck. "You drive."

Wordlessly Wade took his place behind the wheel. Robards swung into the passenger seat, hoisted his weapon, rasped the cocking arm, and set the barrel on the window ledge. "Take it slow."

The closer they drew, the grimmer the picture became. What had been wood was burned to cinders. What had been made of stone was blown to bits. The place reeked of ashes and decay.

They found the clinic by its flagpole. It had stood just north of the village center, just as Wade's directions described. A blackened pole rose before the burned-out hulk of what once had been a long, low structure surrounded by an open veranda. Wade stopped the truck, walked down the ash-strewn path, and climbed the trio of blackened stone steps. There was no movement, no sound save the wind and the cawing crows.

"What happened here?" Wade murmured.

"Somebody got unlucky," Robards replied, climbing the stairs behind him. "Might happen to us if we stick around too long."

Wade turned to scout the silent valley. "You think they could come back?"

"This is a killing ground." Robards kept his eyes trained on the village. "Never want to stay in one longer than absolutely necessary. Somebody comes looking for revenge, or for a lost friend, or loot, they might decide to add us to the list."

"All right, I'm—" Wade stopped, his attention caught by the wind flickering a page tagged to the side wall. He walked over and tore the sheet from the nail.

"What does it say?" Rogue demanded.

"It's in French and the writing is terrible." Wade squinted over the smudged script. "Something about, they came in the night. All the staff managed to escape, but one was wounded. They heard Russian and saw uniforms, then there's something about the patients that I can't make out.

They've decided it would be safer to head for Tbilisi." Wade looked up. "That's the capital of Georgia. It marks the southern end of the Trans-Caucasus Highway."

"You get back to the truck," Robards instructed. "I'll make a quick reccy around this joint."

Five minutes later Robards returned, his face streaked with ash. "All right, time to head on back."

"Did you find anything?"

"Nothing you need to see. You drive."

They left the silent village behind and began the lonely trek back to Carcash. Wade asked, "They were dead, weren't they?"

"Who?"

"The patients. Whoever else you found back there in the clinic."

"Best not to dwell on what you can't help," Robards replied.

"I guess you've seen a lot of stuff like this," Wade said thoughtfully. "I see a little of it in my work. But I don't think I could ever get so casual about death. I think it's important to, well, respect a person's passage."

"You're here until you're not. Respect don't change it any." His tone was clipped. "I've met guys like you everywhere I've been. They get close enough to smell death, they start thinking about what comes next, which leads you to all that God stuff. Let me tell you something, sport. It's a great big world out here. A lot of questions just don't have answers. One place I've been, they keep an empty chair at the table for the dead, leave it there for a year. Another place, folks make up this hefty wooden tablet, cover it with words, keep fruit and fresh flowers in front of it, and bow down to it every time they pass. After a month or so they take it out and burn it, then the spirit's been released to wherever it is spirits are supposed to go. Far as I can see, all that stuff's meant to help the ones left around here, not the spirits." Robards jutted an angry finger at the next curve. "You just keep your mind on the road up ahead, sport. Whoever it was that didn't make it out of there is weeks beyond the point of no return. Talking about it with me ain't going to change things a bit."

Wade drove for a time in silence, then asked, "So what do we do now?"

"That's for you to decide," Robards replied. "But you gotta know that my nickel ends when we get back to the compound."

Wade eased them around a cliff side, determinedly not looking out into the void. "You'd just leave me there alone with two trucks?"

"This is the age of capitalism, in case you haven't noticed. You're just lucky you got yourself somebody who stays bought."

"An honest mercenary."

"There are more of us around than you'd imagine."

"I don't have enough money left to pay you more than what we already agreed on."

"That stuff we're carting around is worth its weight in gold to the right buyer. You give me a script for payment, with a note saying I can take medicines instead of money if that old geezer back in Grozny decides to make trouble." Robards pulled the clip from his gun, flipped out the round in the chamber, and dry-fired the trigger. "So what's it going to be?"

"I've got to think."

"You do that, sport," Robards said, and set the

gun down behind the seat. "Just keep in mind, the meter's running."

When Mikhail saw them coming, he hefted his gun high and shouted something that was lost beneath the engine's rumble.

Rogue climbed down, walked to the other truck, maneuvered it around until it was straight, then motioned Wade to back in beside him. As soon as Wade cut the engine, the old man climbed up on his running board. "I have a favor to ask of you," he said formally.

Surprise filtered through Wade's confusion and fatigue. "Of me?"

"There are members of my clan who live here. One has a sickness, another a cut which has not healed clean." The old man's gaze was strong, direct. "I and my clan would be in your debt."

The stars were welcome strangers when Wade returned from treating Mikhail's kin. He unrolled his bedding behind the truck, and lay enclosed by its captured warmth, too tired to sleep. He searched the silver river overhead, wishing he could leave behind his uncertainty and live with the assurance that ruled Robards' days.

Wade did not awaken until the sun rose over the truck and lanced directly into his face. He squinted against the sudden brilliance, rolled over, and found Robards leaning against the compound wall and cradling a steaming mug with both hands.

"It's almost noon," Robards announced. "Ready for some coffee?"

Wade rolled from his bedding, struggled to his feet, rubbed his face. His three-day growth felt rough as sandpaper. "Noon?"

Robards handed him a mug. "You were doing a right fair imitation of the truck engine."

Wade sipped the scalding brew, rolled the ache from his shoulders. "I was pretty tired."

"There's a bathhouse down the street. Not the cleanest place on earth, but there's plenty of hot water."

Wade scratched at his matted hair. "I could use a shower."

"Better hop to it, then. There was a reception committee here an hour or so ago, but I wouldn't let them wake you. One of them spoke enough English for me to work out the basics. It appears that word has gotten around about your deft touch as a healer." Robards squinted and looked out over the encampment. "Looks like there are a few others who could use a helping hand."

"I'm no doctor," Wade protested, fully awake now.

"You're the closest thing they've got," Robards answered, "and a darn sight better than nothing."

Wade bent over the cooker, poured himself a second cup. "We still haven't talked about what comes next."

"There's time enough for that after you see to your new friends. You go get cleaned up. They'll be back before long."

The bath stalls were rudimentary in the extreme. Generations of insects nested in every corner, and the floors were blanketed with slippery green slime. Still, the water was hot and plentiful. Wade stood and let the water drum down on him and savored the simple pleasure of washing.

The Carcash compound covered the better part of twenty acres and contained almost a thousand trucks. As Wade walked the central avenue, he passed vehicles of every make and vintage. Many had their cowlings opened while grease-stained arms and heads busied themselves with repairs. Guards strung with bandoliers and well-oiled guns lounged with deceptive ease.

The dusty concourse was packed with hawkers. Shepherds tugged at bleating sheep, stopping to haggle with the timeless patience of Asian traders. When a bargain was finally struck, the sheep was lifted and its throat cut with a single motion of a razor-sharp knife. This was done before the buyers to assure the meat was fresh and the blood properly drained according to Muslim tradition. The smells and sounds of death caused a momentary panic among the sheep and chickens not yet sold. Their bleats and shrill cries joined with the laughter and shouts of the buyers, the engine noise, the drunken revelry, the heat, the dust.

As Wade walked the busy passage, he noticed that more attention than normal was being cast his way. Bands of drivers paused in their talk, opened their assemblies to permit his passage, murmured greetings. Wade returned the quiet words and wondered at this courtesy offered to one so evidently a stranger.

Robards waved to him from the midst of a group clustered before their two trucks. "Far as I can make out," he said when Wade walked over, "this is a delegation of drivers. Maybe you'd better take over."

Wade offered them a greeting and saw relief appear on their faces. A gray-bearded man with the unbroken whiteness of one blinded eye said, "It is indeed the blessing of Allah that we find a healer among us who speaks our tongue."

"I am not a doctor," Wade warned.

"Doctors are bloodsuckers," spat a younger man.

"It is said you have the touch of a healer and the voice of a trusted friend," the elder continued. "There are those among us who suffer much."

Wade glanced at Robards, who responded with a grin and the words, "You best get busy making friends and influencing people. We'll leave Mikhail here with the trucks, and I'll tag along long enough to make sure everything's straight."

Wade turned back to the elder and said, "I will come."

In the course of a day, Wade found that his basic medical skills were enough to grant him entry into a secret, unseen world. Entire families, whole clans, traveled together in scores of trucks.

Their tales came out in bits and pieces as he worked. They remained banded together through desperate need. Petrol and spare parts were often impossible to find. Bandits and thieves preyed along the length and breadth of the crumbling empire. Food was a constant problem.

Children were everywhere—silent, watchful, solemn-eyed, never far from an adult. Wade counted it a major accomplishment when he was able to make one smile.

He would be brought in for one problem and find a dozen others. A child with a lingering cough had pus-covered scabs on his legs. A young woman with a poorly set finger had infections in both eyes. Pains that would have crippled a Westerner were endured in silence; here there was no other choice. Wade offered what help he could, and for a time forgot all but the pleasure of giving, of helping, of performing the only act that brought him peace.

They spoke because he showed them the quiet patience of a good listener. They told him of a country that was falling apart at the seams. They described voyages over thousands of miles of empty wilderness, the convoy guards ever vigilant for bandits who nowadays hunted prey from horseback because of a lack of petrol. They talked of distant lands where the Siberian bears and leopards prowled around city perimeters at night and filled the air with their howls. They shared their fears, which were many, and their hopes, which were few and dealt mostly with their children. Their gratitude was humbling in its intensity.

It was dark when Wade made his weary way back to the trucks. Robards received him with open arms. "Got us a regular gold mine here."

Wade dropped down beside the softly glowing stove. "Is there anything to eat?"

"Anything to eat, the man asks." With a flourish Rogue swept back a canvas tarpaulin to expose a vast pile of wealth. "We've got smoked ham. We've got dried beef. Roast lamb, boiled lamb, lamb stew. Two Turkestan carpets. Motor oil. Caviar. Pity you're not a drinking man, on account of we got ourselves almost a case of vodka and some premium Russian champagne."

"It's too much," Wade protested. "These people don't have enough even to feed themselves."

"They're traders," Robards said, settling the canvas back into place. "Traders are the same all the world over—they hate nothing worse than an unpaid debt. Let these people say thanks the only way they know how."

Before the meal was completed, a group of men appeared from the gathering shadows and demanded, "Is this the place of the healer?"

Wade raised his head from his plate and asked wearily, "Can it wait until morning?"

"Perhaps," one of the men replied, coming into the lamplight. He was heavily armed and bore a deep cut running from forehead to chin. The eye that lay in the slashed path was matted shut. "But there is also a chance that he may not see another dawn."

"Careful with this one," Robards hummed with deceptive calm, his eyes remaining on the cup in his hands.

"He's got somebody who may be dying," Wade replied.

"Man's gotta do what he's gotta do," Robards said, his tone almost bored. "Take Mikhail with you for safety's sake."

Wade thought it over, then declared, "One of your men must remain here until my return. And one of my own will accompany me."

The man hesitated only a moment, then nodded. "It will be as you say."

Their way took them far beyond the compound's periphery and into the gloom of a night untouched by public lights. Their flashlights bobbed and wove down litter-strewn paths. Twice they gave way to crowds of drunken men shouting obscenities and seeking trouble. Wade and Mikhail followed the example of their guide and stepped quietly into waiting shadows.

Their destination was a hovel that was part wooden shack, part well-patched tent. A surly voice challenged them as soon as their lights came into view. The guide shouted back and led Wade and Mikhail to where a trio of armed guards kept vigilant watch.

The guide motioned Wade through the low doorway. "In there. Your guard remains here."

Wade hesitated, until he heard a soft groan from within. He nodded to Mikhail and stepped through the door. The stench that greeted him almost drove him out again.

Wade took a gasping breath and forced himself forward. In the candlelight he saw a form curled upon a makeshift bed of burlap matting. There was no furniture. The room's only light came from a sputtering candle. The stench came both from the body on the bed and from a bucket by the far wall. Two other men remained huddled in the far corner, watching him with the dull eyes of bone weariness.

Wade squatted down beside the inert form, gently eased the body over, and saw a young man with pale European features. He turned to the pair against the opposite wall. They too had fair features and watchful Western eyes.

Wade asked, "Do you speak Russian?"

That brought a glint of humor. "What else would we be speaking?"

"What is wrong with this man?"

Instead of replying, the man cocked his head to one side and said softly in heavily accented yet understandable English, "Could this truly be an American who has found his way here?"

The scarred man stepped through the doorway, and immediately the glimmer died in the other man's eyes. He lowered his head to his knees and went on in Russian, "He has food poisoning. You would too if—"

"You talk too much," the guard hissed.

"How long has he been like this?" Wade demanded.

"Four days," the guard replied, his eyes on the other man.

"He has not been able to eat or drink anything for two," the man said to the floor by his feet.

The form on the bed shuddered, moaned, and made a retching sound. Then he subsided.

Wade turned to his satchel. He inserted a thermometer in the man's mouth, checked his pulse, took his blood pressure, fitted a stethoscope and checked lungs and heart. Then he reached for a pen and paper. As he wrote he said, "This man is extremely weak. I must set up an intravenous drip to get some fluids into him." He tore off the sheet, handed it to the guard, said, "Have one of your men take this back to the truck and give it to my friend."

"Your own man—"

"My man stays with me," Wade replied firmly.

"They will never find your truck."

"Then you must go yourself."

The guard glowered at him, started to object. Wade cut him off with a strength he only found when working. "This man is very near death. I do not know if I can save him. Every moment is precious."

The guard spat a bitter curse, then turned and stomped from the room. With electric swiftness, the man who had spoken in English leapt forward, swept up Wade's pen and paper, then returned to huddle in the far corner, his back now to the room. His companion sidled up closer to him and blocked his actions from view.

Outside the hovel the guard barked orders to his men, then marched into the night. Another man, shorter but broader in girth with arms as thick as Wade's thighs, came up and filled the doorway.

Wade prepared one injection of antibiotics and another to stop the nausea. The man made no protest as the shots were administered. Wade turned to the guard and said, "I need water and a clean towel."

The guard hesitated, then retreated a step. As soon as his motion carried him from the doorway, the other man was sliding silently across the floor toward him. But the guard had not left, rather simply told his companion what to bring. The man froze into his position beside Wade as the guard turned back around, then said in a tight voice, "Can you save my friend?"

"I will try," Wade replied, his heart in his throat. "Will you help me strip and wash him?"

"Of course." Together they rolled the inert form over, lifted off the sweat-stained clothes, then bathed the fever-heated body first with water and then with alcohol.

As they were finishing and covering the man with the cleanest of the blankets, the scarred guard pounded up the path. There was a moment's confusion at the door. Clearly the burly guard did not wish to enter too far into the room's fetid depths. As the two men traded places, the Russian slipped the square of paper from the folds of his clothes and into Wade's palm. Wade pocketed the paper with the speed of one handling a live coal.

He set up the drip, taped the needle into place, hung the plastic bag from a nail in the wooden part of the wall, and adjusted the flow. He set two further pouches beside the Russian and said, "You must change the drip when the level reaches here. Just turn this handle so, take off the empty pouch and replace it with a full one."

"I will do as you say," the man replied, his eyes never leaving Wade's face. They shouted a mute appeal.

"And bathe him once more with the alcohol," Wade said, packing up his satchel, wanting nothing more than to be away.

The guard demanded, "Will he live?"

"I will return at dawn," Wade replied. "By then we should know."

Robards listened with the stillness of a hunting cat as Wade described the scene. He then rose and with casual ease checked their periphery. "All clear. The old man's on point guard. Let's see the note."

Wade plucked the slip of paper from his pocket. It was in Russian. He translated, "We were to be delivered to new guides here. They were supposed to pay the men who have brought us this far. They never arrived. We are being held for ransom, but there is now no way for money to reach us here. Save us. We will pay and pay well. Otherwise we shall die."

Robards pulled at his lip. "You say they didn't look like locals?"

"Definitely not. They were Russian. At least the one who talked with me was."

"Did he sound educated?"

"We didn't talk that much. But his Russian was proper. And he spoke at least a little English." Wade reread the paper. "Who do you think they are?"

"Hard to say. The question is, what do you want to do now?"

"What do you mean?"

"Still your show, sport. Long as you're paying for the dance, you call the tune."

Wade examined him. "I just don't understand you."

Rogue smiled. "You're still trying to fit me into some little cubbyhole, aren't you? Still thinking that a man who lives like I do can't be bound by anything as slim as his word."

"I've never met anybody like you in my entire life," Wade replied. "So I don't know what to expect."

"Okay, back to the subject at hand. Like I say, I offered you my services. If I understand you correctly, you want to take up my offer."

"I do," Wade confirmed. "Very much."

"Right. So that leaves us with three questions. First, where are we headed? And second, do we take these joes with us? We can dicker over payment once we figure the first two out."

"You think you can free them?"

"We," Rogue corrected. "Probably. But let's stick to the ifs and the wheres just now and leave the hows for later."

"I think I want to go to Georgia and see if I can find the Red Cross survivors," Wade said slowly.

"I kinda figured that," Robards said. "Well, forward looks about as safe as backward from this point. I've checked the map. We're about as close to halfway as we can get."

"I hate the idea of leaving those men trapped there," Wade said.

"That's the spirit," Rogue said. "Dress up the chance to make a little extra change with some good old-fashioned morals, and all of a sudden the man grows some courage."

Wade threw him a look but did not challenge Rogue's statement. Instead, he confessed, "That guard with the scar really scares me."

"Good. Best chance to stay alive is to have your reflexes sharpened with a little fear."

"So what do we do now?"

"Turn in," Rogue answered. "Tomorrow's early enough to start working on a back door for our friends. You can take top duty."

As Wade was stretching out his bedroll on the truck's canvas roof, Rogue raised himself onto the top of the cab. He spent a moment watching the stars, then said, "I watched you with those folks. You've really got the touch."

Wade slid into the bag. "Touch of what?"

Robards dropped his gaze from the heavens and inspected Wade. "You remind me of somebody I once knew."

"A friend?"

"Probably woulda been," Rogue replied, "if he'd lasted long enough."

"He's dead?"

Rogue nodded. "Took a direct hit in Nam. One meant for me."

"I'm sorry."

"Threads had that way of caring for people. Like you. Had your religion, too. Big, gangly kid. Didn't talk much. All nuts and bolts of different threads, our lieutenant said. That's where he got his tag. Threads. Only time it all came together was when somebody needed help. Then he stopped looking gangly and started..." Rogue shrugged. "He just changed, is all. I don't know how else to explain it."

Rogue's features cut a sharp silhouette from the night's starry swath. "We were up on the line. All of a sudden the gooks were on us from both sides. The caps started going off like crazy. They lobbed in one of their homemade grenades, landed in a puddle maybe ten feet from me. Threads just fell on it."

Rogue's voice held the bleakness of a winter wind. "Man, what a waste. I always felt like something in me died with Threads that day. I came outta that war hating two things more than anything, waste and the lies people put on you to get you to do their dirty work. I decided I was done with waste and I was done with all the lies."

Wade hesitated, then quietly offered, "You could make the best of your friend live again."

The massive frame swiveled around. "What are you talking about?"

Again the hesitation, then, "By accepting what gave his life meaning."

There was a long silence before Rogue turned away. "Threads is dead. That's fact. It's late and I'm tired and we're sitting here jawing about stuff that neither of us knows anything about. That's fact, too. The rest is just your way of trying to fill the vacuum." He slid from the cab's roof. "Get some sleep. Tomorrow's gonna be a big one."

5

"It's too much," Allison murmured as they passed through another timeless university courtyard. "There's no way I can learn everything."

"Of course not," Cyril soothed. "No one expects you to, my dear. What we wish is to introduce you to the topics and terms."

The days had proved to be long and draining. Late each afternoon Cyril met her at Oxford, where one expert after another had droned for endless hours, until her eyelids had weighed ten pounds each, and the voices had taken on the consistency of strawberry jam. "I can't remember a thing anyone has told me."

"I confess that even I find some of these experts to be as interesting as watching snow melt."

At Cyril's direction, Jules brought the car around, and Allison sank back with a sigh of relief. "You don't seem the least bit worried by my lack of expertise."

For some reason her comment momentarily shook his aplomb. He settled into the seat beside her, and murmured, "I continue to forget that you are your father's daughter."

She leaned back in her seat. As the car left the spires of Oxford behind, Allison felt a deep familiar ache. How much this day would have meant to her dad. If only, she reflected sadly, he could have lived long enough to be a part of this with her. As the veil of fatigue rose once again, she found herself recalling another evening, one where Ben Shannon and Cyril Price had gathered with her father. It was the evening when Allison had come to realize that her father was more than the gentle, pipe-smoking professor. That John Taylor had a past filled with mystery upon mystery.

Allison Taylor had positively adored her father. She had been born long after her parents had given up hope of ever having children. From the very beginning, Allison had been her daddy's girl. Her father had been an analyst for a Washington think tank, and had taught international economics at Georgetown. Allison had decided she was going to be an analyst soon after she learned to say the word. Analysts had lots of interesting friends who dropped by day and night. They came from all over the world, and they sat and listened while Allison's father talked in the same soft patient voice he used to answer her own questions.

Allison was seven when she learned of her father's mysterious past. She had discovered that if she hid in the tiny crawl-space behind his filing cabinets, he would sometimes forget that she was there. That afternoon, Cyril Price had come to visit and found her father seated in the study with

Ben. Cyril had brought with him a problem so serious that it had creased her father's face in unnaturally severe lines. For several months after, she had suffered nightmares which began with the words Yom Kippur War. Allison had not understood much of what was said that day, but her young mind discerned that Ben and Cyril placed great weight on what they called her father's experience in the field.

There had never been any question of what Allison would study at college or what she wished to do with her life. She had yearned for the days when the two professors, father and daughter, would stroll across campus, caught up in their glorious shared world of thoughts and dreams and ideas.

Allison had reveled in college life, reinventing herself with people with no memory of her Orphan Annie days. But once a month she had eagerly returned to the easy routine of home. Her mother had stuffed her like the Christmas goose and asked about young men, questions Allison had always avoided. Her father had taken her for long rambling walks in winter-clad forests; she had returned with her cheeks burning and her ears numb and her mind filled to overflowing.

And then her father had dropped dead of a heart attack three days after her final examinations. As soon as Allison had heard her mother's broken voice, she had known. Even before the words were spoken, she had known. The dream of sharing her father's world had been shattered just as it had approached her grasp.

"My dear, is everything all right?"

"I think maybe I've gotten a little too tired." She pushed away the hurt and said, "It will be nice to see Ben again. Pop thought the world of him."

"They met in college, I believe," Cyril offered.

"My father always thought a lot of him," Allison said. "He used to say that Ben was the only one who had the strength to bring their youthful ideals to maturity." She looked over at the gentleman beside her, wondered at what secrets he carried, and how they never seemed to touch the polished surface. "Was that where you two met as well?"

"Who, your father and I? No, our own beginnings were not so commonplace." Cyril glanced at her. "He would be very proud of you, my dear."

"He was a spy for a while, wasn't he?"

Cyril smiled with genuine fondness. "When this is behind us, we shall find a quiet corner, you and I. And I shall fill you to the brim with tales of daring and intrigue."

"Once my initiation is over, right?" When Cyril did not respond, she went on, "Do you know why Ben went off to Aqaba?"

"Not exactly. Your father once told me that medical school had forced Ben into contact with suffering, and that in suffering Ben had found the one thing on earth which intelligence alone could never fathom."

"That sounds just like Pop."

"Your father's wisdom is the salve I place upon his absence from my life," Cyril said.

She said quietly, "I miss him, too."

"You have not seen Ben in quite some time, I take it. No, of course not. He has not returned to Washington since your father's funeral, as far as I am aware. Well, my dear, you will find him much altered. More than either of us might have thought possible."

"In what way?"

"The desert tends to pare men and women down to the basic components of their nature." His gaze became distant. "For some, it brings out the essence of evil; for others, the essence of good. Nowadays I find being around Ben Shannon a very unsettling experience. There is much to him which I wish I had gathered for myself."

"It's not too late to turn back," Robards reminded him the next morning. "Even if the money does sound attractive."

"It's not the money. I don't like the idea of leaving anybody trapped like that," Wade replied. "But I'm worried about taking on anything else until I finish with this assignment."

"In the first place," Robards said, "you did what you were supposed to do. Far as I see it, whatever happens next is going to be a seat-of-the-pants deal anyway. In the second place, the money's always important. Always."

"Then why are you so interested in helping out somebody who might not even be able to pay you?" Wade retorted. "They're in this fix right now because their guide did not arrive with the money."

Rogue nodded. "I've been thinking about that."

"And?"

"And I think maybe we'd be in better shape to collect if we act as guides as well as help them escape."

"You mean, take them to Tbilisi?"

"Like I said," Robards replied, "it's your show."

Wade thought it over. "There's no reason not to take them along, since we're going in that direction already."

"My thoughts exactly."

"But what makes you think you'll be paid then?"

"We," Rogue corrected. "We'll be paid. Those boys were supposed to be met by a guide here for the rest of their trip—somebody who from the looks of things decided to skip town with these other guides' payment in his own pocket. That means they have to have a contact at that end—somebody with dough. So we deliver them to their destination, collect for both jobs, then we're through with the guide-dog business. Simple."

"It sounds okay," Wade said slowly. "Who do you think those Russians are?"

Rogue busied himself with another mug of coffee.

"You know, don't you," Wade pressed. "Or you think you do."

"Just a hunch. Nothing that can't wait until we're safe and all have a little chat," Robards replied. "So what's it going to be?"

"How do we get them out?"

"Is that a yes or not?" It was Rogue's turn to push. "No need to get into details until the go-ahead's been given."

"Does that mean you think we can do it?"

"Wouldn't be wasting time talking about a target like this if I didn't."

"And we can get out of this alive?"

"Those are the only targets that count."

"We can't just leave them, then. Not if you really think we can help."

Rogue waited in catlike stillness, only his eyes showing the faintest glimmer of interest.

Wade took a breath, fought to still a sudden flutter of nerves. "You've got to promise me that nobody is going to get hurt from this."

"I've got no desire to be on the receiving end of a vendetta," Robards answered. "I've met guys like these before; they're the kind that'll follow you to the ends of the earth."

"Okay, then," Wade said. "I guess we should go ahead and do it."

"That's the spirit," Robards said, rising to full height. "I'm going to write a note that you've got to translate and somehow get into their hands."

Wade found his Russian patient much improved, and able to take a few spoonfuls of stew. "I think he is going to survive."

The guard showed no reaction, but one of the other Russians gave a feeble smile. "This is good news."

"I brought enough food for all of you," Wade said, indicating the covered pot. "Try and see if he will eat some more later. And give him as much to drink as he will take."

"I will do this," the Russian agreed. "Thank you."

"He is your friend?"

"No questions," the guard snapped.

Wade busied himself with his satchel. He gave the sick man another pair of injections, then brought out two boxes of medicine. "He needs to take one of these antibiotics three times a day for seven days. It will help protect him from secondary infection."

"Your Russian is very good," the man responded.

Wade handed over the second box. "These tablets should help ease him when the sickness is upon him. Give him one every two hours for as long as necessary." He resisted the urge to glance toward the guard. Instead he looked directly at the Russian and said, "You must carefully read the directions on the box. This is very important."

"I understand," the Russian said, his eyes suddenly filled with the same appeal as the night before.

"Tonight I shall return for a final check." Wade stood. "Until then."

By dusk all was prepared.

Wade walked toward the prisoners' hut on legs that threatened to give way at any moment. The scarred warden grunted his customary greeting and prodded open the door with his boot. "This is your last time," he declared. "The man is well enough, and I will not pay for visits and medicines which he does not require."

Wade stood his ground and spoke as Robards had instructed. "You must give him boiled water and green vegetables. He remains very weak, and if you are not careful, he could still die."

The guard's customary suspicion weakened for a moment. Sullenly he agreed, "It will be as you say. Come."

Wade forced himself forward. He found the same lantern-lit tableau as the night before. The two relatively healthy men squatted in their corner, while the third sprawled on his filthy matting. But three pairs of eyes fastened upon him with singular intensity as soon as he came into view, and Wade knew the morning's note had been read.

The same man crawled over to help as Wade inserted the thermometer. His back to the watchful guard, he looked Wade square in the eye and nodded. Once.

Wade lifted the thermometer and squinted at numbers his nerves would not let him read. "You are doing better," he said loudly and for the guard's benefit. "If you rest and are careful, you will be well."

"Thank you," the sick man said, speaking for the first time. His voice was barely above a whisper, but it held surprising strength.

"I must give you one final injection," Wade said. "You are continuing with the tablets?"

"Just as you said," the helper replied. "Three times this day, one of each, taken with twice-boiled water."

Wade swallowed and resisted the urge to glance at his watch. Time seemed to be dragging by in milliseconds. "You must—"

At that point the promised diversion arrived.

A group of extremely drunken men, Ossetians all, staggered by the front of the hut. Some sang, some argued, others pushed and laughed and milled about and created a vastly noisy confusion.

The scarred lookout snarled a curse and turned to the door. The men staked out on the porch shouted threats and received a chorus of oaths in reply. The yelling became louder still, and the guard took a half-step outside the door.

It was the moment Wade had been waiting for. His heart in his throat, he whispered, "In three hours there will be another diversion. You must break through the back wall, the tent part. Someone will be there waiting for you."

The Russian helper glanced toward the guard, who gesticulated at the drunken crowd with upraised weapon. The helper hissed, "I have leaned on the wall by the chamber pot. It is not just cloth, there is wood beyond. But it gave when I leaned. With luck we can make an opening."

"May luck be with us all," Wade agreed. With hands trembling so badly he could scarcely force a grip, he reached into his bag and extracted a hammer, a short crowbar wrapped in cloth to keep it from clanking, and a long-bladed knife. "Once the opening is seen, others will be there to assist."

The helper stuffed the three implements under the bedding. The sick man lay and watched with a burning gaze. The noise outside mounted in crescendo, then subsided as the drunks began to disperse. The helper asked, "When shall we know to act?"

The guard chose that moment to shift his bulk around. Wade tensed his muscles to still the trembling, lifted the syringe and ampule, and after two tries managed to fit the needle into the opening. He plunged the needle into the man's thigh, released the placebo injection of vitamins, swabbed the place with alcohol, and feared that at any minute the guard would notice the thundering beat of his heart.

But no alarm was sounded. Wade collected his articles, forced his legs to carry him aloft, and steeled himself to meet the guard's hostile gaze. "You must take great care that he eats only food which is fresh and cleanly prepared and drinks only twice-boiled water from a clean cup. He cannot survive a second illness."

The guard nodded. "And for payment?"

"Come and see me at the truck compound tomorrow," Wade replied as Robards had directed. "I have not yet calculated the cost of the medicines used."

As Rogue had predicted, the guard's gaze turned contemptuous. Here was a Westerner who cared so little for money that he put off payment, and thus could be easily taken. "It will be as you say."

The blast, when it came, lit the entire northern sky. Following Robards' directions, Wade had remained on guard duty by the trucks. The compound rocked to its typical night-time revelry. A band of gypsy musicians played beside a great fire, their music rising into the chill night air along with sparks and shouts and drunken laughter.

From his post atop the truck cabin, Wade looked down over the heads of the gathered throng to where two lambs roasted on slowly revolving spits. The meat glistened golden-brown in the flickering light; the tantalizing aroma drifting up past the smell of diesel fumes and road dirt.

But Wade's nerves left no room in his belly for food.

Occasionally men and women whom Wade had helped approached, offered the formal greetings of highlanders, and invited him to join them. Wade declined with quiet thanks. They did not press. There was understanding among such as these for people tending watch. And even more for people who sought the solitude of night.

Then the first flames leapt toward the distant heavens, and all revelry ceased with a series of shouts and cries.

The explosion was not loud, yet even from that distance it pushed at Wade with a powerful *whoof*. Then a great orange ball rose with deceptive slowness, illuminating the entire northern end of town before gradually dying out.

Before the light had faded, a second explosion followed. Shots rang out, sporadic at first, then a long automatic ripping sound. Then a third explosion. A fourth. And a final, larger than all the others combined. The shots continued, and

Wade worried for the man who preferred to take such risks alone.

By then the entire compound was moving. People leapt from trucks, grabbed for weapons, pointed, shouted orders, scooped up children and hustled them to safety, took up guard positions, or scrambled toward the slowly fading explosion.

Wade stayed where he was and doubted seriously that his heart rate could manage a single beat faster.

After what seemed an eternity, yet by his watch was only forty-five minutes, Robards came trotting into view. Wade resisted the urge to race up, grab his arm, and ask what happened. The big man stopped in front of Wade's truck, turned, and pointed back toward the darkened distance. "You see the fireworks?"

"How did it go?" Wade demanded quietly.

"Let's pretend," Rogue replied, his arm still pointing into the distance. "I'll play like I'm filling you in on the light-show, and you play like it's all great fun."

Wade stood on the massive front fender and shielded his eyes and searched the invisible distance. "I feel like a hood ornament."

"Better to play the fool than arouse suspicion," Robards said. "Never can tell when there are watching eyes."

"So how did it go?"

"Without a hitch," Rogue answered. "Long as I can wash off the smell of gasoline before anybody gets too close."

"Can I get down now?"

"Sure. How did it all look?"

"Like that whole side of town was being fire-bombed."

"Biggest Molotov cocktails I ever made," Rogue said with a satisfied grin. "Like to have singed my eyebrows with that last one, though. Didn't make the rag long enough, and the bang was bigger than I expected."

"You smell like a filling station."

"Yeah, got to wash this off. Come on around back." Behind the truck Robards peeled off his shirt. "Your Ossetian buddies sure know how to follow directions. The gasoline canisters and the rags were right there at the back of the empty corral, which ain't no more, in case you're interested. I set the canisters about thirty yards apart in a sort of semicircle around the front of the hut. Good thing that house was set out there by itself."

He poured soap and water into a basin, used his shirt to wash off his upper body, then stripped and doused all his clothes. "After lighting the last rag I skirted around back and watched the guards go blazing away at the night."

"I was worried when I heard the shots," Wade confessed.

"Aw, they were just shooting at smoke," Rogue said, slipping into his dry clothes, "and so blinded by looking straight at those exploding canisters they couldn't have seen me even if I'd walked up and shook their hands. I placed the second and

125

third to either side of the porch. The bombs did just what they were supposed to—sort of invited the guards out into the night before they had a chance to think what was going on."

"The Russians got out all right?"

"Yeah," Rogue said and allowed the satisfied smile to emerge again. "When I made my way round to the back of the hut, those Ossetians stood there like great bearded giants, lifting out these three scrawny dudes, then pushing the wall back inwards, making it look like all the work was done from inside."

"Just like you said," Wade offered.

Rogue nodded. "Might help us make a getaway in one piece, having it appear like they made it out on their own."

"So where are they now?"

"Somewhere safer than they were before, I expect," Rogue replied, rubbing his hair dry. "Where don't matter, long as they're at the pickup point tomorrow."

The weather was still with them the next day. Barely.

By the time the light solidified enough to be truly called another day, it revealed a sky blanketed by heavily laden clouds. The temperature did not rise as it had in mornings past; instead, the air held a biting, metallic feel. Neighboring peaks were lost beneath coverings that threatened to release their dangerous white loads at any moment.

Now there was a different quality to the compound's growing activity. Talk was muted. Men gathered and searched the sky with worried expressions. Children stayed close to their camps. There was none of the casual banter or easy loitering over breakfast fires. Gear was packed and stowed. Movements were purposeful, swift, pressured by what was clearly coming.

The scarred soldier and three of his fellows arrived soon after the dawn. They wore crossed bandoliers and fierce expressions. Two of the men stopped in front of the trucks, arms at the ready. The other pair walked back to where Rogue, Wade, and Mikhail were finishing a breakfast of bread and tea.

Wade stood to greet them. "You will take tea?"

"We will take what is ours," the man snarled in reply.

The old man rose in carefully rehearsed offense at the threat in the man's voice. "My friend has done you a service, and this is how you reply?"

A whistle from the front pair swung the scarred man around. Wade followed his gaze and was surprised to find a delegation of perhaps a dozen armed men walking toward them. An elder whose child Wade had treated two days before for a strep infection called out, "All is well with you this dawn?"

"Thank you, uncle," Wade called back. "All is well."

"The clouds herald a change for the worse," the elder went on, drawing closer. "Which way does your course take you?"

127

"Over the pass and down to Tbilisi," Wade replied.

"Then a swift departure is advised," the elder counseled. "Even a dusting of snow is enough to turn the cursed road ahead to something from your worst nightmare."

"I am grateful for your advice," Wade said.

The elder nodded and turned to face the scarred man square on. In an even voice, he announced simply, "These men are friends."

The scarred man faltered. "I came only to pay for the healer's services."

"Strange that it takes four armed men for such an errand," the elder replied.

"We..." The man hesitated, then continued. "We are missing something of great value. The healer was the only man who approached our house."

"And what might this thing of value be?"

The scarred man gestured toward Wade. "He knows."

Wade turned to Robards and forced his voice to remain even. "He is accusing us of having stolen something from him."

Rogue made an issue of carefully searching the sky before shrugging his unconcern and saying, "They can search the trucks if it'll speed things up any."

Wade turned to the scarred man and said, "The weather presses us. Even so, you are welcome to search our trucks if it will ease our departure."

"There is no need," the elder said, his eyes fixed on the scarred man.

"We have no objections," Wade replied, "if it will help maintain the peace."

The scarred man faltered, then motioned for his men to climb aboard.

"My clan will ensure your honesty," the elder warned. He gestured for several of his own men to move forward and keep watch.

"I thank you," Wade said solemnly.

"My child is much improved," the elder replied. "It is a duty for friends to share the road's burdens."

Within a few minutes the four men were again gathered at the back of the first truck. The elder demanded, "Did you find what you seek?"

"There was nothing," the scarred man muttered, his gaze smoldering. He started forward, beckoning for his men to follow, only to be stopped by the elder and his clansmen.

"There is now the unsettled matter," the elder said, "of payment for the healer's services."

Past winters had chewed great hunks from the road, leaving potholes of ominous depth and edges that were ragged and crumbling. The trucks climbed in an unending stream, grinding abused gears and belching streams of black smoke that rose to join the clouds hovering overhead. Razor-edged peaks jutted aggressively to every side.

They had long since left behind the last sign of green. On either side, in place of trees, loomed piles of crushed rock and scrabble, careless waste heaps dropped by departing glaciers. Their brethren glinted gray-white and ominous upon neighboring peaks, and watched the passing of men with timeless silence. This was their world, cold and harsh and as forbidding as the load that weighed down the clouds.

Wade spotted Mikhail's arm emerging from the truck window ahead to point them both into a lay-by. They passed two round-shouldered buses disgorging weary streams of passengers. In the distance the River Terek poured a milky-white waterfall between two great daggerlike sentinels and down into a chalk-colored pool. The water was almost lost beneath the thundering spume.

Rogue halted his truck beside a battered farm wagon pulled by a muttering tractor. Wade followed his lead and eased in close to the tractor's other side. He joined the pair at the pool's edge, and wondered at the calm with which both Mikhail and Robards looked out over the creamy waters.

Mikhail pointed far in the distance toward the two greatest peaks in the Caucasus range, twin edifices that rose and rose and were finally swallowed by the clouds. "Together they are called El'Brus," he said, "the king and queen of the Caucasus. Five thousand six hundred meters, and still volcanic. The highland Balkars lived at the base there since the dawn of time. But they were all shipped to Khazakstan by the butcher Stalin, may his name be erased. They are now trickling home in twos and threes, with fifty years of bitterness to unleash on those who now occupy their ancestral homes. Today the area belongs to the Karbardino-Balkarija Autonomous Republic and is a part of Russia. For how long, as the Balkar numbers grow once more, is in the hands of fate."

Wade translated for Robards, who nodded thoughtfully, as though taking it all in. He then turned around and said, "I think that should give them enough time."

"Who?" Wade demanded. "For what?"

"Let's hit the road," he replied. "We're racing nature today."

Wade walked to his truck, started the motor, backed out, then drew up to within inches of Robards' bumper. That way, the highway traffic would be forced to grant them both entry at the same time. Together they shouldered the trucks out into an empty pocket, and Wade rammed his way up through the complaining gears. The endless and ever-changing vista of rocks and ancient ice rose and fell before him as the road clambered up and up and up.

Suddenly the covering that separated the cabin from the back of the truck parted slightly, and a voice almost stopped his heart with, "It appears that you are as good at escapes as you are at healing."

Wade whirled about and saw it was the Russian who had helped him care for the sick man. He eased back and fought the wheel around yet another hairpin curve. "You made it, then."

"Yuri Bazarov, at your service," the man said. "And most certainly in your debt."

They encamped toward dusk under a sullen sky. Rogue parked them as far from the gathering of tired and dusty transports as the encircling river would allow. There were a few quiet greetings from some of the other trucks, but no more offers to draw nearer and join in the comfort of a larger group. By then their habits were known. They were marked as loners and left in peace.

While Mikhail made their evening meal, Rogue and Wade worked to construct three tunnels in Wade's truck, walled and roofed by boxes of medicines and floored with the extra beddings. A cramped space was also cleared at the back of the truck, where the trio could gather and sit upright.

The trio of Russians made no protest when Robards suggested they not show themselves, nor even leave the trucks, until well after dark. It was best to expect trouble, Rogue said through Wade, than to have trouble catch them unawares. Yuri spoke for them all when he replied in his rough English that the tunnels were a far better home than the one they had left behind.

After finishing his preparations, Rogue sidled over to where Wade was standing. "Hope you don't mind if I handle the business end of this setup myself," he said. "Having more experience in it and all."

"I've already told you," Wade replied. "I don't want anything."

Rogue inspected him. "What's gotten under your skin?"

"I just wish I knew who they were."

"Three guys on the lam," Rogue answered. "Nothing's changed since we cut them loose except their address."

Wade looked up. "Do you think they're criminals?"

"Not any more than anybody forced to try and survive under impossible conditions," Rogue rejoined. "Bad laws make the best of men crooks in somebody's eyes."

Wade turned his attention back to the fire. "I wish I knew that for sure."

"They're right over there, sport. All you've got to do is ask," Rogue said and turned away.

As Robards climbed into the back of the truck, a figure appeared out of the gloom. He wore the tattered yet clean shirt and trousers and mismatched jacket of a man making a formal call. He clutched the brim of a sweat-stained fedora with both hands. A heavy-duty flashlight protruded from one jacket pocket. "Healer," he called softly. "The blessings of Allah upon you."

"Peace upon you as well."

"My wife has been taken ill. She is with child."

"I am not a doctor," Wade warned, repeating the familiar litany.

"You are all there is," the man replied simply.

Wade reached into the back of his truck for his

133

makeshift satchel. "I will be back as soon as I can," Wade said to a watchful Mikhail. He walked over to where the man was waiting. "Let us go."

It was over an hour before Wade returned, drained more from his lack of medical knowledge than from giving what little help he could. Wade ate dinner with Mikhail while a soft murmur of voices and the muted clink of dinnerware sounded from the back of one truck.

Wade set his dinner plate aside to find the old man's gaze resting steadily on him. "The man was Ingush," Mikhail stated.

"Yes."

"Ossetian and Chechen you treated at our last stop. And now Ingush. Do you seek to make friends of all the world?"

"I saw only need," Wade replied simply.

The old man inspected him. "You are a religious man?"

Wade's fatigue was the greatest truth elixir he had ever known. He shook his head. "I try to be. I wish I were more so."

"What does this mean?"

"I believe. But God has always seemed distant to me."

The old man turned his face back to the fire and was silent for a long while, before saying quietly, "My people claim to be the oldest on earth, with lines that still run pure. Our elders tell how we are descended from the Narts, a tribe from before the measure of time, half giant and half human. There are ruins of Nart villages hidden among our secret mountain valleys. These I have not seen, but my father, he walked as I ride by truck. He spoke of these as real, and I carry his stories with me. Now I am old and face the unseen door. And I seek what before I was content to leave in the hands of priests. I, too, find no answers, save one."

He aimed his gaze back toward Wade. "To seek is in itself a meritorious act. And sometimes the One who is sought speaks when we are not listening. I have watched you as you work your arts of healing, and I have seen a face that knows what I know not. Perhaps you seek what others have found, while all the time the great Lord speaks to you in a different tongue and at a different time."

Their conversation was stopped by the sound of Robards calling from the back of the truck. Wade stood and walked over. Rogue said, "We had a little trouble in the beginning, but this guy's English improves with practice. He's got a question he wants to ask you."

There was a silence, then the one called Yuri spoke up in Russian.

"How do we know we can trust this man?"

"First, I want to know who you are," Wade responded, "and what you are running from."

"We flee an impossible life in a hopeless situation," Yuri replied vaguely.

"I have a right to know," Wade insisted stubbornly.

Yuri exchanged glances with the other two and received some form of silent communication, because he turned back and said, "We are all engineers. We have grown tired of working for ten different bosses, and being ordered to do work made meaningless. We are weary of being paid with paper which will not buy enough to feed our families."

A knell sounded deep and ghostly within him. "Where do you go?"

"We have been promised work," Yuri replied. "Work and enough money to offer our families a life. In the south. That is all we know, and all we know to tell." He nodded at Wade. "And now I ask my own question. How can we trust this giant of a man to do as he says?"

"He is a stranger to me as well," Wade replied. "I met him only a week ago and hired him on the advice of an ally to bring me here. He has done as he said, and more. I believe him to be a man of his word."

The three huddled together to converse among themselves. Then Yuri questioned, "And he will take us where we wish to go?"

As Wade translated, Rogue slid easily from the truck and arched his back. "That's enough talk for one night. We got you gents out, we brought you here. Seems to me that's about the best answer you could find. As to taking you where you want to go, I'll cart you to the gates of Hades itself, long as I don't have to follow you inside." Rogue inspected the darkness, then added, "Looks safe for you three to come on out and stretch your legs."

Yuri and the man who had been sick slid from the truck and followed Rogue out into the surrounding shadows. The third man, the one who had never spoken, walked around to the far side of the fire and sat looking out over the rushing waters. The cloud blanketed all heavenly illumination, leaving only the faintest of ghostly lights to show where the river was. The water's muted roar was a constant call, spoken in the language of the mountains, a tongue held forever secret from the minds and hearts of man.

Wade skirted the fire and squatted down beside the loner. "May I ask your name?"

There was a pause, then, "Ilya."

"You were a prisoner?"

Hard eyes turned his way. "Why do you say this?"

Wade pointed a hesitant finger. "Your hair. And you've lost a lot of weight. Your head looks shrunken around your eyes."

A smirk showed through the shadows. "You are observant. Too observant, perhaps, for your own good."

Wade did not know what to say, so he squatted there in silence. His knees hurt to remain in that position, but something told him it was best not to move just then.

"I was convicted of the crime of trying to leave a country that did not want me in the first place." The man's tone was mild, almost conversational. "I was a technician at one of the military air compounds. A civilian. When Estonia became

137

independent, Russians like myself suddenly became lepers. My wife could not go alone into the marketplace. Nobody would sell her anything. Passers-by would spit upon her and my children. They held elections, and said that because we were Russian we could not vote. No matter that I had been born in Estonia. And my wife. And our children. No matter that I had no other home. We were aliens, and it was only a matter of time before we would be kicked out. So we decided to leave for the West. But when we arrived at the Finnish border, the guards took one look at my documents and sent me to prison."

Wade eased himself down, then ventured quietly, "Because you were a nuclear engineer trained to work on nuclear bombs carried by the Russian fighter aircraft stationed there."

"Too observant," the man repeated quietly.

"I have heard the stories," Wade persisted, "of how Arab states are offering great wealth to attract nuclear engineers. And how Russia and some of the other states have responded by making it illegal for their nuclear technicians to leave the country."

There was a long silence, then, "They took me to Patarei, an old czarist fortress on the outskirts of the capital, Tallinn. For three weeks I was kept in a cage too small for me to even stand up. They fed me slops from a bucket. There was no light, no blanket, a wooden plank for my only furniture. Then I was transferred to a cell with two others, a teenager jailed for three years for stealing twenty rubles and another lad sentenced to two years for stealing a tire. We were let out for fifteen minutes each day. We could walk around a yard with a thousand other men. They played rock music in the yard to keep us from talking. The music was so loud it left my head ringing all the rest of the day."

He fished a cigarette from his pocket. The lighter's flame illuminated haunted eyes. "My wife made a tremendous fuss with the military commander, and he brought my case up before the local tribunal. Finally I was released. Three nights later we escaped into Russia. The Estonian border guards were only too glad to see the backs of one more Russian family. Our papers weren't even checked."

"And now you will go build bombs for the Arab terrorists," Wade said quietly. "And create more suffering for more people."

The Russian pulled hard on his cigarette, sucking his cheeks into hollow caverns. "Tonight my wife and children sleep in a refugee camp in Austria. The same is true for my two friends. We go to where we can make for them a home."

"And what of all the homes your work will destroy? What of the world your children will inherit?" Wade kept his voice quiet, insistent. "You no longer even have patriotism to justify your actions."

"Go away, little man," he said, tossing his cigarette into the fire. "Your questions I do not need."

Wade stood, turned around, and caught sight of Robards' gleaming eyes watching him from across the camp.

The night closed in upon them with a mist so heavy it was almost solid. Every open surface was swiftly drenched. The air was bitter with a wet cold that seeped to the bones. The river's muted roar and the call of other watchmen who could no longer see one another were the only sounds that pierced the stillness. Wade took the first watch, and every few minutes emerged from the cabin's relative dryness to circle the trucks. He was careful to stay close enough to keep touch with the cold metal. His flashlight's beam showed nothing except an impenetrable white wall.

The mist isolated him, for some reason making him think of home. It was a past so distant from that particular place and time that it felt as though it belonged to another person. Wade smiled to himself and knew it was both true and not true. He was different, and yet somehow the same. He carried his thoughts with him into his bedroll, and allowed the voices of his mind and heart to lull him to sleep.

While blackness still reigned, Wade shot awake to the sound of hammering and shouting. He clambered down from the back of the truck just as Robards bolted over the neighboring tailgate, a flashlight in one hand and gun in the other. "What the blazes?"

They came around front to find the man whose

wife Wade had treated the night before beating on the hood with the butt of his automatic rifle while Mikhail watched over him, gun at the ready. "There is little time," the man said. "I saw no movement about your trucks, and my wife said I should come."

Wade was still foggy with sleep. "Time for what?"

"The air begins to freeze," the man replied. "Death stalks above."

"Look!" Robards said. The beam of his flashlight reflected on tiny pinpoints of white. Frozen ice-motes began to dust the windshield. "This what he's talking about?"

"Yes."

"Tell him whatever debt he owed us has just been wiped from the books," Robards said, opening his door and swinging inside. "Let's move out!"

Wade turned back to the stranger. "My friend says—"

The man hefted his gun to stop Wade. "May Allah bless your way with safety, healer. Until our next meeting, farewell!" He turned and vanished into the night.

"Get that truck started!" Rogue yelled over the roar of his own motor.

Yuri's head protruded from the canvas curtain as Wade clambered aboard. "What is it?"

Wade stamped upon the starter pedal, pumped the gas, nursed the choke as the motor faltered, caught, and held. The engine bellowed, eased, roared again. Wade slammed the gears home as Rogue's truck started forward. Then he shouted back over his shoulder, "Snow!"

141

6

As the morning light strengthened into brooding grayness, the trucks crested a rise and confronted two vast cliffs. A narrow slit between the mountains grudgingly permitted passage to both the river and the road. At that moment the softly falling veil of snow lifted unexpectedly, granting passage to brilliant shafts of early sunlight.

Taking it for a signal, Rogue pulled his forward truck into a lay-by nestled close to the right-hand cliff.

By the time Wade climbed from his cabin, Mikhail already had the stove out and was boiling a pot of water for tea. Wade accepted bread torn from a loaf, took more to where the Russians sat in his truck, then joined Robards by the fire.

"Five-minute break," Rogue said, "then we make like the wind. Ask the old man how long the gorge is."

"Twelve kilometers," Mikhail replied when Wade had translated. "This is the Daryal Gorge, known among my people as the Gates of Alan. It is the entrance to South Ossetia, the lands now usurped by the Georgian bandits."

"Georgia," Robards remarked with evident satisfaction. "Does that mean the road starts descending on the other side?"

Mikhail poured tea into glasses and set them by the fire for the tea leaves to steep and settle to the bottom. "Beyond the Gates lies yet one challenge more. After that is safety, at least from the beasts of ice and snow. But ahead we still have the two harshest tests of all. This one first. Here, the road climbs along one cliff wall. Soon it will be a thousand meters up to the heavens and a thousand meters down to the river. Wind blows through the gorge like a funnel, seeking to pluck us from the road and hurl us into the waters below."

"The old man's a real source of light and joy this morning," Robards said, picking up his glass and sipping noisily. "Notice there's no wind."

"Not now," Mikhail warned ominously, "but there is snow. And the highland folk say that one follows the other as smoke follows fire."

"Great," Robards said, not the least affected by the news. "Anything else?"

"Rocks," Mikhail replied. "The winter beasts pluck them from on high and hurl them at the unsuspecting. In the last century a rock fell that weighed a thousand tons and closed this road for more than two years."

Rogue grinned. "If we meet one that big, we won't have long to worry about it."

Mikhail did not wait for a translation. He pointed ahead to a castle perched on the Terek's riverbank just before the entrance to the gorge. "The Fortress of Daryali. A thousand years ago, a line of castles and towers reached all the way across the Caucasus. When invaders swept down from the Russian steppes, fires were lit on their flat roofs to warn the Georgian and Ossetian kings."

"A line of fire and stories from a thousand years ago told like they happened last week. How can anybody not love this place?" Rogue picked up the last three glasses and headed for the trucks. "If you want a second glass, drink fast. Time to go meet the wind."

As though on schedule, the moment they wheeled back into the staggered line of vehicles, the snow closed in. Just before entering the gorge, the road passed over a shaky wooden bridge. Beyond it, the pace of traffic picked up, as though all those who drove before them were pushing themselves to the limit, racing to make it through before the denizens of winter conquered all.

Twisting rock formations rose like guardians of the high kingdom, sweeping in and out of view as the snow danced a silent warning to their passage.

Then the walls closed in around them.

They emerged into another world.

Brilliant sunshine fell upon a wide-open valley of verdant green. A small village of ancient wood and stone spread out in the distance. A flag fluttered in the welcoming breeze, gaily announcing the Georgian border.

Wade slowed in time to Robards' truck and stared out in awe as gusts of wind blew the meadows into paths of frothy silver-green.

Five hours it had taken them to traverse the twelve-kilometer gorge. Five hours of heart-stopping drops, his wheels barely able to remain on the crumbling road. As Mikhail had predicted, the wind had started soon after their entry, and had grown steadily fiercer until it buffeted his truck with angry fists.

Passing other trucks became the stuff of nightmares.

Without warning the veil of blustering snow would part to reveal a marauding behemoth bearing down upon him, horn blaring, the driver's face pressed against the windshield just as Wade himself drove. He had no choice but to move farther and farther toward the verge and the three-thousand-foot drop beyond. Several times he felt the weightless sensation of tires scrambling for a hold on a crumbling edge.

And now this.

Gratefully Wade followed Rogue off the road and onto a lay-by crammed with trucks and people. Laughing, joking, gesticulating, jabbering people. Pointing back up behind them and shouting abuse at the closeness of their escape. Passing communal bottles around. Sharing cigarettes and tea and laughter. Joined together by the lightheaded freedom of having made it through.

145

There were several friendly cries as Wade opened his door and slid down onto legs that seemed barely able to support his weight. He recognized several former patients, including the Ingush driver whose wife had been ill.

He walked unsteadily toward them, grinning as their laughter rose at his faltering gait.

The Ingush offered Wade his hand. "The blessings of Allah upon you, healer."

Wade accepted it in the manner of the East, barely placing pressure upon the man's fingers. "I would not do that again for all the tea in China."

That announcement brought an extended burst of hilarity. "It is far worse for the likes of us," said a stranger, whose own face was split in a gap-toothed grin. "We knew what it was we faced. You entered seeking only adventure."

Wade turned around and looked up at the malevolent peaks. They were enshrouded by clouds that reached from earth to heaven's heights. Here was light and air and the comfort of new friends. There was only darkness and danger.

"The upper realms are closed for yet another year," one spoke, his voice subdued as he too surveyed the higher reaches. "Winter has now come, and where she rules, none may enter and leave again."

"Take, healer," someone said, and offered him a bottle of vodka. "Give some warmth to your bones."

"I do not drink, but thank you just the same," Wade replied.

"If that's what I think it is," Rogue said, walking up behind them, "I'd sure like a slug."

The sound of a foreign tongue provoked yet more hilarity. Rogue grinned to all and sundry, took a long belt from the bottle, roared his satisfaction as he passed it on, and received back-thumping laughter in return.

"Ask your friend what he thinks of the Russian highways now," someone said.

"Not a bad stroll in the park," Rogue replied when Wade had translated. "Coupla times I thought I might have to grow wings real fast."

Wade noticed the Ingush driver standing beyond the group's edge and motioning to him. Wade excused himself and walked over. "Your wife?"

"She is better, thanks be to Allah. I wish to tell you, healer, there is a border station up ahead."

"I have seen the flag."

"Indeed, the Russian dogs who guard this side are eager to rob all who are not seen as regular travelers. Their bribes are heavy at the best of times, but strangers bearing two laden trucks and Western papers will be picked to the bone."

Wade sobered. "What would you suggest?"

"We are seven trucks," the man replied. "Join with us, near the middle, and let two of us drive. We will declare no more than usual, and you can pay your share of the bribes."

"Wait here," Wade said and turned back to find Rogue's piercing gaze holding steady upon him. At Wade's gesture Robards slipped from the group and joined them.

"It's a risk," Robards said when Wade told him of the man's offer, "that they'll save us from the Russians and rob us themselves."

Wade did not disagree. "Even if they don't, we'll pay more than our share of the bribes."

"So what do you think, sport?"

"I say go with them," Wade replied. "You ride in one truck, Mikhail in the other, and I'll hide out in back with the Russians."

"Sounds good." Robards inspected him with a grin. "Wish you could hear yourself."

"What are you talking about?"

"It's been coming on so slowly, you haven't noticed it, have you?"

"Noticed what?"

"You're growing up," Robards replied. "Getting confidence in yourself."

Wade took a step back. "That's silly."

"Sure it is." Robards turned back to the group and the bottle. "Go tell your friend it's fine by me. I've still got a thirst to work off."

They joined the endless line of trucks at the border crossing, one of a group of nine, all driven by dark-skinned Ingush traders. Mikhail sat uneasily in the passenger seat beside the bearded hawk-nosed stranger, showing with every movement of his ancient frame that he neither trusted nor wished to be near this man whose clansmen were his enemies. If the Ingush noticed Mikhail's unease, he gave no sign. He spoke not at all except to turn and solemnly greet Wade, who crouched

148

behind the canvas awning where Yuri had formerly rested. All three Russians were safely holed up in their small tunnels, scarcely breathing.

Suddenly Mikhail hissed a faint warning, and ducked under the dashboard. Hidden by shadows, Wade craned and caught sight of the scarred man standing with two other guards a few paces ahead of the border station. The trio eyed each truck with undisguised hostility, searching for alien Western faces. Wade ducked back into darkness.

The Ingush driver murmured, "Was he not one who came to your truck in the compound and accused you of stealing?"

"Indeed so. Are they looking this way?"

"Why should they?" The Ingush showed vast unconcern. "We are just another cursed Russian truck, barely able to crawl forward another kilometer, driven by a simple trader, in line with his clansmen, bearing meager goods and too many hungry mouths."

"You say it well."

"It is the chant we use before all border stations," the man explained, "one I have heard since before I could walk."

Wade ventured another glance. He could no longer see the scarred man. "Are they gone?"

"They seek you farther back along the line. Who are they?"

"Chechen," Mikhail answered for them both.

"Then they would skin their own clansman for the dregs of his cup," the Ingush replied. "Did one of their own die after you treated him?"

"I don't know," Wade replied truthfully.

"Only two things would force a Chechen to brave the Daryal Gorge at winter's onset," the Ingush said. "Revenge or money."

"The healer is not a thief," Mikhail declared fiercely.

"That much is clear," the Ingush agreed. "Seldom have I seen such an honest face even upon an infant. What brings you to our land, healer?"

"The call of God," Wade replied, grateful for the shadows that hid his reddened face.

"Ah, a holy man," the Ingush said, nodding. "I saw the sign of peace upon you as you dealt with the pains and sicknesses of others."

Mikhail showed surprise. "A Muslim who pays homage to a Christian?"

"I saw what I saw," the Ingush replied stubbornly. "My heart saw as well. The healer is a man who gives from that which is beyond man's vision."

Wade let the flap fall, and spent long minutes inspecting himself in the mirror of the Ingush trader's words.

The village of Kazbegi was rimmed by water and ringed by mountains. It crowned a graceful hillock at one end of the long green valley. Peaks so high they remained white all year round encircled the village, towering giants that glinted proudly in the afternoon sun. The village houses clustered up tightly together, seeking strength and solace from one another in the face of such overwhelming might. The dwellings climbed the hill in orderly rows, their rooftops making a series of ocher steps up to the three church spires.

"The Kazbegi do not care overmuch for us," the Ingush said as he drove on past the graceful village. "They permit our trucks space only beyond the village. They give us air and water, at least until they find a way to make us pay for these as well. For all else we are charged prices higher than the surrounding mountains. What we can do without, we leave until after the true descent is made."

The truck compound was nothing more than a large field too rocky to permit planting. A trio of armed men shouted orders which were lost in the motors' perpetual racket and pointed them to an unoccupied corner. The Ingush gathered their trucks in a tight cluster, with Wade's two trucks at the center. Only when the engines coughed their last did the first trader climb down on tottery legs. It was the man whose wife Wade had treated. Following close on his heels was Rogue.

The big man asked when Wade had descended, "Since we're all here and breathing, I take it the guys didn't spot you."

"I was in the back, and Mikhail was under the dash. What about you?"

Rogue grinned. "It's surprising what a tiny ball this body can make when it has to." He motioned toward the trader. "Tell the man we're in his debt up to our eyeballs."

Wade said to the Ingush, "Our gratitude will remain with us all our days."

"A day when the Chechen dogs are outsmarted is a day to be remembered with great relish," the trader replied. "What did you do to gather such wrath upon your heads?"

Wade's Ingush driver answered for him. "He was gracious enough to treat one of their own, who did not have the grace himself to survive."

Rogue broke in and said, "I sure wish we had the cash to pay for all their bribes."

"I've got an idea," Wade said and ran back to his truck. He reappeared a moment later with a box under each arm, which he offered to the trader. "We shall never be able to repay your kindness. But please do us the honor of accepting this small token of our eternal gratitude."

The trader took one box, split the top with a practiced motion, and widened his eyes at the sight. "Medicines."

"Antibiotics," Wade agreed. "All within the dates of use, as the numbers stamped here state to any who can read the Western script. They should bring you a good price."

"As would gold itself in the right places." A murmur of agreement rose from the gathered traders. The Ingush straightened, accepted the second box, and said, "A worthy gift from worthy friends. I and my clansmen thank you, healer."

"Smart," Rogue agreed. "A good use of what we've got here."

The trader looked around the gathering of his

fellows and apparently received an affirmative, for he said to Wade, "We shall rest here for an hour and then drive up and through the Krestovy Pass."

Wade translated for Rogue, who asked, "They'll take on the pass in the dark?"

The trader pointed toward the cloud-enshrouded mountains behind them. "Tonight the might of winter will reach out to ensnare all this valley and perhaps the pass as well. I would rather drive through a clear night than yet another day of snow, and this one at a thousand meters higher than the gorge."

"Sounds like good advice to me," Rogue said. "You up for another push?"

Wade turned back to the trader and asked, "We would be beholden if a place might be found for our trucks in your caravan."

"There is always room for friends," the trader replied.

"I have yet another request to make," Wade said. "We shall be perhaps the last convoy through this valley before winter. I would like to see if there is a doctor in the village in need of medicines and equipment."

As one, the traders showed astonishment. "You would give such as this away?"

"If he cannot pay," Wade said gamely. "These articles have been given to my charge in order to help doctors in need."

There was a moment's amazed silence, then the driver of Wade's truck proclaimed with pride, "Here is a legend in the making. I shall

153

take him myself, and call myself fortunate this day."

They took one of the Ingush trucks so as to draw less attention in case the scarred man and his fellows still scouted the road. Rogue and Wade refused the traders' offer of help with unloading the supplies. They used their movements as a chance to bring the hidden Russians news and food and water.

The Ingush driver of Wade's truck remained puffed with the privilege of taking him into the village. His enthusiasm infected all the clan, even the children, and they were seen off with waves and happy chatter. Rogue watched the proceedings in brooding silence. His only comment was that if Wade wanted to spend free time driving some more, that was his choice. But it was clear he did not approve of Wade drawing unnecessary attention their way.

Wade hunched below the dash, keeping only his eyes up high enough to watch as the road narrowed and entered the hamlet. The streets were cobblestoned, constricted, and steep. Three times the Ingush stopped and asked for directions, only to be greeted with hostile suspicion. The fourth time, he explained in desperation that he bore a friend approaching death. This time he was reluctantly pointed toward the hovel that contained the village's meager clinic.

"I would not have you lie on my behalf," Wade

chided him as they drew up and stopped before a building whose wide doors indicated previous duty as a stable.

"Do not worry yourself," the trader replied cheerfully. "All men approach death with each breath, healer. You above others should know the truth of such words."

They scouted the street before descending and pushing open the stubborn door. They were greeted with a scratchy female voice declaring from a second room, "Too late, too late! My hours are known by all."

The trader began, "We do not—"

The woman remained unseen as she interrupted with, "I too must sleep and eat and breathe air not infected by the sickness of all. Come back tomorrow."

Wade looked around what apparently served as both waiting area and examining room. As with many of the clinics he had visited in outlying Russian villages, the chamber was pitifully bare. A metal dish contained two ancient glass syringes. The sterilizing tray held perhaps half a dozen needles and a few battered instruments. The medicine shelves were almost empty.

"You must not tell me that the patient shall not last the night unless it is true. I shall not be brought out on a fool's errand." An overweight woman in a stained white jacket strode into the room, and stopped at the alien sight of an Ingush trader alongside a foreigner. "What do you want?"

"Only to help," Wade replied.

"You stay," the trader told him, and headed for the door. "It is not safe for you to be seen."

The woman showed growing confusion. "You are sick?"

Wade shook his head. "Do you need supplies?"

"Ah, another trader bearing the dregs of Russian medicine," she muttered bitterly. Shadows of fatigue gouged deep crevices under her eyes. "Save your strength. I have no money with which to buy even aspirin."

"Then I shall give it to you," Wade replied.

The hostility hardened into anger. "Do not joke with me," she snapped. "I face yet another winter with no news of shipments which are six months late. Six months! Do you know what it is like to treat people with hot water and herbs?"

"Yes," Wade said, and turned as the trader brought in the first load. "Here you will find analgesics. In these two boxes, sterile solutions. And here are two hundred disposable syringes. They can be boiled and reused, but only the needles can go into your sterilizer. The syringes will melt."

The trader departed with a broad grin for the doctor's growing confusion.

"Who are you?" she demanded.

"It does not matter," he replied. When the trader reappeared, Wade went on. "Ampicillin, one hundred doses. Another hundred sulfas. Urinary tract medicines, digestive tract, anesthetics, both local and general. Can you read directions in English?"

The woman sought support from the doorjamb. "You are giving these to me?"

"Yes."

"Do not jest," she pleaded, her voice touched by desperation. "I tell you, I have no money. These people are too poor to pay."

The trader straightened from setting down his load, and declared solemnly, "Woman, I am Ingush. The Ingush do not lie. I tell you truthfully, this is a man of God. Take him at his word." He turned and left the room.

"Here are a few instruments," Wade said. "Not many. Thermometers, scalpels, probes, needles, and gut. I hope it is enough."

"Enough," the woman murmured, her eyes on the boxes.

"This is the last of them," the trader announced, depositing his final load.

"All I ask," Wade told her, "is that whenever a trader or his family enter here, be it night or day, winter or summer, you will give to them from the best of what you know and have."

A single tear escaped from the woman's eye and made its way down the broad features. She whispered, "It will be as you say."

They arrived at the entrance to Krestovy Pass just as the setting sun turned the gathering clouds to burnished gold. "The Georgians call this the Djvari Pass," the Ingush driver explained to Wade. "Djvari means cross. It is here that the Terek River, which flows into Russia, and the

Aragvi, which flows through Georgia, are both born."

From his perch behind the driver, Wade saw glaciers clinging to every visible cliffside. Their passage had carved boulder-strewn scores deep into the alien landscape. From the glaciers' lower reaches poured great flows of whitish-green waters, which gathered in pools and lakes and streams in every direction as far as Wade could see.

The trader had proudly taken charge of Wade's truck before the final onslaught on the pass. Wade had protested, not from a desire to drive himself, but for the sake of the three Russians who remained cooped up within their cramped tunnels. But the Ingush would have none of it. The man of God did not know what lay ahead, he had proclaimed. Otherwise he would not wish to see, much less drive himself. With a nod from Rogue, Wade had agreed.

Out of respect for his years, Wade had insisted that Mikhail take the passenger seat. After checking that the Russians were doing as well as could be expected after almost seven hours in their stuffy burrows, Wade lifted the canvas awning up and out of the way. This would allow more air to filter through and also grant Wade an uninterrupted view.

The road leveled out for its final advance upon the pass. They detoured around what before had been an avalanche tunnel, now smothered by a rockslide so large its lower stones dwarfed the trucks that crawled past. The road deteriorated to a crumbling track, often submerged beneath swiftly running waters. Twice there were great crashing booms as rocks loosened and fell somewhere out of sight. All jollity vanished from the Ingush trader. He drove at a snail's pace and with a white-knuckled intensity.

The road skirted a giant snowdrift frozen into place for countless decades, with only its tip carved away so that vehicles could crawl past. Then came a series of hairpin curves with drops so savage Wade had to struggle not to turn away. And then, with a shout from the trader, the road began to descend. Even Mikhail sighed his relief as descent turned steeper and it became clear that in truth the highest reaches were now behind them.

It was then that the first snowflake descended through the deepening gloom to coast across their windshield. The trader laughed and pointed and said, "See, healer? This is your doing!"

"That is the silliest thing I have ever heard," Wade replied without rancor, glad only to be heading downward.

But the trader was not to be dissuaded. "Allah has protected us. This I know in my bones. Why else would the snows have been held back for our passage?"

Wade was saved from a reply by their line of trucks pulling into a rubble-strewn lay-by. Wearily he clambered down from his perch and took in great drafts of the icy-fresh air.

The Ingush trader approached. "Three hours ahead, the road enters the last Chechen enclave this side of the mountains."

Wade called Rogue over and explained what the trader had said. Robards directed, "Ask him what he would do in our place."

Clearly the man had given the matter great thought. "Two hours further descent will have you beyond winter's reach, so you should have no further need of our help. There is a track which turns off just before the enclave is reached; it is used by Ossetian traders who have no wish to deal with the Chechen."

"I know it well," Mikhail said, coming up alongside.

"There are wars and rumors of wars in these southern Ossetian lands," the Ingush warned.

Wade translated for Rogue, who nodded once. "Thank the man and tell him we'll take his advice."

"What about the wars?"

"If you've got to choose between the bogeyman you can see and the one you can't," Robards answered, "go for the one who might not even be there."

Wade turned back to the trader. "Our debt to you mounts with each passing hour."

The trader who had driven for Wade shouldered his way forward. "The tale of the man of God will brighten firesides for years to come. There is no debt. May Allah guide your footsteps and light your path forever, healer.

These days I shall carry with me to the grave."

It was hot in Amman, hotter than Allison had imagined possible for early autumn. The sun was a blazing orb overhead. Shadows cut spiked angles from the ground. There were no clouds. The air was dry and dusty and sucked the moisture from her skin. Allison walked down the sidewalk outside the airport terminal and searched desperately for a familiar face.

"Over here, Miss Taylor," called a testy voice.

Allison squinted through the glare and found herself looking at a squat little man in a sweat-stained white shirt, a handkerchief knotted over his bald head. "Were you talking to me?"

With an exasperated sigh the little man waddled over, grasped her two cases, and lugged them toward a vintage taxi. "Indeed. Now come along."

The car had the suspension of a trampoline. Every bump in the road threatened to send her through the roof. The driver was a dull-faced Arab who neither returned her greeting nor looked her way. He drove with more use of his horn than his brakes. They raced out of the airport complex, took the highway turnoff on two wheels, and barreled southward at speeds Allison did not care to think about.

The little man swiped the handkerchief from his head and used it to mop his peeling red face. "There was a problem at the clinic," he said with undisguised annoyance. "I was appointed stand-in."

"I'm sorry; I don't believe I caught your name..."

"Smathers. British Embassy. Doesn't matter, really. With luck we shall never need to see each other again."

"You would have preferred it if they had sent someone else," Allison guessed.

"I have long since given up dwelling upon the decisions of the powers-that-be," he said with asperity.

"This wasn't my idea," Allison told him.

"You cannot imagine how much reassurance I find in that," he snapped.

"You don't think this is going to work, do you?" Allison demanded. "Bringing in an outsider like this."

"Quite the contrary," he replied acidly. "Since *professionals* have been chasing down these absurd rumors for more than five weeks and found absolutely nothing, naturally we are grateful for the assistance of someone as qualified as you."

Then it came to her. "You're him, aren't you?"

"I beg your pardon?"

"The guy who Ben Shannon kicked out of the clinic. Cyril Price told me about you on the way to the airport."

The man's complexion darkened. "No doubt it was a cause of amusement to everyone concerned. I cannot wait to hear how you succeed where I have failed."

Allison decided to let that one slip by. She leaned back in her seat, bracing herself with both arms against the jouncing, rocking ride. The highway was a narrow man-made band running through utter desolation. Rock and scrub wilderness stretched out in every direction. Wherever patches of dusty green signaled the presence of underground springs, people appeared. Bedouin tents reached out a variety of multicolored arms as wide as houses. Flocks grazed nearby—sheep, goats, donkeys, camels. Towns were clusters of square concrete blockhouses connected by packed earth tracks. There was little vegetation to soften the harshness of this desert world. The few trees grew stunted and dry and gnarled. Roads to distant settlements were not roads at all, but dusty tracks that rose and fell and twisted like yellow veins on the hard surface.

Closer to Aqaba, the mountains closed in on both sides. Pink and yellow and ocher sandstone cliffs were striated with black volcanic ash and white quartz and brown iron ore, carved into weird shapes by a hundred million years of wind.

The doctor who came out to greet her arrival was both the man she remembered and a different man entirely.

"My dear Allison," Ben Shannon called out, approaching through the compound's open gates. "After all these years. What a delight to see you again."

"Right." The little man from the embassy deposited her two suitcases and his own battered case at her feet. "Break a leg and all that." He climbed back into his taxi and screeched away with a plume of oily smoke.

"He was about the most unpleasant man I've ever met," Allison said, her eyes on the departing taxi.

"The result of a continual diet of subterfuge," Ben replied.

She couldn't stop staring at him. He was strong yet worn to a fine and delicate edge. His face was a chiseled set of firm lines and determined action, his body wiry yet fragile. His eyes, though smudged with weary shadows, were full of peace. "You're not like I remember you. Even your voice is different."

"Ah. That is the Arabic, I suppose. The language is so demanding that it tends to wipe the slate clear as far as other accents are concerned." He led her into the compound.

"You will be a most welcome addition here. Our level of expertise is high, but as with all such clinics, we are underfunded and understaffed. There is always a need for volunteers."

"You expect me to work at the clinic?"

He nodded. "You will be watched constantly. It is the Arab way. Our only protection is to have you carry out normal duties."

Within the clinic grounds, families had gathered. They had set down mats and rugs beneath the trees' meager shade or alongside the building or on the covered walk and set up temporary housekeeping. Women in black tentlike djellabas and head scarves fed squalling children while other youngsters squealed and ran and played in the dust. The compound was as noisy as a schoolyard.

"We deal with numerous stomach and intestinal diseases," he said as they walked. "Infected skin lesions. Infant and childhood ailments. Dehydration. Eye problems. Tooth and gum disease. Some bullet wounds, some beatings, some bomb fragments. But mostly our problems are the result of overcrowding, lack of clean water, and poor sanitation, not war."

"I still don't see what use I'm going to be to you."

"You will." At every step, families looked up and smiled and murmured respectful greetings to him. He led her up the crumbling brick stairs and into the relative cool of the crowded front porch. Rusty metal posts held up overlapping sheets of plastic roofing. The simple concrete floor was packed with mothers tending babies. Men gathered and fingered worry beads and talked in undertones. Everyone paused to inspect Allison as she passed. "It's something of a rambling structure, I'm afraid. We've had to make do with what we had. When there was money, it always seemed there were few construction materials to buy. When we were poor, the market was naturally flooded."

He opened a sheet-metal spring door and ushered her inside a corrugated metal hall with simple benches stretching down both sides. Notices in Arabic plastered the walls. Three large windows had been cut with a torch and then screened. A desultory breeze shifted the heat back and forth through the chamber.

"Our entrances and waiting chambers are castoff shipping containers. They are fine in cooler weather but like ovens in the summer. As you saw, most people prefer to remain outdoors."

He took her through a second door, this one marked "Private," which brought them to an open-air walkway roofed with the same plastic sheeting. Ahead was an ocher-colored building. They walked through the entrance, across a cramped parlor filled with rickety furniture, up a narrow stairway, and down a hall. He stopped before a door marked with an Arabic number. A key dangled from the lock. He opened the door to reveal a clean but austere chamber with an unmade single bed, a sink, a writing desk and chair, a grit-encrusted window, and a bare bulb.

"No doubt it is far from what you are accustomed to," he explained, "but for you to live differently than the rest of our staff would only cause questions."

"It's fine," she said, and meant it. In her weary state, the bed looked immensely inviting.

"Sheets and towels are in the cupboard down the hall, as is the bathroom." He set down her case and said solemnly, "I hope you will be happy here, for as long as it is necessary for you to stay."

She looked at him. "Why are you doing this?"

He regarded her with grave eyes. "There is danger here for us and for all our world. Very great danger. Not just today, but for many years to come. So long as we do not help these people gain a peaceful purpose and clearer vision, we are allowing their world to remain a breeding ground for terrorists."

He looked through the dirty window and continued, "Some people out there seek to take advantage of this misery. They use the guise of their faith to preach of hate and pain and death. Them I oppose—with all that I have, with all that I am."

7

The road away from the Chechen stronghold was little more than a goat track in places, but being on the downhill journey put them all in good spirits. They camped in a meadow an hour or two from the turnoff. When they continued their journey at dawn, Rogue announced that the Russians no longer needed to travel as hidden cargo. The news was received with vast relief.

As they descended into the southern Caucasus, all the world changed—birds, animals, trees, weather. Where the north had been dry and dusty and either overly hot or cold, the south was welcoming. They descended from the dead of winter into a balmy autumn of golden leaves and warm sunshine. The change was staggeringly sudden. In the space of a half-day the world was transformed, and they with it. Birch and fir mounted the steep slopes in friendly welcome to the weary travelers. Wild tulips lined the paths of cheerful streams. Coats were shed, the grim squint through icy winds was lost, the ability to smile returned. For some.

"Now there will be trouble," Yuri muttered when they stopped for a cold lunch of stale bread and goat's cheese and water that tasted of the metal container.

"Don't borrow worries," Robards replied easily. "Keep your weapons ready and hope for peace, that's my motto."

"At least we are avoiding the accursed Chechen," Mikhail agreed when Wade translated, and pointed westward. "All the hills you see in the direction of the setting sun they claim as theirs. The other tribes disagree, of course, we Ossetians most of all. The battles between us have continued for over seven hundred years. War with the Chechen is inevitable."

"Correction," Rogue replied to the translation. "War is inevitable, here or anyplace else."

"What does the warrior say?" Mikhail demanded.

When Wade had translated, the old man grunted. "He speaks a truth. War is man's curse and his destiny and his beginning and his end. I am an old man and have seen much and know there is no other answer."

"I am young," Wade replied quietly, "and yet I believe you are wrong. With respect, I must say that I feel you are wrong."

The old man turned glittering eyes his way. "Tell the warrior that this is a land where time is not measured as elsewhere. Here the Khevsur tribesmen still have shrines to their tree gods. Here the Eti fought in chain mail and great

169

swords until Stalin swept through here in the thirties and showed them that modern war has no concern for battle honor, only blood."

Robards accepted this news in silence. "What got this started?"

"It wasn't—"

"Tell him these mountains contain the great fortress of Shatili," the old man continued, his sharp gaze now shooting from one to the other. "The only fortress in the world never taken in battle, although the Chechen, their mortal enemies, whom they call the Kistebi, tried for more than eight hundred years to overrun its defenses. Tell him that here the word of honor dominates all else. Disgrace and offenses to the family name are held as matters of revenge for three and four and five hundred years. Here men still show their strength as warriors by abducting brides from enemy villages in the bright of day."

Instead of being troubled by the news, Robards leaned back against the stone wall, crossed his legs, and released a satisfied sigh. "Been looking for a place like this all my life and never thought I'd find it."

"So tell me," Mikhail demanded of Wade. "Where does this peace of yours fit into my world?"

They traveled through a countryside that spoke vivid tales of bygone days.

Tucked here and there amidst the green landscape and softly layered hills lay deserted villages, ruined by passing wrath and conquering armies. Piles of rubble buried what once had been cobblestone thoroughfares, the cinders and sorrow gentled by forty years of weeds and wind and rain. Testimony to Stalin's determination to wipe out all allegiance to anything save the great Soviet Empire.

And yet elsewhere remained hamlets of a dozen or so houses, untouched by the red tide of Soviet power. They were peaceful places, rich in produce and beautiful to behold. Vineyards glistened in the early sunlight, their orderly rows pointing toward ancient villages. Chapels nestled beneath trees so old that their girth could not be spanned by six grown men. Churches and monasteries crowned distant hilltops, majestic in their timelessness. The houses had been built before Western Europe had formed itself into nations, and had served as homes to more than twenty generations, often of the same family. Living history dwelled among the citizens of such places, reminders of what had been, beacons to what was yet to come.

Women sat in doorways and hand-spun the hair of goats into thread, most of which would be used within the community. The local wool, Mikhail told them at their next stop, made clothes with the softness of silk, yet was waxy enough to keep skin dry through the hardest of storms. Wade waved as they passed and wished them well from the fullness of an adventurous life.

Yuri and Mikhail rode in Rogue's lead truck, while Ilya and Alexis, the man who had been ill, traveled with Wade. Ilya remained the loner, content to stay in the back of the truck and doze. Alexis, on the other hand, reveled in his regained good health. He was thin by nature, and his illness had left him little more than skin and bones. He bore the air of an ascetic, his light blue eyes glorying in all they saw, his cheeks sunken and arms almost skeletal, his copper-colored hair and three-day beard in unnoticed disarray.

As they drove, Alexis turned from gazing out the side window to demand, "You are a religious man?"

"He is a fool for God," Ilya called from the back, speaking for the first time that day. "He seeks to grow peace in soil where only war can take root."

"My mother was religious," Alexis said, taking no heed of Ilya's bitterness. "I thought of her often when the illness had me."

"Be glad the fool stays silent," Ilya shouted over the road noise. "Otherwise he may ask questions for which there are no answers."

"There is more to be learned from the silence of some than the ceaseless talk of others," Alexis countered.

Ilya cursed and subsided. There was a silence until Alexis announced quietly, "I lived in Polygon."

"I don't think I've ever heard of it," Wade replied.

"It is Russian for nightmare." The sunlight streaming in the truck window turned his stubbled features into a deeply shadowed visage. "And if it is not, it should be."

"Where—"

"Moscow 400, that was our only address. We were more than two thousand kilometers from the capital, but letters went first there, even if sent from a neighboring village. Every letter was screened by the KGB. A telephone call to the outside world meant applying for a pass and waiting a day, a week, sometimes months. Travel outside was tightly restricted. Everything was restricted."

"Why did you stay?" Wade asked.

"Because I was ordered to." Blue eyes glinted with bitter humor. "Of course, that is something one raised in a land of freedom like you would not understand."

"Perhaps not," Wade agreed.

"Life was not so bad. We were well paid, by Soviet standards. We had good housing, by Soviet standards. We had access to goods that were not available to the average citizen. My work was granted high priority, which meant that almost anything I felt was required, I received. There were twenty thousand of us, all either specialists or soldiers or spies. We used to joke that Polygon was a comfortable model of the great Soviet state—a prison within a prison."

"What did you do there—I mean, what was your work?"

Alexis replied simply, "Object 100."

"What?"

"A miniature nuclear reactor. A propulsion system for an atomic-powered rocket." He stretched his legs out as far as the cabin area would permit. "Your American scientists had such a project, but it was dropped in 1979 as too costly. There were also environmental questions, although we have since proven them to be unfounded. We were on our way to Mars. We were just ten years away, and then... "

"And then everything changed," Wade said.

"Before I left, we had teams of American scientists visiting, looking, taking pictures, asking questions." His tone turned bitter. "We were required to stand and be polite because suddenly there was no more money. Our research was at a standstill. Our stores were empty. Our homes had no heat. The Americans walked around as if they were shopping at a local bazaar. Then they left, and we heard nothing further. We wondered if perhaps they had decided to take all our years of research, return to their warm comfortable homes in America, and do their work in bright new American factories. We asked, and we wrote, and we begged, and still we heard nothing."

"What shame you must have felt," Wade offered softly. "What humiliation."

"So now you ask why I go to build bombs for strangers, yes?" Alexis smiled sadly. "Tell me, have you ever watched your life's work lie in ruins? Have you ever had to beg for assistance, only to be ignored? Have you ever seen your children go hungry?"

Slowly Wade shook his head. "No."

"Then what right have you to judge me?"

"None," Wade said quietly. "I have no right."

"No?" Alexis turned back toward the front windshield. "Then why do you bother me with the questions in your eyes?"

"A hope only," Wade said. "That you would stop and think of other families, families who also only wish to live in peace."

Alexis was silent so long that Wade thought the conversation had ended. But as the truck bounced and rumbled its way around another bend, Alexis said to the window, "Can you also tell me why I hear such questions asked by my heart to my head? Can you tell me why there are no answers?"

They approached yet another nameless hamlet as the sun softened and cooled and touched the highland peaks. Robards pulled from the road and pointed. Nearby fields had been torn apart by dual troughs, which ran in irregular patterns around the nearest houses. "Tanks."

Mikhail walked ahead on foot and returned in the last light of day. "I have found us safe refuge," he announced.

"The trucks?" Rogue demanded when Wade had translated.

"There is a stable," Mikhail replied, swinging

into the truck. "Come. My belly is becoming too neighborly with my spine."

The village houses were constructed of rocks slathered with concrete and laid roughly in place. The roofs were all jagged slate. Other than the single main road in and out of town, the tracks were mud layered by stones upon which donkeys and people could find safe footing. At the high point of the village rose an ancient watchtower. A church huddled up against it, as much in abject submission to the region's brutal ways as for protection against invaders.

The house where Mikhail led them was of concrete and brick. One side of the house was in shambles. A deep trench split an old oak standing between the house and stables. The trench continued on through the living-room wall and ended upon the opposite wall, a violent fiery comet whose reddish tail splashed up and around the ceiling.

"Three weeks ago we were hit by a rocket attack," the woman of the house told them dully. Her five young children clustered about her with expressions of weary sadness. "The rocket did not explode. Otherwise we would all be dead. My aged father and mother came and dug it out while we waited in the woods. They said their lives were closer to an end, and so they took the risk of it blowing up in their faces."

Robards inspected the plastic tarp that covered the gaping hole and asked, "Where is her husband?"

"Away," she replied through Wade. "Fighting these past four months."

Wade did not need to ask for details to explain further, "When Georgia declared independence from the Soviet Union, South Ossetia declared independence from Georgia."

"That was asking for trouble," Rogue commented.

"I do not know where he is," the woman went on in her toneless drone, "or even if he is alive. I have no way of finding out. When the Georgians last came through here, they demanded that I hand over my husband. When I said that he was not here, they did this and ordered me to leave my own homeland."

"Ossetia was divided by Stalin," Wade continued to Rogue after translating. "The lower half was joined to Georgia to split up the patriotic Ossetians and to make the Georgian border look straighter. They don't have the same language as the Georgians, not even the same alphabet. North Ossetia has been made a semi-independent enclave inside Russia. South Ossetia wants to join up with its other half."

Wade gestured at the ruptured wall. "The result is war. All of South Ossetia has been split into villages either full of Georgians or Ossetians."

"You are speaking of my lands?" Mikhail demanded.

"Yes," Wade replied, and explained what he had said.

"How is it that you know so much of our struggle?"

"I listen," Wade said simply.

"You listen and you hear with compassion," the old man corrected. "It is a pity that others do not do the same."

The woman declared, "There is little in our house to eat."

When Wade translated, Robards replied, "Tell her we'll eat from our stores, and we'll leave her more food in return for lodging. Ask her if there is bread to be had in this village."

"For those with money," she replied.

Wade handed her a few rubles. "We have little cash, but we will pay for your hospitality with goods that can be easily traded as well as with food."

She nodded, and then volunteered, "The next three villages are Georgian held, and they shoot anyone coming from this area. You will need to go south on a trail I can show you in the morning."

"For such information," Wade replied, "we shall pay even more."

She handed the money to her daughter, who leapt up and ran out the door. She then turned and spoke sharply to her eldest son, who nodded and left without a word. She explained, "He will go and sleep in your trucks."

"I was planning to do that," Robards said when Wade had translated.

"Do so," she replied. "But let him be there also. He has the eyes of a night bird and knows all who live here, who is foe and who friend. There are not many friends."

After the meal, the woman and her children retired to the back room, leaving the men sprawled about the drafty living chamber with its single flickering bulb. The three Russians smoked their foul-smelling *papyrosi* cigarettes, enjoying the moment's relative freedom. Robards cast a glance at the wall's open wound and declared, "This whole region's a patchwork quilt of little wars."

Wade translated for the others, and there was no dissent. "It is the same story over much of the former Soviet Union," Yuri said, speaking in Russian so all but Rogue could understand. "The local tribes have suffered much."

"Not to mention we Russians," Ilya muttered.

"The usurpers of ancient tribal lands have no rights," Mikhail countered, but without heat.

"I, a usurper?" Ilya snorted. "I was born in Estonia. My parents were forced there, given fifteen minutes to pack and shoved upon a cattle car and sent off on a voyage that lasted two weeks and almost killed my mother. I am the product of modern Russia, a man who belongs nowhere."

"The villagers have never been concerned with Tbilisi or Moscow or politics or the world," Yuri said. "They live life on a different level. They want to know, what is the price of bread? How will I heat my home this winter? Will there be medicine for my sick child?"

Rogue demanded, "How has the military been handling the crisis?"

Yuri looked at him with a cynic's eye. "You wish to know if it would be possible to add product to your cargo of people?"

"Not this trip," Robards replied, unruffled by the man's tone. "Maybe later, though. A little material, maybe. Something small enough to carry."

"Just go to the right gate and ask the right person," Yuri replied bitterly. "The one with hunger in his eyes."

"I've heard things were bad," Rogue said conversationally.

"Listen, and I will tell you how bad," Yuri's voice was overlaid with venom. "For I was stationed at a military compound meant for collecting and holding nuclear weapons."

"Sounds like I've come to the right man," Rogue said easily.

"Families with cash bribe those sent to look for absent conscripts," Yuri continued. "The officers responsible for rounding up draft dodgers put down one illness or another, because they too have hunger stalking their doorsteps. Those conscripts who do show up find there are no uniforms, no weapons for training, and little food. An admiral was imprisoned for starving naval conscripts to death, and his response was, how can I give what I myself do not have? Every base in Russia overflows with men brought in from former Soviet lands, and none of them have clearly assigned duties. It is chaos. Total chaos."

Yuri nodded to himself, his face etched deeply by the shadows of the room and the memories of what he fled. "You want to steal weapons-grade nuclear materials? Fine. Go to such a base, carry dollars, and seek out the hungry man."

Rogue chewed thoughtfully on his twig. "Sounds to me like a good time to get out."

"A normal country, that is all I seek," Yuri replied.

The next morning Wade accepted his cup of tea and hunk of breakfast bread from his unsmiling hostess and took it out to where Alexis stood by the cracked oak. The man looked more haggard than usual. When he was up close Wade asked him, "How are you feeling?"

Startled, the man swung around, "Oh, it's you. I did not hear you approach."

"Are you sick again?"

"No, thanks to you," Alexis gave his gentle, sad smile. "I simply found my sleep disturbed last night by your questions—and by ones rising within my own heart."

Wade sipped from his tea. "My whole life is full of unanswered questions and unsolved mysteries."

"Yes," Alexis murmured, his eyes returning to the bomb-shattered tree. "Perhaps that is why I find it easy to speak with you, this honest sharing of doubt."

"It should be quite a change," Wade offered tentatively, "working in the desert."

Alexis examined him. "You have visited the great northern steppes?"

"No."

"In winter it is so cold that snow freezes hard and sharp as broken glass. The ground is like iron, the wind a knife that tears through your skin. There is nothing to see for hundreds of miles in every direction except snow and ice and more snow and more ice." He returned his gaze to the damaged house. "I do not think the desert will be so great a change."

Wade hesitated, then quietly asked, "Where are you going, Alexis?"

It was as though the man had been waiting for the question. There was not even a moment's delay before he demanded, "Do you know the city of Aqaba?"

"I don't think so."

"I found it on a map just before my departure. It is in Jordan. We were intended to rendezvous there for transport to Baghdad. The guides who failed to meet us were to bring us to Tbilisi. From there transport was supposed to be a matter of buying a ticket to Jordan, then overland to our destination."

Wade stared at Alexis. "You are to go and build bombs for Iraq?"

The man's eyes were haunted, his reply without strength. "Iraq or Iran, Russia or America—what difference does it make so long as my wife and child are fed?"

"You really don't care?"

"A flight to Amman via Istanbul," Alexis replied, his voice echoing the doubts that plagued his gaze. "A night there, then down to Aqaba—just another Russian tourist taking in a few days by the sea. There is a group operating there, far from the listening ears and watchful eyes in Amman. They will transport me along desert ways to Iraq. Either that, or a boat to Iran. Or so it appears."

"But do you really want to do this?" Wade pressed.

"Yes," Alexis replied. "And no." The sadness in his eyes threatened to spill over. "This I have agreed to do, this I must do. There is no other way."

"Couldn't you—"

"No more questions," Alexis interrupted. "Please. My head and heart are full to bursting." He turned and walked away.

Wade started at the sound of approaching footsteps, and turned to find Rogue towering over him. "What'd you say that got him so worked up?"

"Nothing."

"Didn't look like nothing to me."

"I just asked where he was going," Wade said. "And why."

"He's going where he's going," Robards answered. "That's all you need to know, long as we get paid."

"Yes, I know you're here for the money," Wade accused. "But what about the casualties? What about all the pain and grief and hardship that happens when bombs blow up and worlds end? What about cities blown apart and families torn up and little children starving or killed? Doesn't that bother you even a little?"

Robards inspected him with a strange mix of amusement and irritation. "What happened to the shy little guy I started this trip with?"

"I don't know what you mean."

"Sure you do. You're speaking up. Charting your own course. And it's not one I care too much for, either. You better keep your nose out of this business, sport. We got too much riding on this to start digging around where we don't belong."

The tone rankled deep. "I thought you said I was calling the shots here."

"Sure you are, long as you don't start aiming to shoot yourself in the foot. Might end up shooting me as well."

"I don't think that's what I'm doing."

"Maybe that's the problem." Rogue changed course with, "Were you planning on giving medicines to the old lady to help pay for our stay?"

"Yes."

Rogue shook his head. "Bad idea. It'd be leaving a clear trail for anybody who might be after us."

"She won't tell anybody."

"Maybe not, but it's a risk we don't need to take. You've got cash left. At least enough for my second payment."

"Not much more than that."

"Go ahead and use it now," Robards urged. "I'll take my share in medicines. It's safer."

For some reason he could not explain, Wade found himself resisting the idea. "I planned to keep the cash with us—for a crisis."

"Brother, if traveling through a war zone ain't a crisis, I don't know what is."

"I'm also planning to stop at every village with a doctor and leave supplies," Wade said stubbornly.

Robards inspected him, his face set in lines as hard as granite. "If you were a man under me—"

"But I'm not," Wade replied, with a strength he did not feel. "Shouldn't we be getting under way?"

Allison arose before the day's heat became a burden. From some unseen grove came the fragrance of ripening fruit. The early morning air was alive with scents—nutty smoke, blooming herbs, dark bitter coffee. She opened her window as far as the stubborn hinges would allow and drank in the aroma.

The window faced east and south. Allison was able to look out over a series of rooftops and catch sight of a sliver of sea. The water looked impossibly blue, as did the sky. In fact, the whole landscape was brilliant with color. Silver-green olive trees softened distant hills. Tiny rivulets furrowed the dry earth, their paths lined by brilliant yellow flowers. Allison watched the dawn strengthen and felt an awakening sense of excitement over the beauty and mystery of this land.

She arrived in the kitchen after everyone else had eaten. A communal pot contained coffee of gluelike consistency. A metal serving tray was piled high with cold pita bread. A vat of butter and half-gallon jar of marmalade stood alongside, both covered by cheesecloth to ward against the flies.

As she served herself, someone glanced in, spotted her, and left. Soon afterward, Ben arrived and greeted her with a smile. "I hope you slept well."

Allison nodded around her mouthful. The bread was utterly tasteless and had the consistency of boiled leather. "Fine. I had a visitor here a minute ago, but I scared him away."

"Oh, that was probably the clinic's driver, Fareed. He's a product of the old school. He will be friendly enough once he has been properly introduced to this attractive new foreign lady." He watched her set down the half-eaten bread and push the plate to one side. "If you are finished with breakfast, perhaps I can show you around."

Beyond the cramped waiting room, the clinic opened into a series of largish rough-hewn chambers. Ben led her down a side hall and explained, "This was formerly a tea warehouse, which was very good for us as it meant that at least a modicum of cleanliness was maintained." He pushed open a door. "This is your office."

The closet-sized room was jammed full with a desk, chair, and two filing cabinets. Papers were strewn about the desk, piled on every surface, littered across the tiny floor. There was no window.

"We lost our administrative assistant three months ago," he said. "I am afraid we have permitted things to get a little behind."

"A little," she agreed.

"We deal with the poorest of the poor," he went on. "People who are disowned by clan and society. Bedouins, Palestinians from the more impoverished neighborhoods, workers within the truck compound and harbor, illegal guest workers from other Arab states who cannot afford a licensed doctor's fee. Our money comes from various missionary and hospital associations. Forms for this, and the stock lists, will make up the majority of your work. I also make rounds through outlying areas. I shall expect you to accompany me."

She nodded her understanding. "Granting me entry to closed-off areas."

In response, Ben pushed her gently into the office. By scrunching up beside her, he managed to close the door. In a low voice he said, "You would be well advised to say as little about that as possible."

She stared at him. "You have spies working in the clinic?"

"One of whom we know for certain. His name is Ali, and I alternate between thinking that he is a delightful young man and a pestilent little demon."

"But if you know who he is, why don't you get rid of him?"

"Because any outside group such as ours will be carefully watched. That Ali is both young and overly vocal suggests they consider us to be relatively harmless."

The thought of such subterfuge at close range chilled her. "But there might be others."

"Certainly others whose sympathies lie more with the fundamentalists than with the West," he replied quietly. "But they are excellent workers and willing to consider compassion as an alternative to hatred. So I remain certain only about Ali."

"I'll be careful," she said solemnly.

When Ben excused himself to see to his rounds, Allison sought refuge where she had always been most comfortable—in work. It was slow going at first, but by midday she was beginning to orient herself.

The first requirement was to establish order, and order was something she was very good at. A box was found. File drawers were inspected, and outdated files stored away. Then Allison began gathering the piles of paper littering her office, sorting them the best she could, and stowing them in the freed file space.

She was so involved in her work that the knock on her door made her jump. "Yes?"

The door creaked open to reveal a sprite crowned

with a bounty of dark curly locks. "You Miss Allison?"

"That's right."

"I am Ali. Dr. Ben, he say, you no eat?"

Allison glanced at her watch. "I didn't realize how late it had become."

"You are hungry, yes? You wait, I bring."

Within a few minutes he was back, bearing a tray with a sandwich, some dates, and a Pepsi. Ali set it down, looked around the room, and observed, "You work hard, Western lady."

"Thank you for the food," she said, suddenly very hungry. "Do you know where I can find a broom and some cleaning rags?"

"Don't worry. I bring." But Ali stayed where he was. "You are American?"

"Yes?"

"Why you come here to Aqaba?"

She inspected the boy as she took a bite of the sandwich—processed cheese on white bread, no butter, no nothing. Ali was small and wiry, probably about eighteen or nineteen. Certainly not what she had expected as a spy. "My father and Dr. Shannon were friends."

"Ah." He nodded. Family ties were clearly something he could understand. "So very nice to see you here, Western lady. You are sleeping good?"

"Quite well, thank you."

"*Insh 'Allah Sulameh*—thanks be to Allah for your well-being. I am so very glad for you. Yes, so nice."

She took a bite of the tasteless sandwich. "And how are you doing?"

"Thanks be to Allah, life is good. Yes. You will take something else?"

"Not just now, thank you."

"You need, you call me. I help." He surveyed the office once more. "All people are saying you do big work. I think yes, is so."

"A lot needed to be done," Allison agreed.

"Yes, work is going very smooth." He nodded. "Allah must smile on your work, I think."

She pushed her plate to one side, picked up the next form, and said, "I'm not sure how much Allah had to do with this."

Ali scoffed. "This is opinion of who? You? You are expert? You have witnessed all life?"

"No," she said, determined to work despite the interruption. Maybe he would get the idea and leave. "But I'm just not sure how the hand of Allah has been busy in this office."

"This is something not yet revealed," Ali agreed. "Maybe sometime in future, all will be told for you, but not yet."

Ben chose that moment to step into view outside her doorway. "Ali, are you bothering Miss Taylor?"

The young man looked positively offended. "I am only standing here. Bring lunch and cool drink. I wonder how you can throw on me such accuses."

"I think your services are required elsewhere," Ben said.

Allison finished her Pepsi and stood. "Thank you for the lunch, Ali."

"You good lady," Ali decided, taking the tray. "We talk more."

"Ali tends to linger where he is not wanted," Ben said.

"So I've noticed. Still, I think I just passed inspection." Allison pointed at her overflowing out box. "All these need are for you to look them over and sign, and then I can get them in the mail."

"Later," he replied. "I want to take you into the desert this afternoon, and for that we need to make an early start."

They stopped at several villages along the way, all cut from the same depressing mold. The houses were square and squat and flat-roofed, all constructed of concrete blocks. The wealthier dwellings were encircled by concrete block fences topped with broken glass. Around every house, goats and camels and donkeys searched for meager shrubs. There were no trees. Children in filthy djellabas played in the dust. Everyone stopped to stare at the strangers. Ben flitted from house to house, then quickly returned, and they were off again. Every twenty minutes, Allison made note of their whereabouts.

They were inspected twice, once by blue-shirted policemen and once by the army. In both cases the uniformed men spoke in gentle tones barely above a murmur. Fareed, Ben's driver, answered the same way. When Allison remarked on their almost effeminate voices, Ben replied simply, "It is the desert. Quiet breeds quiet."

Beyond the third village, they passed through the final army checkpoint and left the highway. Soon the world consisted only of rock and sun and sand and wind.

They traveled a washboard road, and the ride was too noisy to permit talk. They rattled and bounced their way between steep-sided mountains, the surrounding desert ever changing and ever the same.

At a spot where one of the gnarled akashi trees grew large enough to offer shade, they stopped. "Time for a breather," Ben said.

Allison got out, stretched her back, and gazed at a scene void of anything familiar. "You know," she said quietly, "I've heard about this part of the world all my life, and even studied it, but I never imagined what it is really like."

"I call this the land of thyme," he said. "Do you know your Plato?"

She shook her head no, her thoughts filled with the sound of wind.

" 'Just as bees derive honey from thyme, the strongest and driest of herbs, so too does man gain great rewards from mastering the difficulties of this world.' " He stood for a moment, sharing with her the vastness of their landscape, then turned back to the car. "We must be getting on."

The mountain faces were nature's artboards, molded into fantastic dreamscapes and painted a thousand hues. Eagles called out their desert songs, as much at home in these empty reaches as the wind. Plants grew in scattered profusion, their twisted branches as white as bones.

"The rock is smoothed by sand, not water," Ben told her at their next stop. He pointed up to a semicircular cave. "Bits of sand become trapped in hollows, and over millions of years of wind carves out caves. The Bedouins use them as dwellings during the worst of storms, pushing their herds in before them."

He led her by foot around a spit of rock to where the mountains clenched in together. As they started into the cleft, Allison noticed a sweetness to the dry air. "What is that I smell?"

"Water. Even after just a few hours here, our senses become more attuned to its presence." He pointed to where the passage was blocked by barbed wire. "Up ahead is a Bedouin spring. Rights to its use have been passed through the local Hawaitaat tribe for countless generations."

He stopped before the remains of a fire and tested the ashes with his shoe. A plume of dust rose at his touch. "Stone cold. They haven't been here for days. All right, we must search elsewhere."

"You don't know where they are?"

"Of course I do." He waved an expansive arm, taking in the rocks and mountains and sky. "Somewhere out there."

Beyond the narrow passage, the mountains opened into a vast yellow sea of sand. Rock islands pushed up at odd intervals. For some reason, their presence amplified her sense of aching emptiness.

The Land Rover lurched its way over a sand track of dips and curves and bumps. Fareed released his two-handed grip on the wheel long enough to turn on the radio. Arabic music filled the car. Allison continued her vigil out the windows and found the music to be in harmony with all that surrounded her.

They spotted the camels first.

At the sound of their approach, the animals sauntered over a ridge, vanishing from view. Fareed topped the slope and cut off the engine. In the sudden silence, Allison heard the bleating of goats and the shrill calls of children.

There were perhaps a dozen tents, each about thirty feet long and half as wide. A cluster of akashi trees marked the presence of water. A trio of old trucks were pulled up nearby.

"In twenty years this way of life may be gone forever," Ben said, leading her toward the camp on foot. "As the old generation dies off, more and more of the Bedouins are choosing to settle in permanent villages like the ones we just visited. It is a far easier life, but I for one will be sad to see this world disappear."

Allison followed Ben into the central dwelling, where a toothless old grayhead croaked a welcome and waved them in. Ben shook hands with a hawk-nosed younger man, whom he introduced as Mahmoud.

"He is the effective leader of the clan," Ben explained, seating himself gracefully on the carpet-covered ground and motioning for Allison to join him. "His father rules in name only."

At the center of the tent was a rectangular dugout lined with coals, over which rested the ever-present brass coffeepot. A woman entered, murmured greetings to Ben, knelt, and poured them thimble-size cups. Allison accepted hers and tried not to stare at the intricate tattoo that ran across the woman's forehead and down over the bridge of her nose, and across her lips, ending at her chin. She was perhaps nineteen or twenty years old.

"Tradition requires you to accept three refills," Ben murmured. "Shake your cup from side to side when you have had enough."

The two Arab men wore the *keffiyeh,* or checkered headdress, and Western-style jackets over their robes. An interminable discussion ensued, all in Arabic. Allison sipped her coffee, watched the men talk as much with their hands as with their mouths, and took in her surroundings.

Around the tent's periphery were low cushions covered with soft carpets. Taller square cushions were set at intervals, upon which arms and bodies were leaned. The tent's interior was surprisingly cool.

Abruptly Ben stood and announced, "Time to begin."

They made their way from tent to tent trailing an entourage of chattering children. With each woman and child patient, Allison stood in quiet attendance. When the sick person was a man, she waited outside. As they walked through the camp, Ben told her quietly, "They have heard of new smugglers operating through the desert routes."

"Smuggling what?" Allison stopped. "Going where?"

"Walk with me, please." When she had caught up, he went on. "They can only find out so much without forcing dangerous attention their way. The smugglers and the local Bedouins live an uneasy truce. Those camels you see out there are nowadays kept more as signs of wealth than as a means of transport. The only time they are worked is when the Bedouins become competition for the smugglers. Camels are harder to track on radar than trucks and do not leave tire treads on sand. A full-grown camel can carry five or six televisions roped to each side."

"That's what they think the new smugglers are carrying?" Allison asked. "Just televisions?"

Ben shook his head. "Not this time. Smugglers tend to specialize—one tribe takes radios and televisions and computers to Saudi Arabia, another carries Lebanese hashish to the wealthier Gulf states and sometimes for the West, and so on. But these new people are different. Mahmoud called them shadows, since he had not seen any of them, only signs of their passage. That and a strange rumor from other tribes."

"But what—"

"Men," he said, turning to face her full on. "The rumor he hears is that these newcomers are smuggling Westerners into Iraq. Which troubles him most of all, for what profit could there be in this, unless they are people intent on war?"

8

The trucks arrived at the main road to Beloti around midafternoon. Fifty yards before the turning, Rogue halted the trucks and waited. Once an hour, their hostess had told them, Russian-led convoys drove through, headed for villages still controlled by the enemy. Otherwise, the roads belonged to the Ossetians.

They took a late lunch and waited behind the high hedges until a deep rumbling announced the convoy's arrival. They watched through the leaves as a pair of Russian tanks rolled into view. Behind these came several armored personnel carriers, and following them was a hodgepodge of vehicles—trucks, buses, autos, ambulances, farm transports piled to the brim with produce, even an occasional horse-drawn wagon.

"Russian troops were brought in to protect the enclaves held by non-Ossetians," Wade explained in an undertone. "Stalin emptied a lot of villages. He hated the Ossetians' patriotism, so he shipped more than a hundred thousand either to Siberia or Kazakhstan."

"And imported Russians to fill in the holes," Rogue finished.

"Georgians, too," Wade added. "Stalin wanted to scatter them around as well."

"So why don't the Georgians have something to say about these Russian troops being around here? Didn't you tell me they claimed this territory for their own?"

Wade nodded. "It's not as simple as that."

"Yeah, I kinda figured."

"The Georgians have been tied up fighting a civil war with the Abkhazi tribe farther to the east. That area has been a part of Georgia for more than a thousand years, and the Abkhazis make up less than fifteen percent of the total population. This trouble started before Georgia actually became a nation, and the Russian troops arrived long before independence. So the Georgians sort of turn a blind eye to the Russians' still being here."

"From the sound of it," Rogue agreed, "they need all the help they can get."

Wade translated this conversation for the impatient old man. The Russian engineers listened with the intensity of those whose fate rested in the hands of others.

Mikhail nodded his agreement to Wade's explanation and added, "Thus the conflict of South Ossetia has neither front nor cohesion. The Russians have no way to plan an attack. The Ossetian militia fights roving battles. Newly returned transportees gather arms and attack whatever village had once been their own. There is no central command. We are a hundred different armies, unified only by our desire for an Ossetian homeland."

"With a lot of old hatreds added in just to make things interesting," Robards amended, watching a third tank roll by at the end of the convoy. "Okay, road's clear as it's going to get. Let's head out."

At the village outskirts Rogue pulled over and waved Wade in behind him. Just ahead, a pair of battered jeeps had been parked to partially block the road. Heavily armed men clustered around them. Wade cut his motor and walked over to Rogue. They watched as Mikhail approached the men, calling out loud greetings and proffering all their papers in outstretched hands.

Wade asked, "Is everything all right?"

"We'll find out soon enough. Get a load of the man in charge."

The soldier examining their papers had a distinctly raffish air. Instead of a helmet, he wore a black Stetson with its wide brim pulled down low over his eyes. His hollow cheeks bore the three-day growth cultivated by Western male models. He wore a hand-stitched leather hunting vest over a dark green flannel shirt, with regulation camouflage trousers tucked into lace-up doeskin boots. Over his back was slung a machine gun. Around front hung a machine pistol with polished burl handle.

Rogue snorted. "He looks like the Marlboro man, Russian style."

"He's not Russian," Wade corrected. "He's Ossetian."

"Doesn't matter," Robards said easily. "What you see there is just another trendy trekker. Anybody that concerned with looking the part isn't a problem. If he started shooting, his first concern would be how to keep his hair neat."

The man was taking his time over their papers. Wade swallowed nervously. "Looks dangerous enough to me."

"Aw, he's just another style bandit. Look over there, see the guy in the black leather gloves with the silver studs?"

"Yes."

"Another wannabe warrior. These days, you find them around every little war. They're mostly guys bored with the normal life. Probably locals, Russians or Georgians or Ossetians, but you see the type everywhere. The former Yugoslavia is full of cowboys these days." Rogue pointed with a jutting chin. "Look, see that one? Black outfit, matching boots and blackened bayonet, probably got some local woman who washes and presses his uniform at night. They get these Skorpion machine pistols and wear them down real low, like a Dodge City gunslinger. Problem is, every time they have to run anywhere the doggone thing gets caught between their legs."

Robards waved cheerily as a cluster of guards walked toward them. "Gucci warriors, the lot of them. Look at the black bandanna. Means take no prisoners. Reason is, the first sign of trouble they'd be raising dust from here to Moscow. Take a look at those aviator shades—gold Ray Bans. Probably set him back a year's pay."

Wade glanced at Robards. "What's the difference between them and you?"

"Ten years and a lotta miles," Robards responded easily. "I guess you could say I've been distilled. I'm the essence of what these guys wish they could be."

"A mercenary."

"I prefer realist. Besides, life on the edge has its advantages. Take an honest look at yourself. Tell me the last time you've ever felt so alive."

The search was perfunctory, with Mikhail proclaiming friendship in the inspectors' own tongue and Rogue hovering around with smiling menace. The three Russian engineers were too cowed to appear a threat and received less notice than did the two Americans, which was not much at all. Clearly the Ossetians saw them as just another strange group attracted by the rough-and-tumble lawlessness of a world at war. Two bottles of vodka were passed over, apparently the customary bribe from the way they were accepted, and the trucks were waved through.

They entered the village a few minutes shy of the next hour, in time to watch all life vanish. Rogue followed suit by pulling over to the curb and waving Wade in behind him. They hunkered down below the dashboards and waited for the Russian convoy to pass. When the grinding of the tanks died away, the streets returned to bustling activity.

Every so often they came upon the burned-out hulk of a truck or bus or car, pushed far enough to one side so as not to impede traffic. At least one building in each block had been bombed to smithereens. Children played in the ruins, while vendors filled the front spaces with their stalls.

Everywhere were signs of life without order. Cars raced down streets with total disregard to lanes or speed or traffic signs. Occasional bursts of machine-gun fire ripped through the air; pedestrians stopped in mid-breath, searched their surroundings, then returned to matters at hand. Motorcycles zigzagged down sidewalks at thirty or forty miles per hour, the pedestrians simply stepping aside. Cafes took advantage of the fine autumn weather by moving tables out onto the sidewalks and into the streets; customers paid little heed to the cars and motorcycles and pedestrians who threaded their way among the tables.

Twice their own progress was halted by roving bands of armed men who threatened the lead truck. Mikhail's loud exhortations and Rogue's imposing presence eased them through.

The town's only hotel was situated on the central square. They rented the only room with a private bath—not because anyone would sleep there, but so they all could get clean. Rogue and

Wade pulled the trucks into the neighboring alleyway, and Robards offered to take first watch. Mikhail and the three Russians headed upstairs to wash. Wade asked the desk clerk for directions to the city's clinic, then returned to the trucks.

Rogue demanded, "Why aren't you upstairs?"

"I'm going to see if the local doctor needs anything," Wade replied. "If there is a doctor."

Robards shook his head. "Not a wise move. All you'll be doing is telling every gunslinger within a hundred miles what we've got on these trucks."

"People are fighting and dying all around here. They need this stuff. What if you were wounded and in danger of losing a limb because there weren't any antibiotics? What if you had to have surgery and there weren't any anesthetics?"

"I'm not," Robards replied with his false ease. "I'm here and I'm fit and that's all there is to it. A man can't build a life on worrying about all the what-ifs."

"And have you ever considered the possibility that there might be something more important than yourself?"

Rogue leaned his back against the near truck and sighed up at the heavens. "Don't I recall having pretty much this same conversation with you the other day?"

"You're doing great now," Wade persisted. "But what happens when your own strength isn't enough?"

"Then I'm dead," Rogue said flatly. "That's part of the price you pay for living a real life."

"Carting people around so they can go build bombs for terrorists doesn't seem all that real to me."

"Oh, it's real, all right," Rogue drawled. "You know what your problem is, sport? You never had enough confidence in yourself to make it on your own."

"Reality is living each day with compassion for others," Wade answered steadily.

"Sick, sick, sick," Robards responded. "Shame we don't carry any medicine for delusions."

Wade said quietly, "I am going to go see if there is a clinic in need of supplies."

Robards inspected him for a moment, then declared, "If you head out on this goodwill mission of yours, all bets are off."

Wade did not understand what was meant, but nodded acceptance all the same. "I'll see you when I get back."

Once again, the doctor's gratitude was almost pathetic. He was a slender man with the long graceful fingers of a classical pianist. His dark eyes opened wide as Wade led him to the back of the truck and pointed out the various things on offer. His two aides rushed to unload the chosen boxes, moving as fast as they could, determined to take everything possible before this crazy man returned to his senses and demanded a payment they did not have.

All I ask in return, Wade had said upon departure, is that you do not speak of this for several days. The doctor had nodded an abstract reply, unable to look beyond the largess which littered his waiting room. Yet when Wade turned to leave, he noticed that one of the aides was nowhere to be found. He returned to the hotel with a faint sense of disquiet.

When he pulled up alongside the hotel, Wade discovered that the other truck was not there. He was almost certain his comrades had gone in search of gasoline, but no amount of internal reassurance could still his jangling nerves. He bounded up the stairs, rushed down the dimly lit hall, pushed open the door, and felt his heart stop when all he found to greet him was a note propped upon the crumpled bed.

With shaking hands, Wade lifted the paper and read, "I gave them a choice, sport. Everybody decided to come along when I announced I was pulling out. Mikhail says Tbilisi is a hundred klicks or so straight down the south road. I've taken the truck and its load as payment in full. Rogue."

Voices from outside drew him to the open window. He stuck his head out and felt his blood freeze at the sight of a dozen or so armed men crowding in and around his truck.

He shouted a protest and was answered by the clinic's aide, who turned and pointed and shouted back. Four armed men broke off and headed for the hotel's front door.

Wade fled out the door and down the hall, but stopped at the sound of heavy boots clumping up the stairs. He craned and searched and realized there was no other way out.

He turned to the nearest door, twisted the knob and pushed. It was locked. The boots clumped ever closer. He tried the next door, and when he found it locked as well, gave a panicked shove with his shoulder. The flimsy lock gave with almost no noise. Wade entered and leaned against the door and listened as the men hastened up the final stairs, fearful that his breathing was loud enough to alert them.

When the footsteps had passed his door, Wade turned and flew to the window. Four meters below protruded the roof over the hotel's dining room. Wade slid himself out. He hung from his fingers, then released and dropped the final meter with a thud he was sure would be heard in the next village.

He stumbled over to the roof's edge, shifted and slid and dropped to the street.

Feeling every instant that the cry of alarm would be raised, Wade fled as fast as his feet would take him.

The name Petra, Allison learned from her guidebook, was derived from the Greek word for rock, and never had a city better deserved its name. The ancient ruins were reached by way of a *siq*, a narrow chasm two miles long, in places no more than six feet wide, with walls rising four hundred feet above her head.

Although much of the city had been destroyed

in the earthquake of A.D.747, what remained was still spectacular.

Eight- and nine-story buildings had been carved from the surrounding cliffs. Temples, treasuries, granaries, spice markets—all such designations were guesses, as the Nabateans had left few records. Allison did not mind the mystery.

The larger halls had been carved from multicolored sandstone, as had the pillars and building edifices. Lanes were further canyons extending from the central valley. Caves that had once been used as pantries for rock-hewn houses now served as teahouses and museums.

Allison walked past temple steps more than three thousand years old, following the terse message which an embassy staffer had passed on, when she had called to report their findings in the desert. She glanced at her watch, found she still had almost an hour until her appointed meeting time with Cyril. As she continued along the ancient cobblestone way, Allison found herself reflecting back over recent relationships. She smiled to herself, as much from relief as regret. She had an amazing ability to pick the wrong guy.

From the safety of these distant lands, it seemed to Allison that the men in her past had always been a little less than her. A little less bright, a little less witty, a little less successful. In each relationship she became the driving force, and the men depended upon her. But in order to reinforce their own masculinity, they spent time putting her down. As a result, even though she knew she had a lot going for her, she wound up being the weaker partner. She was the one who sat by the phone. She was the one who waited for hours when the guy was late, then accepted weak excuses for inexcusable behavior, only because she knew that was all she was going to get. She *accommodated* them. And tore herself down in the process.

The reflection grew a little too painful; Allison sought to escape her thoughts by moving up close to a passing tour group. She heard the guide relate, "The Nabateans were famous traders, and over the centuries they borrowed architectural ideas from quite a variety of lands with whom they dealt—Egypt, Persia, Greece, even China. Then came the Romans, but even here the wily Nabatean traders did not give up easily. There was one local hero by the name of Sikarius. When the Romans under Augustus tried to take control of the region, he pretended to be a traitor and offered to lead them into this fortified city by a secret back route. He led them around in circles for six months, then left them to die in the desert. The Jordanians hold Sikarius up as their sort of David against the Goliath of other, greater nations. What they don't bother to mention is that Augustus responded to the trickery with a Roman style of economic sanctions; he moved the spice and silk route so that it bypassed the Nabateans entirely. In thirty years the Nabatean Empire was decimated, and they accepted incorporation into the Roman Empire, coming to be known as the state of Arabia Petra."

Allison broke off from the group as they came upon the stairs leading to the high temple, the place Cyril had set for their meeting. The steps were carved from the mountainside, and had been smoothed by millions of feet over the previous three thousand years. She climbed up one cliffside, made a series of sharp turnings, and continued on to breathtaking heights. Every supposed pinnacle proved at its summit to be nothing more than the base for yet another climb. The steps numbered well over two thousand. With each sharp turning the views became more spectacular and her breath harder to find.

She finally crested the last rise to find herself standing in a flat space carved from the very top of the mountain. Cyril rose from his seated position and dusted off his trousers. "My dear Allison, how lovely to see you. Do come sit down."

She allowed herself to be guided to the ledge and seated, her lungs still pumping like overworked bellows. Her shirt was plastered to her back, her hair sticking to the perspiration that streamed down from her sun hat and down her neck and face. Cyril looked neat as a pin and untouched by the heat. She could have shoved him over the edge.

"We are now standing in the triclinium," he said, politely ignoring her efforts to compose herself, "a three-sided gathering place for worshipers. The carved stone there at the center of the forefront dais area is called a *djinn*, or god-block. Probably in the late Mesolithic or early Neolithic times, people began taking the unformed stones which they worshiped and shaping them. From these crude square blocks later came the formation of statues and idols. But not here—at least, not as far as we know. Here it appears that the people remained content to offer their sacrifices upon the *djinn*."

Allison turned and looked over the ledge at the magnificent vista. "I feel as though I can see to the ends of the earth."

"Probably why the high places were originally chosen as places of worship; the view granted people the feeling that they were closer to their gods." Cyril pointed again to the god-block. "Of course, this is a perfect example of one of the high places destroyed by King Josiah. Do you know your Bible, my dear?"

Allison lifted her hat and pushed the hair back from her face. The desert wind had already dried her skin. "Why did you bring me here?"

Cyril pointed back down the stairs. "Security, my dear. Anyone following you up the ceremonial way, as it is called, would long since have shown themselves."

Allison stood and walked over to where she had emerged from the stairway. "Who would they be following, you or me?"

"Do come back and sit down by me." Cyril raised a thermos from his carry-sack. "Would you care for some tea?"

"I would prefer some answers."

"Very well." He replaced the thermos. "I can only tell you what I know. We think you are being trailed, but we cannot say for sure. We had thought that perhaps this little trip today would flush them out."

She nodded. Her suspicions of the past week were becoming as solid as the surrounding peaks. "You're using me as bait."

"My dear Allison, I would never dream of referring to you as anything so crass as bait."

"A decoy, then." Now that it was out in the open, she found she did not really mind. "It's the only thing that makes sense. Ben is perfectly capable of keeping watch on his own. You wanted to draw attention to your search and see what or who pops out of the woodwork."

Cyril did not bother to deny it. "You are clearly your father's daughter," he said approvingly.

"I just hope you are keeping a careful eye on me."

"Rest assured," he replied. "You are better watched than the crown jewels."

She continued her guessing game. "I also give Ben a convenient out, don't I? If all of this ever comes to light, he can deny all knowledge of anything."

"His work helps so many," Cyril agreed. "It would be a great pity if his assistance with our efforts forced him to make an untimely departure." He reached into his sack once again and extracted a thin circular object about two inches in diameter. "I think it would be a good idea if you were to carry this upon your person at all times."

Allison accepted the object and inspected its smooth black surface. The only marking was a switch embedded into one side. "What is it?"

"A satellite tracking device." Cyril pointed to the switch. "In case you are ever unsure of your safety, you should immediately switch this on. Do not hesitate, my dear. It would be far better to have a few false alarms than once to have you wait a bit too long."

"All right." She slid the object into her pocket. "So what do we do now?"

"We wait. Wait and hope that our efforts will not go unnoticed."

"And if I flush them out?" Allison pressed. "What then?"

"Then you flee," he replied gravely, "just as fast as your feet will carry you."

9

Two days later, Wade arrived at the outskirts of Tbilisi, footsore and filthy.

His pack was a burlap feed sack, compliments of the farmer who had picked him up outside Beloti. Wade had raced out of a side alley, almost colliding with the farmer's donkey cart, and had pleaded for a ride with the urgency of one frightened for his very life. The farmer had been returning from market, more than a little drunk. His cart had been empty of anything worth stealing, so he had waved Wade on board and offered him a drink from an almost-empty vodka bottle. Wade had politely declined, and had crammed a tattered straw hat he had found under the seat down hard on his head. The farmer had thought that hilarious. Three minutes later, a jeep had roared by in pursuit of a young man now masquerading as a farmer's helper.

After a night in a smelly barn with a donkey for company, Wade bathed in the horse trough and walked back to the main road. While waiting for a ride, he opened the money belt still firmly attached to his waist, pulled out a few dollars, and rolled them in the dirt. This gave them the look of Western currency hoarded for years and given up only as a last resort.

As he expected, the truck driver who stopped demanded money for the ride. In such lands where gasoline was scarce as diamonds, drivers often stopped for paying passengers. Still standing on the road, Wade argued the fare down to half the asking price—to do otherwise would attract attention. The driver heard his accent and asked if he was a Latvian down seeking work. Wade responded with a half-nod, half-shrug. The driver snorted his derision at a fool who would travel in any other direction than westward, but he opened the truck door for Wade to clamber in.

The road leading into Tskhinvali, the capital of South Ossetia, was barricaded with sandbags and barbed wire and guarded by machine guns and mobile rocket launchers. To Wade's astonishment, the barricades came in two distinct sections—the first guarded by the Russians and the second, a hundred meters later, by the Ossetians. When asked about the double barricade, the driver replied that the Russians wanted to pretend they controlled the capital city, and the Ossetians were not fool enough to openly attack the Russians—not yet, anyway.

From Tskhinvali, Wade obtained, with more dollars, a ride in what once had been a proud Communist limousine. A hard life and countless kilometers had reduced it to a rattling junk heap with fenders held in place with baling wire, two plastic sheets for side windows, no lights, and a faulty exhaust that sent continuous foul puffs up into his face as he wallowed on the springless backseat.

The town of Gori was thoroughly Georgian and relatively safe. It was best known for having produced the half-Georgian, half-Ossetian man named at birth as Josif Vissarionovich Dzhugash-vili, and whom the world knew as Joseph Stalin. Wade used a few more dollars to obtain a bed and his first decent meal in two days. By then his clothes resembled those of the Georgians around him, dirty and nondescript, and in this land of swarthy features and numerous accents he was taken simply as another northerner.

After eating, Wade stretched out on the first bed he had felt since Grozny. His time at the clinic now seemed like ages ago. He stared up into the darkness of a strange room in a strange town, more alone than he had ever been in his life, and wondered at all the mistakes that had brought him to this point. Yet as he lay and tried to condemn himself, something as all-enveloping as the darkness closed in, granting him a peace he could not understand.

When he arrived at the outskirts of Tbilisi, Wade was of two minds. On the one hand, he had no idea what he should do next. On the other, there was a growing sense of ordered process, of a clear purpose rising from the chaos and confusion of his circumstances. Wade sat in the rear of the empty produce truck, jounced heavily by every bump in the road, surrounded by choking clouds of dust and diesel fumes, thirstier than he had ever been in his life, yet retaining a strong sense of determination and direction.

Tbilisi's architecture spoke of two distinct and clashing cultures. Ancient buildings climbed the steep-sided hills in the pattern of formerly walled enclaves, covering every possible inch of available land. Streets were narrow and winding and ever in shadows. The multistoried dwellings were brightly painted and well kept. Delicate balustrades curved into ornate balconies. Yet sharing the streets with these fairy-tale houses stood newer Communist structures, squat and stolid and featureless as a tombstone. The newer buildings dominated much of the city like the foreign rule they represented—alien, unwanted, hated, scorned.

The buildings along the main thoroughfares showed scars from recent conflict. Windows blown to gaping holes. Façades stripped of paint and punctured by thousands of bullet holes. Whole structures reduced to ashes.

Also along these main streets were shops where men gathered and smoked and drank innumerable glasses of spiced tea. The truck halted outside a tumbledown department store. Wade climbed down, thanked the driver, and headed into the cool depths of the nearest cafe.

Everyone spoke simultaneously. Faces were grim yet spirited. There were few smiles, yet none of the resigned hopelessness Wade had often seen in Russia.

Wade accepted his bread and tea from the counter and carried it back to a table by the wall. His arrival brought the usual frank stares. He responded with a greeting in Russian, this time strengthening his American accent as much as he knew how.

His efforts had the desired effect. After a proper pause for him to sip his tea and taste his bread, the nearest man, a grizzled elder with the nose of a hawk, asked, "The stranger is not Russian?"

Wade shook his head. "American."

"Ah." The news brought around the head of the other person at the old man's table, a younger man with the wiry strength of an underpaid day worker. The old man continued his queries. "Truly you are from the United States?"

"Yes." Wade took another tentative sip from his steaming glass. "Forgive me for not speaking your own language, but I have just arrived in Georgia."

"My own language was seldom heard outside the home for many years, and even now I speak the Russian tongue better," the old man confessed. In the ways of his world, too many direct questions would be an offense, so he simply commented, "I have never had the pleasure of speaking with an American. Is it normal for

Americans to know the tongue of our former oppressors?"

"I come from Grozny," Wade said, supplying the desired information. "I worked with the sick and wounded."

This the old man could understand. "We have many such in these troubled times."

"My own brother lies wounded in the central hospital," the younger man confirmed. "He has just this week been returned from the Abkhazi front."

"It is a difficult time for our nation," the old man agreed. "And yet at least we are a nation once again."

"I have heard that yours is a land with a long and glorious heritage," Wade said politely.

"Sarkatvelo, it was known in the dim reaches of man and memory," the old man replied, his eyes alight. "The land of the Kartvelian tribes. It was the very first of the northern lands to accept Christianity, when our king was converted in the year 337. Since that time, Georgia has had its own Orthodox church, its own Patriarch, its own struggle against foes who sought to bury its name and its nationhood forever."

Through the open door Wade could see a fire-blackened shopfront before which rested the remains of a burned-out bus. "You have had a hard struggle."

"Indeed. Schevardnaze rules not one nation, but twenty, with all the old tribes now saying, since we cannot trust Tbilisi to govern us fairly, then we will govern ourselves."

"Civil war," Wade interpreted.

"Chaos," the old man moaned. "Chaos and bloodshed and hatred from which this land may never recover."

Wade finished his tea and asked, "Where would I find the main hospital?"

"Just off the Rustaveli Avenue, not a kilometer from here," the younger man replied. "And may you bring peace and healing to those who are in need."

Before the trauma of independence, Rustaveli Avenue had been a main artery of Tbilisi. Its great trees had shaded thousands as they took their regular evening strolls. But recent battles had transformed the city's heart. Nowadays Rustaveli Avenue was a bombed and gutted ruin. Its length was no longer littered with the smoke-stained hulks of cars and buses and tanks and bodies, refuse from the civil war which brought Schevardnaze to power. Yet scarcely a building was left unscarred by shells and smoke. The central government building at the avenue's end was little more than a blackened skeleton.

Wade turned off the main boulevard, and a hundred meters farther entered the central hospital's main gates. After an interminable wait he was allowed to see one of the head doctors, a heavyset man with the girth and hands and rumbling voice of a human bear. Swiftly Wade explained his mission and asked if Red Cross personnel had appeared from the highlands.

"They were here," the man replied, his eyes bearing the same fatigue smudges as every doctor Wade had met in these war-torn lands. "But they returned to the West."

"When?"

The man shrugged. "Soon after they arrived. One was slightly wounded, and they stayed until she was well enough to travel on." Clearly the exact date was unimportant to him. That they had left was all that mattered. "Are you a doctor?"

Wade shook his head. "A nurse."

"Yes?" Gray eyes took on renewed interest. "We have much need for trained personnel. You will be staying?"

Wade hesitated, but not for long. "If I do, I would be honored to work with you."

"Honored, yes," the doctor sighed. He understood the answer for what it was. He rose to his feet. "You must excuse me, then, I am seeing to the work of ten."

Wade made his way out of the hospital and faltered.

He understood that even to hesitate meant to choose. He could not back away, could not turn around, could not ignore that simple fact. He could certainly refuse the challenge. He could pretend that it was none of his concern and do nothing. He could turn away from the silent call. But he was too honest to lie to himself, to believe that anyone else would pick up the fallen baton. It was him or nobody.

It was hard to cast off the blanket of anonymity that had sheltered him all his life. Harder still to see the cliff's edge there before him, and step off.

So very hard.

His connecting flight from Istanbul was delayed, so Wade arrived in Amman long after the last bus had departed. The plane ticket had cost him almost every cent he had left, leaving him enough for bus fare to Aqaba and perhaps a few sparse meals. He purchased a sweet cake and Pepsi from one of the airport vendors and settled himself as comfortably as possible in a corner.

After the final tourist hordes had been processed and gathered and sent to their hotels, the airport belonged to the Arabs. Desert travelers too poor to afford city prices bedded down in family clusters. From time to time one of their number would approach a short-tempered clerk to whine and plead and shake fistfuls of grimy tickets and beg for things that Wade could not understand. Each departing traveler was escorted by huge extended families who had brought comfortable-looking carpets, copper-lidded food containers, radios, and even several goats. The air was full of smoke and talk and wailing babies. Wade ate his sugary supper, leaned back, cast a final glance around the cluttered hall, and fell asleep.

He awoke the next morning with every muscle complaining from the hard floor. Bright sunshine lanced through the smoke-filled air. The hall was already filled with bustling, jabbering, scurrying figures who paid scant attention to yet another road-worn traveler.

Wade collected his meager belongings and made his way to the toilet. After scrubbing his face and the back of his neck he raised his head and stopped. For a long moment he stood and stared in the mirror, and wondered who was staring back.

Dark brown hair had been slicked back by countless motions of grimy hands too busy to bother with a brush. The bandanna knotted around his neck was matted with sweat and dirt. Hard travel and poor diet had honed down his features, giving his face a leaner, tougher cast. His nose and cheeks were splotched by multiple bouts of sunburn. His five-day growth covered a jaw set in alien, determined lines.

But it was his eyes that held his attention. They burned with a resolute light. There was none of the doubt that had plagued his life for so many years, none of the hesitant worry. There was no longer room for any of that.

The wind still blew from the southwest—never varying, never ceasing. All the clinic staff spoke of it and complained of the accompanying heat. To Allison, the reddish dust, blown in from the distant African plains, was a far greater trial. It was red and fine and irritated her throat and nose. Her eyes looked as though she suffered from a perpetual cold. She kept a plastic bottle of mineral water by her at all times, so that she could sip continually and ease the dryness caused by breathing dust. But the bottle had to be kept tightly capped; otherwise a thin red sheen would quickly appear across the water's surface. The dust coated every surface, even her papers, and left her hands and face and clothes feeling perpetually grimy. The dust made the hottest part of the day almost unbearable.

The knock did not raise Allison's attention from the dusty pile of forms. Someone was always coming by, asking in that pleading tone she hated for things she could not understand. She was in the middle of counting down a long line of figures, so when the knock was followed by the sound of someone clearing his throat, she impatiently waved the person away.

But when the unseen stranger spoke, the sound of an American accent pushed the numbers from her mind. "What?"

"I asked," the bearded, dirty young man asked, "if you were a doctor."

"No, I'm, that is..." She hesitated. The young man exuded mystery. His clothes were battered beyond belief. His features were chiseled, his air raffish, his look tremendously determined. "Who are you?"

"My name is Wade Waters." His voice was soft, almost apologetic. "I was wondering if you needed help—at the clinic, I mean."

His appearance was a strange mixture. Piercing eyes, yet gentle voice. Rugged good looks, a determined presence and an air of urgency.

She immediately assumed he was a doctor. "You are American?"

He nodded. "I've just—"

"I am Doctor Shannon," said a voice from down the hall. "Can I help you?"

The young man turned and said, "I was wondering if I could work for you."

Ben stepped into view, surveyed the young man, and asked, "Why?"

"I'm trained as a nurse, and," the young man hesitated, then finished, "I'm hungry."

Ben smiled. "That we can remedy. Forgive me for pressing, but a young American nurse appears out of nowhere seeking work—you must admit that a few questions are in order."

"I trained in Illinois," Wade responded. "I have a BA, a BSN, and two years experience at a U.S. hospital. For over a year now I have been a missionary nurse..." Again the hesitation.

"Where," Ben pressed.

"Grozny," the young man replied, almost a surrender. "It is the capital of Chechenya, north of the Caucasus Mountains."

Dr. Shannon's eyes widened considerably. "Not exactly a place from which I might obtain a recommendation."

The internal struggle subsided. "I am a good nurse, Doctor Shannon. Personal reasons have brought me here, that's all I can say. I don't know how long I will need to stay, probably several months. But I will work hard at whatever duties you give me."

"We are terrifically understaffed," Ben admitted. "But I cannot pay you anything more than room and board."

"That is enough."

"You will be watched carefully," Ben warned, "and not allowed to take on a number of duties unattended."

"I understand."

"Well, I am tempted, but I shall have to think more on this before making a decision. In the meantime." He turned to where Ali had appeared and waited just outside the door. "Take this young man over to the house and have Esa prepare him something to eat."

"And soap and a razor, if possible," Wade added quietly. "All my belongings have been stolen."

"Really? At the airport?"

"No." A moment's indecision, then the softly spoken words, "Near Tshkinvali."

"I beg your pardon?"

"It is the capital of South Ossetia. I was delivering Red Cross supplies to clinics along the battlefields, and my truck was stolen."

"And you came here from—what was that city called?"

Wade shook his head. "I flew to Amman from Tbilisi via Istanbul."

"So you traveled all the way from a war zone in Georgia to Aqaba in southern Jordan," the doctor said, and waited. But the young man gave no reply.

"I see," the doctor murmured. "Well, I suppose it will not hurt anything to offer our mysterious young man a meal and some soap. Ali?"

"This way," Ali said.

"You won't regret this," Wade promised as he turned away.

"I hope and pray not, young man," Ben Shannon said doubtfully. He gave an eloquent shrug to Allison and walked back down the hall.

Allison leaned back in her chair and cast a bemused look around her empty office. Suddenly everything seemed so quiet, as though a powerful and unexpected storm had just passed through.

Mentally she caught herself and pulled back hard. Allison returned to her work with a sigh. She always was attracted to the wrong sort of man.

10

Wade made his way from the clinic toward the local souk, which bordered the enormous truck compound. Aqaba's port traffic had exploded since the Iraq war, and the compound for trucks ferrying goods to and from the harbor was now a city in itself. He hoped that a little of what he had gained from his time in Russia would apply here as well. If so, then the market would not be simply a place to buy, but a focal point for community life, a magnet for all, a central gathering place for both people and information.

What he could possibly learn, neither knowing the language nor having the first contact, he had no idea. But he had to try.

The foremost ranks of stalls catered to the tourist trade—in this case, truckers from distant lands. There were the usual sorts of mementos on display—coffee urns, etched plates, brightly colored blankets, hookahs, rugs, hats, straw camels, leather gear, carvings. Wade walked past these offerings and searched for he knew not what. His obvious lack of money saved him from the worst of the sales pressure.

Past these outer ranks was the heart of the old market, row upon row of spindly stalls selling a vast variety of items. Sheep and goats and chickens kept up a panic-stricken cacophony at the row of butcher stalls. Fruit and spices and animals colored the enclosed air with intense fragrances. Flies swarmed everywhere. Dust settled on everything and everyone. The heat was fierce.

The cramped alleyway opened into an ancient central square. Tired donkeys and a few camels were lined up under a makeshift straw shelter. Some munched from feedbags; others drank from leather buckets held by ragamuffin youths in threadbare robes. A series of tea shops lined the opposite wall. Wade counted through his meager change and decided one glass would do no harm.

But before he could seat himself he felt a hand grasp his elbow. "Not there, Mister Wade. He will cheat you and serve bad food, make you sick. Come here, over here. My friend, he treat you better."

"I only wanted a tea," Wade protested. The young man from the clinic was called Ali, that much he recalled.

"Here, over here," Ali insisted, and led him to the corner shop. "What you like, I order for you."

"Just tea. I don't have much money."

"Is okay, Mister Wade. Today I buy. Another day you do same, yes?"

Wade shrugged. "Another day I still might not have money."

"Okay, okay, you buy when you can."

"Fine," he consented. "Whatever you say."

"Good." When they were seated, Ali launched a barrage at the hovering waiter, who remained utterly unmoved. When Ali stopped, he scooped up a pair of dirty glasses, ignored the overflowing ashtray, gave his filthy towel a single flick at the covering of dust, and slouched away. Ali turned back to Wade with, "Is good place, you see."

"The clinic pays you enough for you to eat in restaurants?" Wade asked.

The young man's eyes flickered everywhere but directly at Wade. "I already tell you. My friend, he own this place. I get special price."

"I see."

"For you too, when you come back. Just say you are friend of Ali, and all will be first-rate. You see."

"Thank you for your kindness," Wade replied.

Dark eyes turned and searched suspiciously for sarcasm, found nothing, and darted away. Ali reached inside his robes, extracted a pack of cigarettes. "You like?"

"I don't smoke, thank you."

He lit one for himself, drew on it with fierce intensity. He pulled his hand back in a jerky arc, threw the ashes out into the street with impatient gestures. Blasted the smoke from mouth and nose, paused to make smoke rings, drew again. An adolescent bundle of nerves. "You come from Russia, yes?"

"How did you hear that?"

"I hear," Ali assured him proudly. "All things in clinic, Ali know."

"I see." Wade nodded his thanks as the waiter deposited a glass of steaming tea in front of him, the mint leaves floating on the top, and a piece of rock sugar set upon the saucer. He had seen this in several Muslim cafes, where the men would place the sugar in their cheeks and suck on it as they drank their tea.

"Russia is far from Aqaba," Ali persisted. "Why you come?"

Wade knew the question had to be asked and answered. He knew also that he would not, could not, lie. But there was no way of knowing for whom Ali asked—for the clinic, or for others. "I am looking for a man," he said.

The smoking grew more intense, the eyes darted ever swifter. "Arab man?"

"No," Wade replied. "An American. He stole something from me. Something important."

"Money?"

Wade shook his head. "A truckload of medical supplies I was supposed to use to help the poor. And the truck."

"Whole truck of medicines," Ali mused aloud. "Worth much money."

"It was very hard to bring those supplies in," Wade continued. "A lot of people in dire need could have been helped."

"So why you look for American man in Aqaba?"

"A rumor," Wade replied. "It is all I have to go on."

The cigarette was already down to the filter. Ali took a final drag and flicked the remains out into the sunlit square.

"Maybe I help," he offered. "What he look like, this man?"

"Big," Wade replied. "Two meters tall, heavy, dark hair, blue eyes, very dangerous. Trained as a soldier."

Ali was not impressed. "There are many soldiers here. Some in army, most not. What his name?"

"Robards," Wade replied. "But most people call him Rogue."

Allison went through the motions of preparing for bed, but her mind remained fixed upon the day—and on the strange young man called Wade.

She could find no reason whatsoever to justify her interest, except perhaps the mystery surrounding him. He had cleaned up to reveal a fairly attractive person with nice, even features. The only remarkable thing about him, as far as she could tell, was the single-minded intensity that surrounded all his actions—that and his silence.

The one time she had seen him discard his reserve had been that afternoon. He had been assigned work in the men's ward. Ben had allotted Wade only the most menial of duties— changing sheets, prepping patients for surgery, bathing and feeding them—and those only under strict supervision. He was not to approach either the children's or the women's wards nor to touch any medicines. He was never to be left alone for an instant. Wade had accepted it all, including the ward nurse's evident hostility, with apparent indifference.

Yet when Allison was restocking cabinets that afternoon, she had caught sight of the nurse looking back toward the end of the hall, a bemused smile on her face. The nurse was a battle-hardened ward sister seldom given to any expression except a perpetual grimace. Curious, Allison had risen to her feet and looked down the hall to see Wade seated beside an old Bedouin trapped in the fever dreams of pleurisy. The old man had dribbled a broken stream of Arabic; Wade had responded with a continual croon of English, bathing his face and upper body with a cooling mixture of alcohol and water. His motions had been calm, steady, and patient—infinitely patient.

But it was the expression on his face that had captured Allison. The naked compassion reminded her of the way a mother might watch her own newborn. Allison had watched as the old man calmed, quieted, drifted into deeper sleep. Only then had Wade relaxed from his bent-over position, dropped the sponge into the basin, gently pulled up the sheets, and risen to his feet.

Instantly a querulous voice had reached out from another bed. Again Wade had responded with gentle patience, clearly not understanding what the man was asking, but in no hurry to leave until the request was discerned and answered.

"He says his bandages are uncomfortable," the nurse called out, making no move to approach.

Wade looked around and spotted a metal basin on a nearby table bearing new bandages, scissors, antiseptic, and tape.

He did not roll the patient over as much as help him turn at his own pace, soothing the occasional groan with a murmur of his own. Only when the man was resting comfortably on his side did Wade begin the laborious process of pulling away the soiled bandage. Blood had clotted the cloth, sealing it to the skin. Wade comforted not with words, but rather with his entire being. He plucked, waited, spoke, sponged, pulled again, his face filled with a compassionate sharing of the man's pain.

By then the families gathered at neighboring beds were watching, many faces bearing the same gentle smile as the nurse. They murmured their sympathy as the man jerked in response to Wade's last pulling tug. The man basked in the attention and relaxed under a touch he had come to realize would give him not an instant's more discomfort than was absolutely required.

The ward nurse happened to glance over at Allison. Something in her expression caused the nurse's smile to alter to a knowing smirk. Allison blushed without knowing why and fled back to her office.

Within a few minutes Ali was lounging in the doorway. "What you think of this man, this nurse?"

"I have work to do, Ali," she replied automatically.

"I ate with him," he announced. "We talked. He told me things."

She resisted the urge to raise her head. "What things?"

"Things," he repeated. "He comes from Russia."

She had learned it was best not to show too much interest in what Ali had to say. If she did, he treated it as a negotiable property, only to be traded for something in return. "I already knew that."

"Sure, Western lady. But did you know he was here looking for a man?"

She inspected a paper she scarcely saw and replied in a bored tone, "I don't think he mentioned that."

"American man," Ali confirmed. "Stole his truck. And medicines. This man Wade thinks is here."

"Seems strange that he would follow another American from Russia to Aqaba," she ventured idly, drawing designs on her pad.

"Yes, I think, too. Is crazy. Just another Western man with no idea of where he go in life." Ali turned from the door. "I tell Doctor Ben."

Allison carried that bit of news and the look on Wade's face with her through the rest of that day. She thought of it as she washed her face and brushed her hair. But it was only after turning out the light and climbing into bed that a new thought struck her. It came unbidden, and she could see no logical reason for it. But it came with such force that it left her shaken and unable to sleep.

The thought was that this young man would change her entire life, if only she would let him in.

By the end of the week, Wade's presence in the clinic was an established fact. He worked the long hours, accepted the basic conditions and standard fare and lack of pay without complaint. Constant emergencies and an overworked staff soon dissolved his restrictions. He moved freely through the men's and children's wards, carefully avoiding the women's rooms out of respect for the clinic codes. This too won looks of approval from the other staff. He handled medicines with precision, gave careful attention to duties both major and menial, accepted orders without argument, yet also showed he could think on his own. By week's end, even Dr. Shannon greeted him with a smile.

The mysterious errand that had brought this young man to Aqaba was much discussed. Opinions varied. Some thought him foolish, Ali included. Many of the nursing staff, however, took note of his abilities and his quiet demeanor, and accepted his single-minded determination as just another part of his makeup.

Wade was assigned to the morning shift, which was by far the busiest; it included both breakfast and lunch, the doctor's morning rounds, surgery prep, processing new patients, bathing and cleaning and dressing wounds. Wade finished sometime between two and five each afternoon, depending on how the day progressed. Then he returned to his room, changed clothes, rested, ate, and began his endless searching in the cool of the dying day.

He had registered his complaint with the local police, whose only interest was sparked by the idea of one American following another American from Russia to the tail end of Jordan. Now he mostly walked and looked—and daily resisted giving in to the futility of his search.

Dr. Shannon called Wade in after the clinic's Sunday worship service and asked him to be seated. "I have heard, as has everyone here, that you are here looking for another American who stole a truck from you in Russia."

Wade nodded reluctantly.

"And you really think the man you seek is here?"

"It's all I have to go on."

"He told you himself where he was going?"

"No." Wade hesitated, then added, "It was one of his companions."

"Then he's not alone?"

"I'm not sure, but I don't think so."

Ben Shannon examined him carefully. "The Arabs are the world's experts at saying much through the silences between words, so I have become skilled at listening for what is not being said. I have the distinct impression that you are leaving out more than you are telling."

Wade tensed, then forced himself to relax. "I have told you all I can."

"Tell me this," Ben insisted. "Is it possible that your search could endanger this clinic?"

Again there was the inward struggle, then Wade conceded, "Rogue Robards is a very powerful man."

It was Ben's turn to deliberate. "You are one of the finest nurses I have ever had occasion to work with. That much is clear after just five days. And it is true that the workload here is pushing us beyond our limits. But before I can allow you to remain, I must have your solemn word that you will do everything possible not to endanger our work."

"You have it," Wade replied earnestly.

"Wait, there's more." Ben bore down on him. "I also have the impression that more is involved than just a stolen truck. If I am to trust you with the lives of my patients, I feel I have a right to ask what this is."

Wade dropped his eyes to his hands, and replied quietly, "I'm sorry, but I just can't tell you."

Ben regarded him steadily, and said, "Tuesdays and Thursdays I make rounds within the local camps. I want you to come and assist. I want you to observe me very carefully. After you have gone with me, if you decide that I am worthy of your trust, I ask that you tell me what you are leaving unsaid. However, if you feel that I cannot be trusted with your secret, then I must ask you to leave at the end of the week."

"I guess I don't have any choice," Wade said bleakly.

"On the contrary," Ben replied. "Choice is all we are speaking of. For you, and for me."

That night Wade accepted last-minute duty to replace an ill staff member. He slept late the next morning and ate his breakfast alone. Heavily burdened both by a sense of futility and the impending choice, Wade took a purposeless walk down into the souk. At the central square he took a table just inside the shop's open doorway. When the same bored waiter appeared, he purchased his seat for the price of a tea.

He sat and watched the dust drift in the brilliant sunshine, while various half-formed ideas flitted through his troubled mind. Overriding every thought was a feeling as intense as the rising heat—that it was all a mistake. That he had no business being there, and all would result in futility.

Which made the sound behind him even more shocking.

"You're making yourself a real nuisance, sport," said the unseen man. "There's a knife aimed at your gizzard. Calm and easy, now, I want you to—"

Wade acted without conscious thought. In a single electrified movement he threw his glass back over his shoulder and dived through the doorway.

Behind him echoed a roar of rage and pain.

Wade did a three-point scramble in the dust, arms akimbo and legs flailing wildly, and fled down the nearest shop-lined alley.

Allison was just climbing into the clinic's battered Land Rover when a very dusty Wade came racing into view. "Where are you going?" he demanded breathlessly.

"Just our normal supply run to Amman. Why?"

"Take me with you," he burst out. The focused power to his gaze shone with feverish intensity.

"What's the matter?"

"Please," he said, pressing with more than just his words. "It's really important."

"Are you in some kind of trouble?" Allison had a sudden thought. "Did you find that man?"

Wade shot a glance over at where the clinic's driver sat stoically behind the wheel. All he said was, "Please."

Allison pondered briefly. It was standard policy for all clinic staff to be granted lifts wherever official business took anyone, so long as there was room. "We'll be stuffed to the gills on the way back."

"No problem. I'm used to cramped quarters."

She shrugged. "I guess it's okay, then." She cast a glance over his rumpled form. "Do you want to change or anything?"

"No, I—" he stopped. "My passport! I'll be right back."

Allison stared after his departing back and felt a faint tingle of alarm. The only place she could think of where a passport would be required was entry into the American Embassy.

Judith Armstead strode impatiently out of the US embassy in Amman, crossed the dead space and entered the guardhouse, where all nonembassy personnel were required to sign in. She greeted her friend with "What took you so long?"

"I was lunching with the ambassador and the foreign minister," Cyril Price replied. "What on earth is the matter? Our meeting with Allison is not for another hour."

"You'll see." Judith managed a quick glance at her watch as Cyril surrendered his passport and signed the passbook. "Come on, we've got to get this finished before Allison shows up."

He nodded his thanks as the Marine guard waved him through the security gate, then crossed the open parking lot and hurried up the US embassy stairs. "Don't tell me there's trouble."

"I'm not saying another word," Judith replied. She hustled her British counterpart through the main entrance, across the foyer, and down the long hallway. "I want you to hear this straight from the horse's mouth."

She opened the door leading to the small conference room and let Cyril enter first. Seated within was a decidedly scruffy young man, dusty and sweaty and clearly the worse for wear. But his expression was resolute and he measured Cyril with a cautious eye.

"Wade Waters," Judith began, "this is—well, let's just leave out any introductions for the moment, okay? This man is the primary contact in these parts for activities such as what you have been describing."

"If I'm to trust him," Wade replied, his voice as steady as his gaze, "I want to know who he is."

"Cyril Price at your service," Cyril said, taking a seat across from the young man. "Judith says you have something of interest to tell me. I have known Judith for a number of years and have learned to trust her implicitly."

"Cyril's the real thing," Judith said, seating herself beside Cyril. "Why don't you just take it from the top and tell him exactly what you told me."

When Wade finished, Cyril sat in stunned silence. "I confess," he said finally, "I am at an utter loss."

A smile appeared on Judith's face. "That is a first."

"Would you permit me," Cyril asked, "to return to a few minor points?"

"Sure," Wade replied.

"Judith, how much time before our next appointment?"

"Fifteen minutes, tops."

"We shall simply have to reconvene another day. Would you mind returning to Amman later in the week, Mr. Waters?"

"If I have time off," Wade replied. "And if I can find enough money for the trip."

"That's right," Cyril recalled. "You spent virtually every cent you had after losing your truck in... what was the name of that town once again?"

"Beloti," Wade replied. "About twenty-five kilometers north of Tskhinvali."

"Ah, yes. And that is..."

"The capital of South Ossetia," Wade replied. "A contested region currently held by Georgia."

"You do not, I hope, take offense by my returning to such points," Cyril said. "My memory, you understand—an attribute of age."

"I understand perfectly," Wade replied calmly. "I have spent more than a year in places where strangers are tested as a matter of habit."

Cyril's gaze turned keener. "Ah, yes. You were in Grozny, I believe." And with that he switched to a passable Russian. "You were no doubt instructed in the local tongue."

"Many of the locals," Wade countered, also in Russian, "would dispute your calling this language their own."

"Indeed," Cyril said, returning to English. "Most interesting. Well, I suppose that brings us to asking for a description of the three men."

"Four," Judith corrected. "Don't forget the American. I was just finishing up the descriptions when you arrived."

Wade asked, "Is there any chance you could find me a job or something where I can earn my keep?" Swiftly he explained the problem with Ben Shannon.

"It so happens that I know Dr. Shannon," Cyril replied, avoiding any eye contact with Judith. "Quite well, as a matter of fact. I shall write a note for you to carry back with you to clear things up."

"That would be great," Wade said, visibly relieved.

"If I were in your position," Cyril went on, "I should trust Ben Shannon with everything you know. He is both well connected and extremely trustworthy."

"I was worried that somebody that close to the locals might pass on word."

Both Cyril and Judith shook their heads to that. "Not a chance," Judith stated flatly.

"I quite agree," Cyril said. "Ben Shannon positively loathes the activities of terrorists. You will do well to trust him with your secrets, young man."

"While we're at it," Judith interjected, "it probably wouldn't hurt to supply you with a little pocket money."

"An excellent idea." Cyril rose to his feet. "I am afraid that a prior appointment forces us to end our discussions for now. I suggest that we plan to meet again on," he thought for a moment, then asked, "Would Thursday suit both of you?"

"Thursday's fine with me," Judith said.

"If I can get off work," Wade said.

"Trust Ben Shannon with your secret," Cyril said, "and you will find any number of impediments disappearing from your course. And rest assured that we shall in the meantime make every effort to seek out the men you have described."

He offered Wade his hand. "As my colleague mentioned, it is very seldom that people surprise me. You, young man, have succeeded in doing so. I shall look forward with anticipation to our next meeting."

After Wade's departure, the pair stood and watched the closed door for a time before Cyril murmured, "Most remarkable."

Judith took that as her cue. "You're going to use him as bait too, aren't you?"

Cyril nodded. "Now that all else has failed, it may be the only way to draw the lion from its lair."

"You're not going to warn him to stay out of harm's way?"

"Oh, I am certain he will remain enclosed and relatively safe for a time." Cyril smiled frostily. "Perhaps even as long as a day or two."

"And then?"

"Then the same determination that has brought him this far will push him out into the open yet again."

"They'll be waiting."

"And so shall we. You must double the guard at the clinic."

"That will just about strip the cupboard bare."

"The cupboard has up to now produced nothing of substance," Cyril replied. "Let us place all our resources where we have the best chance of succeeding. Allison and this lad must be watched every step of the way."

Judith smiled. "I know that look."

"What on earth are you talking about?"

"You do have plans for this young man, don't you?"

"Yes, well. It is so very seldom these days that one finds a person who combines a talent for adventurous derring-do with an ability to think on his or her feet."

"What about Allison?"

"Oh, our young lady has all that and more." He gave a fond smile of remembrance. "Her father would be so very proud of her."

Judith watched him with wise eyes. "They would make quite a team, wouldn't they?"

"I find it is best not to raise my hopes too high," Cyril replied. "But yes, I admit the thought has crossed my mind. And yes, they would make a truly formidable pair."

"So will you tell her about him?"

Cyril thought it over. "I think not. This is Ben's turf, at least within the clinic. It should be his decision." The glint of humor resurfaced. "Besides, not telling them should grant our dear Dr. Shannon yet another reason to be irritated with me. That should please him no end."

The three-hour trip back to Aqaba that afternoon was long and hot and far too quiet. The Land Rover's air conditioning provided a fitful stream that blew only when the truck was coasting downhill. The trip left Allison feeling sticky, dirty, and frayed around the edges. But that was not what bothered her the most.

It was Wade's total lack of interest in her that really hit where it hurt. Not that he was anything like her ideal man. Yet here she was, upset because Wade sat and stared straight ahead, not speaking with her, not noticing her at all.

She didn't know anything about him. He probably had a girlfriend. Maybe he was even married. She checked as unobtrusively as she could—no ring. Not that it meant anything these days.

Allison looked out at the arid landscape and could almost hear her girlfriend's condescending voice. A male nurse—are you kidding? The bartender at Clyde's would be a big step up. Yet she could not deny she was attracted to him.

Since Wade's attention remained focused outside the car, Allison took the opportunity to furtively inspect him.

Nice hair. Beautiful green eyes—his best feature, really, with that strong, purposeful gaze. Not too strong a chin, but he was so determined it was hard to notice.

Clearly not a snappy dresser. But Aqaba was not a place that attracted men from the pages of *GQ*.

Great teeth. She wondered what his smile would look like.

Then she recalled his caring attitude toward the patients, and felt that little catch to her breath once more.

Was she really interested in a relationship with him? She pushed the thought away as hard as she could. Definitely another Mister Wrong, to be avoided at all costs.

And yet there was something to him that she could not put her finger on. Something that called to the heart's small voice. Something that would not be denied, no matter how hard and loud her mind might object.

Allison risked another furtive glance at her silent neighbor and wondered at the emotions welling up inside.

Wade was immensely relieved when they arrived back at the clinic. As soon as the Land Rover pulled up to the main gates, he bolted as though flung from an ejector seat.

Sitting next to Allison the entire way to and from Amman had been sheer agony.

She was without a doubt the most beautiful woman he had ever met. And because of that, she was utterly beyond his reach.

Wade had tried as hard as he could to hold his attention to the matters at hand, but with Allison beside him it had been impossible. The fact that she had been so close and yet so unreachable had left him hollow.

Wade found Ben in his cramped office, working his way through a pile of forms. He knocked on the open door. "Can I bother you for a moment?"

"Only if it's good news," Ben replied, giving him a tired smile. "I've had one of those days."

"I'm not sure whether this is good or not," Wade ventured doubtfully. "Maybe I should wait until tomorrow."

"What, and leave me free to worry all night?" Ben shook his head. "Too late for that. Come in and sit down." When Wade had done so, Ben asked, "What's on your mind?"

Wade offered him the note from Cyril. "Maybe you ought to read this first."

"Read what?" Ben opened the letter. He read the note a second time, growing grimmer by the minute. Finally he said to no one in particular, "Is this his idea of a joke?"

"He told me you would understand."

"Oh, I understand, all right. I understand my old friend suffers from an overdose of international intrigue." He focused on Wade. "Go find Allison and bring her here, please."

"But I'm not—"

"Now," Ben said.

Wade departed in utter confusion. He found Allison in the dining room, glumly passed on the message, and responded to her query with a shrug. He followed her back into Ben's office and allowed himself to be guided into a seat.

"All right," Ben said. "I will start the ball rolling. Allison Taylor is here at the request of Cyril Price." He ignored Allison as she bolted upright in her chair. "She is assisting British and American Intelligence in trying to track down smugglers of nuclear scientists."

Allison protested, "Why are—"

Ben stopped her with an upraised palm, his eyes never leaving Wade's face. "Now it's your turn."

"I'm not sure—"

"I am," Ben interrupted. "These shenanigans will not extend to cat-and-mouse games inside my clinic. Now then." He folded his arms across his chest. "You trust me, you trust her."

Resigned to his fate, Wade gave them a scaled-down version of his experiences over the past month. When he finished, he risked a glance at Allison. She stared at him in open-mouthed shock.

Ben, on the other hand, responded with a grin. "That tale is far to wild to be a lie."

"I've told you the truth," Wade responded quietly.

"Yes, I believe you have." Ben eyed him with newfound respect. "And what would you call the coincidence that has brought you to this particular clinic at this particular time?"

"A miracle," Wade said softly, warmed by Allison's uninterrupted gaze.

11

Allison was awakened by a knock on her door. "Sorry to trouble you so early," Ben said. "There's been a change in plans. If you want to come with us, you need to be ready in ten minutes."

She struggled to blink away the sand still clinging to her eyelids. She scratched her head and instantly regretted it. Her hair still felt stiff, despite three washings that had turned the shower floor brown. "Come where?"

But he was already moving away. "I'll have someone bring you a cup of coffee. Please hurry."

The afternoon before, the skies had darkened and shadows lengthened and dogs howled, and evening had descended hours early. Then the southwest wind had delivered a deluge of fine red dust that was finer than sugar frosting, lighter than face powder. Swiftly every flat surface—floors, desks, cabinets, shelves, beds, and patients—was layered with the stuff. The clinic staff was kept frantically busy trying to keep damp cloths over the mouths of patients—an almost impossible task, since a perfectly clean pail of water was polluted with silt ten minutes after being filled.

Late that night, when the wind began to settle, they found the dust would not. The slightest footstep sent rust-colored plumes wafting to the ceiling. The only way to clean it up was with a damp cloth, on hands and knees, scouring away at everything. Stripping all the beds. Washing down every surface. Sterilizing all the equipment. It had even managed to infiltrate half of their refrigerators.

Allison had finally pleaded exhaustion and stumbled to bed around two that morning.

She arrived downstairs to find three men already in the Land Rover. When she appeared in the doorway the driver fired up the motor. She slid into the backseat beside Wade, taking meager satisfaction from the fact that he looked as tired as she felt.

"What's going on?"

Wade shrugged a weary reply. Ben waved the driver on and said, "We have to hurry. The boat leaves in less than half an hour."

"What boat?" she asked, then gave up as the engine bellowed and cut off further talk.

They flew down the hillside, weaving in and out of traffic, driving as much by the horn as the wheel, scattering dogs and people. Women hiked the hems of their djellabas and scampered to safety, children in tow. Allison saw no angry gestures at their passage, only waves; clearly the locals were accustomed to the doctor's quick getaways.

Buildings grew higher and streets broader the closer they came to the sea. Hotels sprouted balconies and names in both Arabic and English. Trees rose alongside the boulevards. Shops bore signs advertising Swiss watches and Italian suits and French perfumes. White-limbed tourists paused to inspect prices and take one another's pictures. Allison felt as though she was catching a fleeting glimpse of another world.

They took the main boulevard around to the port. Traffic ground to a halt behind an endless line of trucks. Ben threw open his door, said, "We'll have to go the rest of the way on foot."

"But where—"

"No time!" Ben was already striding down the sidewalk, motioning for them to follow.

She looked a question at Wade, who spoke for the first time. "I don't know any more than you do. But it looks like if we're going, we'd better do it now."

They slid from the Land Rover and hastened to catch up with Ben. Their path edged past three battered steamers unloading sacks and bales of goods, both by crane and by endless lines of sweating men. Ben dodged through the lines, hustled down a long, littered passage, and finally stopped at a windowless gatehouse. Beyond swarmed a mass of humanity. Farther still rose the filthiest boat Allison had ever seen.

The officers staffing the guardhouse clearly knew Ben. All three rose from their sullen lethargy and offered smiles and outstretched hands. Ben returned the greetings, motioned Wade and Allison forward, talked rapidly in Arabic.

At that moment the ship's whistle wailed. The people not yet on board responded with a cry of their own, and surged forward. Over the clamor, Ben indicated to the officers that they wanted to board. Allison looked from Ben to the struggling, shouting people and from them to the foul boat. She opened her mouth to say they could give her place to somebody else.

Before she could speak, two of the officers hefted long wooden batons and gestured for them to follow. Allison grabbed for Ben's shoulder, wanting to turn him around and tell him she had changed her mind, that she would wait in the truck. He mistook the gesture, grasped her hand tightly with one of his, and stepped forward. Immediately Wade moved up close, gripping her with one hand and Ben with the other. She was well and truly trapped.

The two officers used their batons to form a wedge. They pressed forward, shouting fiercely. Turbaned men and kerchiefed women turned angrily to see who was shoving them, recognized the uniforms, and stepped meekly aside. Ben drew himself and Allison and Wade up close behind the officers, so that they moved in virtual lockstep. As soon as they passed, the opening closed up behind them, swallowing them up into the noisy, smelly throng.

People closest to the gangway held money and tickets and passports aloft, screaming continuously at the two sailors barring their way. The officers pressed grimly forward until they were directly in front of the gangway. The noise was deafening. The sailors were not impressed by the guards' uniforms, and gesticulated that there was no more room. But the officers had not come that far only to be turned away. Angrily they pushed the sailors aside and formed a narrow passage between them. Ben ducked his head and slipped through, pulling the pair along behind.

The sailors shouted a protest but were kept from following by the crowd, who saw an opportunity for themselves and massed forward. Arriving at the top of the gangplank, Allison looked back to see the horde funnel into the gap, carrying both officers and sailors with them. But three more sailors pushed by Allison to join their mates, and together they forced the crowd back down. The whistle hooted, the sailors retreated, the gangplank was removed, and the boat chugged away.

"I had expected for us to travel to Nuweibi tomorrow."

Ben stopped to wipe his brow. "I only heard at the last minute that the boat had been rescheduled to leave today."

Allison turned to Wade and explained, "We heard a rumor that this place might be used as a staging point."

"More than rumor, less than fact," Ben added. "Nuweibi is an Egyptian port on the Sinai Peninsula, about halfway down the Gulf of Aqaba. The full name is Nuweibi al-Muzayyinah. Because smuggling has become so serious a problem, all sea travel between Jordan and Egypt and Saudi Arabia has been limited to these weekly ferries. They don't hold to a set departure date, in order to lessen the crowds."

"Their plan isn't working," Wade offered.

"It is far better than it might have been." He gestured for them to follow. "Come, we'll be more comfortable in the bow."

Once the boat was well underway, the clamor died. Those who had made it on board swiftly settled into the relaxed activity of people long used to endless waiting. Bedrolls and prayer rugs and frayed carpets were laid out, marking clan territory. Lines formed at two kiosk windows selling lukewarm drinks and coffee and platters of unidentifiable food. Men lounged and chattered and smoked. Women gathered and tended children. All eyes marked the Westerners' gradual progress.

Allison did not see another white face.

Conversations stopped as they approached the bow, and everyone turned to stare. Ben responded with a nod, a wave, and words in Arabic that resulted in a blooming of delighted smiles. Room was made for them at the railing. Ben had been right about one thing; here the air was indeed better. It blew directly off the sea, uncontaminated by the countless bodies crowded in behind Allison.

When curiosity about the three white passengers abated, Ben turned to Allison and Wade. "Are you both all right?"

Wade nodded. Allison declared, "I never want to go through anything like that, not ever again."

"I am truly sorry," Ben replied. "It is always such a press for these ferries, and with the new travel restrictions the situation has become almost impossible." Ben motioned at the boatload behind them. "The people you see here come from Egypt, Sudan, Libya, Chad, Niger, Mali, even as far away as Morocco. They come from small desert villages that are often a hundred miles from the nearest electric light or running water. But still they hear of the money to be made in these richer lands. So they hoard their pennies or sell their livestock or barter a prayer rug that has been in their family for generations. They walk the days or weeks to the nearest big road, buy a ticket for the bus or the train, and make their way to Nuweibi.

"For some the trip lasts a week, for others up to three months. They gather there, where corrupt agents squeeze out the people's last remaining pennies in exchange for work contracts the majority cannot read. These agents of course collect their commissions from those hiring, but such agents do not rise to the rank of flesh peddlers unless they are utterly consumed by greed."

Ben's face grew stern, his eyes lost their light, his voice cut like a rapier's sweep. "So the guest workers board the ferries and go to work as street sweepers and janitors and dishwashers and ditch diggers. They work six, sometimes seven days a week. They are paid a pittance, but it is a fortune by the standards of their homelands. They often do not return until their contract is completed. They do not see their families for as long as ten years, and their families are almost never allowed to join them. They often live in appalling conditions. But they have no recourse, no one to turn to. No local or international agency sees to their rights. It is a practice that has existed for a thousand years, and is accepted by almost everyone here. The argument is that the guest workers are so much better off, even under these circumstances, than they would be at home. And because this is tragically true, the people keep coming."

Allison demanded, "What are we looking for?"

Ben responded with a glance toward Wade. "I will do a quick check of the four local clinics. That is normal for me. I try to come over every few months to see what they need. Our way will take us along the central thoroughfares. Search the markets, the cafes, the streets. Be extremely careful not to become separated, both of you. And watch out for thieves."

The voyage was long and hot and monotonous. Allison watched hill after desert-colored hill pass until the sun's glare became too strong. Ben then found them a place to sit and doze by a shaded bulkhead.

When they arrived at the port, the chaotic scramble occurred in reverse. At Ben's direction they hung back and watched passengers push and shove and shout and scramble off the boat. When the worst of the crush was over, he slipped away, then returned a few minutes later and motioned them to follow.

"Where did you go?" she asked.

"To ensure our return passage. We must hurry. There isn't much time."

The port area was a series of dilapidated metal and concrete warehouses lining a red-clay street. Their way was often blocked by crowds gathered about hawkers who had set up impromptu stalls wherever foot traffic was heaviest.

The dust was as fierce as the heat. Following Ben, they sidled around packed throngs of gawking Arabs and Africans. Their shirts swiftly became plastered hard to their backs and coated with the reddish sand. Where possible they stayed to the shadows; entry into daylight meant being struck by hammer blows of heat. Wade searched in vigilant silence, his eyes constantly on the move.

Nuweibi looked just like what it was—a poor Egyptian village overwhelmed by a flood of humanity. The original blockhouse structures were now merely a centerpoint to a sprawling city of shacks and shanties and tenements. There was little electricity, less running water, the most rudimentary of sewage. The only saving grace for most of the people was that they would not be staying long. Those who lived there permanently were drawn from life's very dregs.

Allison passed gatherings from three dozen different tribes representing the length and breadth of Africa. Many of the darker men and women had faces deeply marked with tribal scars—patterns cut into cheeks and foreheads with ritual knives during coming-of-age ceremonies. Headdresses varied as widely as stature and faces and dress, ranging from simple rags to elaborate coiffures of brightly colored cloth and beads and silver pins.

Ben knew exactly where he was going, and he did not tarry. He led them past great open spaces where men harangued gatherings and waved papers bearing fancy script. He ignored the cries of stall holders and the smells of cooking and the plucking arms of beggars. His calls on the clinics were in-and-out affairs. He was clearly uneasy being in Nuweibi, and was determined to cover the ground in the least amount of time possible.

It was while he was in the third clinic that the bandits struck.

Like many of the older structures, the clinic was built upon a raised foundation that lifted it above the worst of the rainy-season mud. A narrow sidewalk fronted it and the businesses to either side. The walkway had not been built to handle the foot traffic now inundating the town. Stopping and standing proved difficult because it forced people to shove around them. Allison did so anyway, as the sidewalk offered them shade.

At first the tug on her shoulder bag was so gentle that she simply took it for someone's robe having snagged it in passing. But when she pulled back, the tug became sharper. She tightened her grip and jerked, then felt the grimy hand weaseling around her fingers.

Allison tried to reach over with her other hand, but the crowd was especially thick just then, and suddenly there was another body blocking her movement, another pair of hands reaching for a hold on her arms.

Her call for help almost came too late. But the knife's blade caught a glimmer of the sun. As her grip loosened, Allison folded in and around the bag and screamed as loudly as she could.

Suddenly a whirlwind erupted around her.

The pull on her bag loosened as swiftly as it had come. The crowd parted, no match for the force that assaulted it. Allison looked up, still tensed into her half-crouch, and saw Wade shove a second man off the sidewalk and into the dust, then turn and barrel into a third.

It all took place in less than three breaths.

Ben appeared in the doorway. "What is—"

"Come on!" Wade shouted. He reached and plucked up Allison with a surprising strength for his slender frame. "Back to the boat!"

While the crowd was still collecting itself, Wade drew Allison up next to him and jammed them through. Not quite a run, but fast enough to jar.

Aggressive. Hard and sharp and as determined as his gaze. The crowd parted before them.

"What happened," Ben demanded, hustling to keep up with Wade.

"A thief tried to take my bag," Allison said, gradually recovering. The vision of the knife blade still swam before her eyes, and she was grateful for Wade's supporting arm.

"It wasn't just a grab," Wade said, not slowing down. "And it wasn't just a thief. There were a lot of them, and it was slick. They separated us before I even knew what was going on. Just a tight group of people, sliding us apart one half-step at a time, and if she hadn't yelled I wouldn't have noticed what was going on until too late."

"Take this left," Ben directed. "How can you be so certain it wasn't just a thief taking advantage of the situation? We haven't finished covering the ground yet."

"I don't know how I'm sure," Wade said stubbornly. "But I am. And I'm not going to let her risk staying around here any longer."

Let me risk staying. Normally Allison would have bristled at the sound of someone looking out for her like that. But just then it sounded nice. Warm and comforting. Something a friend would do. Let her be weak for a moment. *The knife.*

"I'm still not clear—"

Wade slammed to a stop so sharp that Allison almost lost her footing and Ben rammed into them from behind. Ben protested but was cut off by Wade's upraised hand. "I thought I heard something," he said, and squinted into the shadows of a rank and narrow alley.

Then Allison heard it too. A voice. Speaking in a tongue she had heard before but could not understand. Soft and sibilant and musical. Wade answered in kind.

She asked, "Is that Russian?"

The voice from the shadows said once more, "Can this truly be the man who has robbed me of my nights?"

"Alexis," Wade said, his heart hammering hard. "Is that you?"

"Rogue said he had found you in Aqaba, but I could believe it only because of the anger he shows when speaking your name. I have both hoped for and feared this moment." The Russian stepped forward far enough to reveal himself, then slipped back again. "All night I hear your voice, my friend. There alongside the calls of my wife and child. Asking me questions for which I have no answers."

"What are you doing here?"

"Yes," Alexis agreed. "That is one of them. And others. Many others. Too many. I find I cannot go on, but I also do not know where I might go instead."

"Is Robards after you?"

"If they already know of my absence," Alexis replied, "then you are speaking to a dead man. I saw you and your friends from my window, and I slipped out. They leave me alone much of the time, you see. I have not been well. I lie in bed much of the day, trying to regain what you have taken from my nights."

"Will you come with us?"

Still he hesitated. "I am defeated. I cannot go and do what I know is wrong. It would kill me. But where else can I go? You have given me so many questions, now answer one. What can I do? I will not go back to Russia, that is certain. Where else is there for me? How can I bring my family together again?"

"I don't know," Wade replied honestly. "But I will try to help."

Alexis thought on this, and decided. "Then I will come."

A cry was raised behind them. Wade started, wheeled around, and saw the man he had shoved from the sidewalk heading a gang that stalked the alley toward them. "We must flee!" he cried, for a moment not even aware that he still spoke Russian. "To the boat!"

Whatever the language, they all understood. They raced down the alley and across the central square, dodging through the throngs gathered about the various job peddlers. And it was the crowd that saved them. Where four white-faced foreigners were given the leeway to scramble through, a gang of local ruffians were caught like a beast in quicksand. One pushed someone, who hit another, who pushed back, and soon the entire clearing was a mass of cursing, heaving, jostling humanity.

Together the four of them raced down the central port road, skirted the hawkers, rushed past the guards, and ran up the gangway to the boat.

And safety.

<u>12</u>

The next afternoon, Allison found Wade waiting in Ben's empty office. "Did he call for you too?"

"Oh." At the sound of her voice, Wade leapt to his feet. "I mean, hello."

His shy uncertainty was such an incredible difference from the take-charge attitude he had shown the day before.

"I'd like to thank you for what you did yesterday."

"I didn't really do anything..."

"Don't say that," she said, determined not to be put off by his reserve. She took the seat next to him, then waited for him to settle. "If you hadn't moved so fast, I might not be here today."

Wade looked down at his hands. "I don't know what came over me," he said quietly. "When I heard you call—"

She repressed a shudder at the memory and said lightly, "A lot of good my homing device would have been."

"Your what?"

"Oh, something Cyril gave me. He said I should switch it on if I was ever in trouble." She sobered at the reality of how close the encounter truly had been. "I could have been—"

"Don't say it," Wade told her. "Don't even think it."

"All right." More softly, "At any rate, I do thank you."

"Oh good, you're both here," Ben Shannon said briskly, entering and closing the door behind him. "I have something to discuss with you."

"Did they find anything in Nuweibi?" Allison demanded.

"As I understand it," Ben replied, seating himself behind his desk, "the preliminary search last night was unsuccessful. But with the information Alexis supplied, the Egyptian authorities are again combing the area, and no doubt they will soon have everything under lock and key. Alexis himself is now safely ensconced in a hotel in Amman." He looked from one to the other. "I now feel that your work here at the clinic has come to a close."

Allison found herself with nothing to say. She looked at Wade. The young man observed the doctor with quiet intensity and said, "You were frightened."

"But you knew about this risk before we started," Allison protested.

"I did," Ben concurred. "Yet I did not truly come face-to-face with the possible danger until yesterday. I am in the business of running a clinic, not chasing after international smugglers and terrorists. I could not sleep last night from the thought of what might have happened."

"We're willing to take that risk," Allison responded.

"Perhaps, but I am not." Ben sighed. "Now these terrorists in Egypt know of us and probably know of my clinic. Whose lives have we put at risk? What will keep them from attacking us here?"

"We understand," Wade said quietly. "We'll pack and depart this afternoon."

"We will?" Allison demanded.

Wade turned her way and nodded slowly. "Could you really stay if he doesn't want you here anymore?"

"Allison, your administrative work is impeccable. Wade, you are one of the finest healers I have ever had occasion to work with. I would love to keep you both on in these capacities, and simply ask you to stop with the intrigue. But I can't. I hope you understand that. It has gone too far. I simply cannot put you or my patients or my other staff at risk."

Wade stood and lifted Allison with his gaze. "You have other responsibilities."

Ben did not rise. He kept his gaze on his desk, clearly unhappy with the turn of events. "I will stop in and see you both again before you go."

Wade followed her from the room. Once the door had closed behind them, she demanded, "Why wouldn't you let me argue with him?"

"Because it was tearing him apart," Wade replied softly. "His mind was made up. He was doing what he thought was correct, and he was doing it for valid reasons. What right did we have to try and force him to do something different?"

They walked outside and entered the brilliant sunshine. "I guess I better go pack," Wade said.

"Wait," said Allison. Someone was standing by the front gate, talking with Fareed and gesticulating urgently. "I think I know him."

"Who?"

Then it came to her. "That's Mahmoud. He's a Bedouin leader and a friend of Ben's." She started walking. "Come on."

Mahmoud was so fiercely involved in his discussion that he did not notice their approach. Then he saw Allison, shouted, and waved her over.

Allison demanded of the driver, "What's he saying?"

"Mahmoud, he say he must talk to Doctor Ben and right now."

"The doctor's tied up," Allison replied. "What's the matter?"

"He say, men come at dawn, set up camp. Another truck arrive later. He not know them, but one was tall white man who moved like a soldier. Two others spoke a different language, he thinks Russian."

"How can he be so sure?" Wade said, his voice taut.

Another rapid exchange, then, "Before were many Russian soldiers in desert, here with

Jordanians, with Iraquis. Make much trouble. He say maybe are people you seek."

Allison said, "Ben is going to stay tied up pretty much all day. Ask Mahmoud if he will take us with him now."

"But Doctor Ben, he say—"

"It's all right," Wade chimed in.

"We just spoke with him," Allison went on. "He can't be disturbed today. So we'll take care of it. Ask Mahmoud if that's okay with him."

Ben's driver posed the question. Mahmoud responded by turning and striding toward where his dusty truck was parked.

"Tell him I have to write Ben a note and pack a couple of things," she said to Fareed, then to Wade, "Let's get moving."

"Where are we going?" Wade said, hurrying to catch up.

"The desert!"

Night painted the desert with a mystic's brush. The half-moon competed with a million stars for their attention. The sands glowed as though lit by soft, silver fires. The mountains were great dark djinn, silver and still as the night, watchful as the stars, timeless as the wind.

Wade sat with his back to the camp, so he did not know of her approach until he heard the soft footfall. "Can I join you?"

He nodded, then realized she could not see him. "Please do."

"It's so beautiful," she said, sinking down

beside him. "Like another world."

"It is another world," he said quietly.

Mahmoud had brought them to the Bedouin camp just before sunset. Together they had paid respects to his father, talked with several of the men, arranged for Allison to bed down in one tent with the women and Wade in another, then Mahmoud had taken off again. He had not yet returned.

She looked at Wade. The campfire behind them cast half her face in the softest golden hues. "Are you afraid?"

It took him a while to answer. "I've been frightened for so long, I guess I've grown used to it."

"I don't think I could ever grow used to fear—or want to," she replied, then asked, "Would you tell me the whole story of how you came to Jordan?"

Because she asked with the tone of a friend, because they shared the exquisite aloneness of an empty desert night, because their fear was a bond between them, he told her. All of it.

She watched him intently while he talked, her gaze large and solemn, so quiet that Wade did not notice her shivering until he was almost done.

He interrupted himself with, "You're cold. Why didn't you say something?"

"I'm fine, really. Please don't stop."

But he was already up and moving toward the camp. He returned with a heavy blanket, which he flipped open and draped around her shoulders. "It's amazing how cold it gets out here at night."

As he settled back down, Allison lifted the edge toward him. "Come share."

Wade slid closer, and allowed her to drape the blanket around his back.

"Okay, now finish your story."

He did so, acutely aware of her warmth and the memory of her touch on his shoulder. He spoke, but scarcely heard himself. He was too full of her closeness and the night and the scent of her.

"So you used the church's money and followed them down here," Allison said when he fell silent. "Amazing. And you're sure it was the same man behind you in the Aqaba souk? What was his name?"

"Rogue Robards. And yes, I'm sure." Once again he was chilled by the memory of Rogue's words. A knife. He pushed the thought away by telling her the whole story of Alexis.

After a silence, Wade heard a new tone. With the voice of a woman-child, Allison asked him, "Did you leave a girl behind in—whatever that city was called?"

"Grozny." And because of the vulnerability in her voice, and because of the night and the stars and the wind, Wade found the courage to speak from the yearnings of his heart. "I've never had someone I really, you know, loved."

She backed off far enough to inspect his face. Wade turned to meet her gaze, although it was hard. With a wisdom that transcended his feeble words and her own awkwardness, Allison's gaze opened, filled with compassionate understanding.

And slowly, ever so slowly, she drew closer to him, stopping now to study his eyes, finding the reassurance she sought, moving closer, closer still, until her lips met his.

Wade awoke to a desert choir in full performance.

Donkeys brayed. Camels groaned. Goats bleated. Desert sparrows relished the power the echoes gave their chirps. Behind his tent a group of men chanted their morning prayers. Other voices murmured and called and even sang in their desert tongue. Baby goats cried like a band of hungry young children.

He rolled from his bedding, looked around, saw that all the other men of his tent were up and started with their day. He combed back his hair with his fingers, tucked in his shirt, flipped open the tent cover, and blinked in the glare.

"Good morning, sleepyhead." Wade squinted and saw Allison approach with a smile and a glass of tea. "I was just coming to wake you up."

Gingerly he accepted the steaming glass, grasping it around the rim. "How long have you been up?"

"Oh, hours." She smiled. "Truthfully, about fifteen minutes. Mahmoud wants to tell us something. He's waiting in the main tent."

Wade sipped his tea, struggled to find the proper way to say, "Our talk last night was, uh, really..."

"Me, too." The touch she gave his arm was as

soft as her gaze. "But we probably should save the rest for later. Mahmoud looked like a man in a hurry."

At their approach Mahmoud rose and offered them a formal greeting, to which they nodded in thanks, then he waved them to seats. His father blessed them with a toothless grin and chanted words they could not understand.

Mahmoud gestured with hands to the side of his head, asking how Wade had slept. Wade leaned forward and patted the stones lining the tent's central fire. Like a rock. The old man cackled with delight, then heaved his chest full with a deep breath. The desert air. Wade nodded his agreement and sipped at his tea. It was good to be alive.

By the tent's outer corner an older woman sat where she could remain in the shadows, yet still watch the children play. She combed shreds of thick goat's hair with a pair of wire brushes, then gathered the strands and spun them into black thread on a portable spindle. Beyond her, children laughed and squealed and rolled a pair of inflated goatskins back and forth between them. The children were beautifully bright, their intelligent faces so full of character that they looked more like miniature adults than true children. Then Wade heard the sloshing liquid inside the skins, and realized they were making curds from goat's milk.

Mahmoud brushed the sand before him flat and smooth, then drew a line and pointed to the eastern hills. He made a humping motion. Up and over to the other side. The old man nodded and spoke a running commentary as Mahmoud drew a slit running partway through the line—a narrow passage leading to the mountain's other side. Here he drew a circle, then pointed around him. A camp.

Next Mahmoud pointed to his own truck, pointed at the sun, drew a wavering line toward the sun. Then he pointed higher in the sky, drew another wavering line from a different direction. A third time the finger raised to point directly overhead, then a third line drew in toward the camp. Wade nodded and spoke to Allison, "I think he means he watched trucks come in yesterday at different times, from different directions."

"A meeting point," Allison said, slightly breathless with the sudden excitement.

Again Mahmoud pointed at his truck, then showed an open palm. Five vehicles. He then tapped the nearest stone, hands held over his head, squinted, looked around, shrugged. This time Wade looked confused; Mahmoud repeated the gesture. Then Allison understood. "He's saying the chasm has ledges so that the camp can't be detected from above."

Wade asked Mahmoud, "Bedouin?"

Mahmoud balanced his hands in the air. He was not sure. Then he pointed to his chest and shook his head. Definitely not of his tribe. He pointed at Wade and nodded vigorously. "Foreigners in the camp," Allison said.

Mahmoud stood. *"Jallah?"* We go?

Wade rose to his feet, and Allison followed. "Jallah," he agreed.

Before starting out, Mahmoud had them don old Jordanian army jackets—camouflage against prying eyes. He then brought out a pair of men's headdresses and insisted on fitting them both personally. The white-and-red-checked keffiyeh was set on the head, held in place with a black thong twisted into a figure eight then folded into a double loop. Mahmoud pointed from it to the camel's hoofs, indicating that it was also used for hobbling the animals in an emergency. Then the keffiyeh's two tasseled ends were crossed behind the head and tucked into the hoops.

By that time most of the camp had gathered to watch and see them off. They smiled and murmured approval when Wade was equipped, and joined in delighted laughter when Allison's headdress was set in place. They laughed even harder when the camels were led up.

Mahmoud showed them how to mount the animals, sitting side-saddle with their front leg cocked up and around the wooden saddle horn. The camels rose in stages, rocking like a small craft buffeted by heavy seas. They shared smiles as the Bedouins lifted hands and shouted *"Humdi-'lah"* in approval, their grins as bright as the sun.

Their passage over the desert took the better part of the day, a lurching journey over harsh and beautiful terrain. The wind was a constant force. It buffeted. It probed. It etched. It moaned a sibilant voice into Wade's ears, teaching him of the desert in a tongue only his heart could fathom.

The wind and the sun and the camel's rocking had a stupefying effect. Wade's whole body swayed in time to the motion. He found it increasingly difficult to keep his eyes open. At one point he drifted off entirely, only to be startled awake by a tap from Mahmoud's riding crop. The Bedouin pointed at the ground in warning. It was a long way to fall.

They stopped twice for water and unleavened bread and olives and goat cheese. Mahmoud would not let them tarry long, however, and made his fingers walk up while pointing to a setting sun. They must climb the hills ahead of them before dark.

The desert shadows were already slanting when they entered a maze of interlocking chasms. Mahmoud motioned to his lips—from here on they should not speak. As the cliffs closed in around them, they were granted welcome relief from the sun. Wade soon understood why they had not taken the truck; the sandstone walls tightened so that he could touch both sides at once.

As the sky began to darken overhead, they entered a sand-bottomed cul-de-sac containing an almost empty pool and a single tree. When Mahmoud made his camel kneel, Wade sank gratefully to the ground and walked about loosening his sore muscles. He glanced at Allison.

Her face was set in tired yet resolute lines.

While the camels slurped greedily at the pool's scummy water, Mahmoud pointed at one of the cul-de-sac's side walls and traced the upward passage they were to take. Wade immediately saw why they had raced the sun. Their climb would start upon a crevice fashioned into irregular stairs, then continue along a slender walk which had crumbled in places, reducing it to narrow toeholds. From there a kind of rough rock ladder ascended another forty, perhaps fifty meters.

Wade swallowed hard and refused the urge to simply sit down and give up.

Mahmoud turned to Allison and motioned that she should stay with the camels.

Although her face had turned pale beneath its coating of dust, she whispered, "I'm going with you," and pointed sharply first at herself, then at the wall.

Wade protested quietly, "Two of us—"

"Save your breath. I'm going, and that's all there is to it."

Wade turned back to Mahmoud, who responded with an eloquent shrug. He then walked to the crevice and started to climb.

The steps in the crevice were waist high and far from level. Wade climbed with hands as well as feet. Because the stone had been shaped by sand and wind instead of by water, the rock was very porous and offered good grips.

Mahmoud stopped them at the top of the stairs. Wade leaned his back against the rock and looked out, up, across—anywhere but down.

"Are you all right?" Allison whispered.

"I don't have much of a head for climbing," he admitted.

She bit down hard on a smile. "My pop would say this will either kill you or cure you."

"Thanks a lot."

Mahmoud hissed them to silence and started out along the ledge. Wade forced his muscles to unclench and followed. The ledge narrowed, then narrowed further, until they were progressing in a sideways crawl with their faces crammed up against the rock and their heels over the edge.

Then Mahmoud began to climb again, ascending the rock ladder. Wade clung grimly to the ledge until Mahmoud's boots were up above his head, then started up immediately. Anything was better than hanging on where he was.

One moment Mahmoud's boots were scrambling up above him, sending a shower of dust and stones down on his head with each step, and the next he was gone. Wade scrambled up the last few rungs, grateful for the strong arms waiting to help him over the ledge, then he was up. Sitting in safety. Helping Allison over the cliff's edge. Willing his legs to stop their trembling. Breathing great gulps of desert air and feeling the wind on his face. Safe.

They sat upon the roof of their desert world. The sun's ruddy orb touched distant peaks and began to dissolve into another evening. A thousand hues of orange and red and violet and deep blue painted the sky. Besides their own rasping breaths, the only sound they heard was the wind. Wade looked about, waited for his stuttering heart to quieten, and gloried in the boundless view.

Mahmoud turned from his inspection of the sunset to give them both a gold-toothed smile. He whispered, "Goot, yiss?"

"Good," Wade softly agreed. "Very, very good."

Allison nodded and looked around their plateau. It was a level space about twenty feet to a side, as though the peak had been sawed off. She pointed to the carved blocks set to one side and whispered, "This looks like another high place."

"A what?"

"You know, for sacrifices." Her brow furrowed in concentration. "Like the ones the king—I forget his name—struck down."

"Josiah," Wade replied, looking at her anew.

Mahmoud hissed from the plateau's opposite side, motioning for them to move over and stay low. They walked at a stoop, then sank to their knees and looked over the edge.

A narrow path crept down the mountainside from where they lay, making a series of jinking turns as it descended to where the chasm's sides joined. There a broad stone shelf jutted out, forming a natural protective barrier from any low-flying planes.

Allison pointed to the path and whispered, "The ceremonial way. The worshipers probably came up this side."

Mahmoud silenced her with an upraised hand. He then motioned with one finger to his nose, and breathed in. Wade smelled the wind, and nodded. Smoke.

Mahmoud pointed back to where the sun had descended behind the clouds and made a motion up and over the sky, then pointed down and traced a trail leading away from the rock overhang. When it was fully dark, the trucks would drive away.

They watched for a time as the darkness gathered. Twice Wade heard the muffled clank of metal upon metal; once he thought he heard the murmur of voices. But no one came into view.

Then he had an idea, and before fear could stop him he whispered, "Do you still have the homing device?"

"Yes, but what—"

"Show me how it works."

"There's just a switch to start the signal," Allison said, handing it over. Wade sidled along to where the path started its descent. Mahmoud started as though to rise up and protest, but Wade stopped him with a look. Confused and worried, the Bedouin sank back down.

Wade crept down the path, his heart thundering so loud he feared the men down below might hear. His hands kept to the cliffside, holding tightly onto nooks and crannies in case he slid. He did not. He made it down to the overhang just as the moon's first sliver appeared over the far peaks.

Wade dropped to his belly and slid toward the lip of the overhang. Holding his breath, he gradually eased himself out the last few inches until the hoods of five trucks came into view.

They were parked facing outward and crammed in so closely together that they completely filled the chasm's mouth. There was just enough light to see that the sandy ground leading into the gorge had been brushed to clear away the truck treads. A single guard sat on the hood of the central truck, busily eating from a tin plate in his lap, a carbine resting on the hood beside him.

A voice called softly from the unseen spaces behind the trucks. The guard swiveled, and instantly Wade slid back out of sight, holding his breath, steeled against the call of alarm. But he had not been seen. He heard the tread of boots over metal, and after a wait he risked another look.

The guard was gone.

From the back came louder sounds of people moving about, objects being shifted, murmured conversation. In the dying light Wade could see an old-fashioned metal lockbox welded to the front bumper of one truck. It was open, revealing tools and an oil canister and rags used for emergency repairs.

Moving quietly, pushed to hurry by the fading light, Wade slid over until he was perched directly above the truck. He leaned backward, slipped off one shoe, and slid off his sock. He pulled the homing device from his pocket, thumbed the switch, and slipped it into the sock. Then he balled the sock up tightly, reached over the ledge, held his breath, and took as careful aim as he could. Then he let go.

The sock dropped into the box with a muffled thud.

Wade slid back out of sight, rolled over, and lay looking up at the stars with his mouth open, breathing great silent gasps and feeling the sweat trickle down the sides of his face toward his ears.

The noises gathered, and metal scraped against metal as the trucks were rocked against one another by bodies sliding up and into place. Then one by one the motors started, roaring loudly in the confined space. Then the first one moved out, followed by its fellows. Traveling slowly, without headlights.

Wade waited until the engines' noise had drifted away, then rose to his feet and began his slow return to the top.

Judith Armstead and Cyril Price arrived at the American Embassy within moments of each other. He demanded, "Do you know what this is all about?"

"No," she replied grimly. "But if it's another false alarm, you are about to witness the demise of last night's duty officer. In any case, it appears that your bait has slipped off the hook."

"Yes," Cyril agreed tiredly, nodding to the Marine who passed him with a salute. "A bit tedious, that. I can only say how relieved I am that I don't have to face Allison's late father with this news."

"That's right. You used to work with Dr. Taylor, didn't you. Back in the good old days."

"Those days were many things, none of which I would describe as good." Cyril climbed the embassy stairs and held the great doors open for her. "Yes, John and I happened to be quite close. He had a way of dressing one down that practically flayed skin from bone, all without raising his voice."

"I seem to recall an instructor who shared that ability," Judith told him. "It made the experience all the more painful to have it done in such genteel tones."

"You can't possibly be referring to me," Cyril replied, tasting a small smile. "Still, I shudder to think what he would say to the news that I had managed to lose his daughter."

"In the Jordanian desert, no less." Judith keyed in the elevator doors. "How is Ben Shannon taking it?"

"The poor man is pulling out what little hair he has left. Fareed traveled out with our people and finally located the Bedouin encampment, far to the east of their normal grazing territories. The pair were nowhere to be found. Interestingly enough, their leader, Mahmoud, was also not there."

"It sounds—"

The door to the nearby stairwell slammed open. A young technician with glasses and tie askew announced, "We've got a reading on the homing transmitter!"

Cyril bolted forward as though electrocuted. "Tally ho, lads! The prey has been sighted!"

13

Wade and Allison dined that night at a sidewalk restaurant near the Gulf.

They had spent the night before in the high place, huddled together against the cold and watching the stars parade overhead in timeless grace. They had dozed, and awakened, and dozed again, warmed by each other's closeness and by the knowledge that everything possible had been done. The hunt was out of their hands.

At daybreak they had climbed down and started the long journey back to camp. Toward midmorning the desert stillness had been shattered by eight helicopters thundering by in close formation. Two hours later one had returned, circled them, then descended to earth. Cyril had alighted amid the rotors' noisy hurricane.

Two Russian nuclear scientists had been captured, he reported, and the men matched the descriptions Wade had supplied. Along with the scientists, they had seized three truckloads of components for making bombs and several lead-lined containers holding what he suspected was weapons-grade fissionable materials. Quite a haul.

When asked about Rogue Robards, Cyril had shaken his head. Several of the Bedouin guides had managed to escape, so perhaps he had vanished with them. Wade found himself both relieved and troubled by the news.

Cyril had been on his way back to Amman, where the scientists would be held for questioning. He offered the pair a ride back to Aqaba. They had bid Mahmoud solemn thanks and farewells, then returned to the port city by chopper.

"I'm a little sorry it's all over," she confessed. "It's been the most exciting time of my life."

"I'm sorry, too," he agreed, his eyes locked on hers, "but for different reasons."

The remains of their repast had been pushed to one side so that a way was clear between them. People smoked and talked and walked about the tables. Traffic hummed along the nearby street. In the distance, great cargo vessels and tankers vied for places in the crowded port. They saw none of it. Their attention moved no farther than the borders of their table.

"All that's happened," she shook her head. "I wonder if I'll wake up in a couple of weeks and decide it was all a dream."

Wade was silent for a moment, then said, "Can I ask you something?"

"Anything."

He hesitated, then asked, "Is there someone waiting for you?"

"No." She smiled without humor. "I'm afraid my love life has been sort of a mess."

"Do you want to tell me about it?"

"I guess it's like the song says, I was looking for love in all the wrong places."

"At least you were looking," Wade murmured.

"I didn't understand that having a man want you because he loves you is different from having him want you because he's weak and lazy." She hesitated, startled into silence by her own unexpected honesty. But Wade remained as he was, silent and focused upon every word. So she swallowed and went on, "I always defined myself by what he needed. You know. Typing his résumé. Cleaning up his apartment. Buying his birthday gift for his mother. Always ready to help out when he ran short of cash. All I ended up doing was trying too hard to overcompensate for the fact that he really didn't care that much at all. Caring takes effort. Caring means responsibility. And those are things a lazy sort of guy avoids at all costs. I was left feeling weak and dependent on someone who didn't want to help me, since that meant too much effort as well." Allison stopped once more and dropped her head, raw and ashamed and hurting by the confession.

He asked softly, "So what about giving to someone who needs you and loves you as well?"

"I can't tell you about what I've never known,"

she replied, still unable to lift her head. "More than anything, I guess I just want to feel wanted."

He reached out, took her hand, enveloped it in both of his. "What about someone who needs your strength but wants to give back from what little he has himself?"

"You have more than you give yourself credit for," she said, raising up now, finding his gaze as open as her own. "But to answer your question, I think I'd be a little afraid that I was only kidding myself. That I was only repeating the same old patterns and that sooner or later I'd drive this person away too, just like all the others."

"No chance," he said softly. "No chance at all."

They sat without speaking for a long moment. Then she asked, her eyes luminescent, "Tell me about your dreams."

"Just now," he replied, "it's hard to see much beyond the dream here in front of me."

"Tell me," she pressed.

"I think I want to go back to medical school. There's so much more I need to learn. But..." and there he hesitated.

"But you're afraid."

"Very," he admitted.

"At least now," she said, "you won't have to take that step alone."

They paid and rose and clasped hands. He asked, "Do you want to walk awhile?"

"Sure." Reluctantly she let go of his hand. "Just a moment, I'll be right back."

But when she returned from the restaurant's interior, Wade was no longer there.

Wade stood waiting for Allison at the restaurant's periphery, intoxicated by the night. The traffic was thinning with the hour, yet each time a car passed he had to resist the urge to smile and wave. His feelings were almost too powerful to hold inside. He had to share them, and since Allison wasn't there just then, anyone would do. He had happiness to spare.

Then came a hand from the dark, gripping his throat with the pressure of a vise. His feet were lifted almost clear of the ground. His own hands clutched at an arm as solid as a steel girder.

The voice. "Time for paying dues, sport."

And then blackness.

14

"Until the moment we are having all informations," the Jordanian officer crossly informed his three Western visitors, "we wait."

"What if you wait too long, and," Allison could not say it. To even come that close to the thought pierced her heart with an ice dagger.

She had searched the restaurant and the street, calling his name with increasingly frantic strength. The waiters in the restaurant where they had eaten had observed her theatrics with growing concern. Finally one of them had approached, fearful, knowing without being told that he took great risk involving himself even this much. Still, he had observed their talk and their affection, and now he observed her panic and her pain.

The waiter had not spoken much English, just enough to say that Wade had met a man. Big man. Yes, English man or American, but big. Very big. And strong. No, he had no idea where they had gone. Only that Wade had vanished into the night, taken by the big, big man.

Fareed and Ben had driven her to Amman that very night. Judith Armstead and Cyril had gathered at Ben's request, and the search had begun. In Allison's mind, there was no room for question. Wade had been taken by Rogue Robards. Kidnapped.

Because the crime had taken place on Jordanian soil, Cyril had felt obliged to inform the local authorities. The Jordanian general had been most sympathetic. After all, Allison and the missing young man had been largely responsible for the international coup that already was reaping such benefits as press visits and interviews and urgent cables from Washington and London and elsewhere. The general had assigned an officer whom he claimed to be his best man.

But the officer assigned to them did not want to look for a missing young American. He wanted to be involved in the uncovering of the cache of nuclear weaponry. And he did not like Allison at all. He was Jordanian, he was Arab, he was military, and he had no time for her borderline hysterics. He treated her with the contempt he reserved for pushy Western women.

And Allison had started off on the wrong foot from the very first moment. She had almost screamed at the officer when confronted with his reluctance even to move from his office. Allison had caustically pointed out that the two Russian scientists were being held in the same military compound; why couldn't they ask them if they knew of safe houses anywhere in Jordan where Wade might be held.

The Russian scientists had responded to their questions with sullen silence, and the Jordanian officer had been vastly pleased by this result.

They were now standing in the front hall of the compound's main building. Arguing. Getting nowhere fast, while seconds ticked away, and Wade might be hurting.

"I cannot see any problem to wait," the officer announced pompously, his gaze brooking no further argument.

Allison was having none of it. "No problem? He's been kidnapped and you see—"

"Yes, kidnap. Is much kidnapping here. Question is, for what did this? Is only one answer."

"Ransom," Cyril said quietly.

"Is correct." The officer nodded in Cyril's direction as if to say here, look, observe a professional. "If you add this plus this, is only one answer. For money."

"And if you're wrong?" Allison found it painfully hard not to scream the words. "What if he wants something else? Like revenge?"

"We already have this before many times," the officer replied laconically. "Almost never are problems. Your man here say he pay. We set up for pay only for the live man. He gets money, we get man. Is almost never problem."

Allison turned to Cyril and pleaded, "Can't you get him to understand?"

"Yes, yes, I see very clear," the officer snapped. "Is everything out in open now. Now you do what should be first day, you talk to Jordanian military. Is Jordanian matter. Has always been."

"This is an international issue," Cyril argued, "involving Russians and Americans and possibly Iraqis—"

"On Jordanian soil," the officer finished for him. "So now we do what Jordanian military say, with experience over years. We wait." He pointed at Allison. "Why this woman come along? She is civilian, yes?"

"She happens to have been in on this since the beginning," Cyril replied. "She is a field agent working with both our governments and has been indispensable in ferreting out these criminals. Miss Taylor has as much right to be here as anyone."

The officer glared first at Cyril, then at Allison. "I say who has right. I say this woman not belong."

"Your superior officer happens to feel otherwise," Cyril replied at his frostiest.

That did not sit well at all. "I am speaking with them this day. Then we see."

"Indeed we shall. Now, can we please get on with the matters at hand?"

"Yes. We do." The officer drew himself up and pronounced, "We wait."

"Fine," Cyril's tone was icy. "We will do our waiting at the American Embassy, in case the man attempts to contact us there. You won't object if we stop by the hotel where the third Russian is being kept and ask him a question or two? No, of course not." Not allowing the officer time to respond, Cyril ushered the two women toward the doors. "Come along then, we mustn't keep the busy officer any longer. Good-day to you, sir.

But Alexis proved equally unhelpful. He spent the entire time staring blindly from his window, responding to their questions only with silence. Allison thought his own sorrowful face mirrored how her heart felt.

"We have so very little to go on," Judith Armstead told Allison on their way back to the embassy. "Unless this Robards slips up and lets himself be seen—"

"No chance," Allison said morosely. "Wade always referred to him as the professional's professional."

"—or tries to take Wade out of the country, we just have to wait." Cyril had succumbed to the heat and the morning's pressure, and folded his coat in his lap and loosened his tie a notch. "We can only hope that this Robards fellow will seek to gain from us what he failed to receive from our opponents."

"And if he doesn't?" Allison pressed. "What if his motive really was revenge?"

"In that case, my dear," Cyril shook his head and turned toward the window. There was nothing more to be said.

The car slowed and halted at the embassy's guarded entry. Allison used the temporary stop as an opportunity to throw open her door and alight. She leaned back down and said, "You two can hang around here waiting for the phone to ring. I have to at least try to do something. I *have* to."

When the door had slammed shut behind her, Judith asked, "You're going to let her go?"

"We can hardly hold her against her will," Cyril replied. "Besides, she and her young man have already worked wonders. Perhaps she can once again uncover what remains lost to us."

Neither the Western security men nor the two Jordanian military guards questioned Allison's right to visit Alexis in his downtown hotel room a second time. Allison had already appeared once that morning with Price and Armstead. So when she showed up by herself and asked to speak with Alexis alone, a note was made in the logbook, the door was unlocked, and she was permitted entry.

Alexis was not actually under arrest. He had broken no laws except that of leaving Russia, for which he could not be extradited under international law. He was therefore not held with the other two scientists, who had been caught transporting weapons-grade nuclear fuel. He was not, however, free. A half-dozen nations clamored for the chance, according to Cyril, to grill him and his companions for what they knew about the international nuclear arms smuggling operations—how had they heard of the jobs, what form the offer had taken, who, where, when.

When Allison entered the hotel room, Alexis was sitting just as she had left him an hour earlier. The room's single comfortable chair was pulled up close to the window, angled so that he could remain hidden from view and still watch the street below. His face wore the only expression she had seen on him—that of blank despair. Life held little hope for him and less purpose. He remained motionless as Allison crossed the room, pulled up a straight-backed chair, and seated herself. He appeared totally unconcerned as to whether she came, went, stayed, sat, or danced on her hands. He was lost in the defeat that filled his gaze.

"I need your help," she said, filling her voice with all the quiet urgency she could muster. "Not the government. Not the others. Me. Just me. I have to find him."

"Slow, speak slow," Alexis said. "Little English."

"Wade has talked to me about how you met. He saved your life."

"Yes? Save from what? For what? What I do now with this life he save? What about my wife, my child?" Alexis turned back to his window. "Too much questions."

"Alexis, please. I..." She had to stop and swallow hard. "I love him."

That brought his gaze back to her. He searched Allison's face long and hard before saying quietly, "He good man."

"I know," she said and blinked back hard at the sudden burning in her eyes.

"Not just good. In old Russia, we have *staret*. Not know English word. People with problem, they go to—what is church where people live?"

"Monastery," she offered.

"So. People with big problem, they go there and speak to *staret*. Sometime he answer with words, sometime with silence. But the people, they come back with answer in heart, because *staret* share wisdom. Is from heart to heart." Alexis showed her the agony of his choice. "Your man, he show me first answer with his silence, but now I have new questions. Too many."

"I want him back, Alexis. I need him back." *I need him. I need him.*

"Perhaps he come and speak with me again, yes?"

Allison felt the first electric thrill of hope. "Or perhaps we can arrange for you to go and speak with him."

"I can go? I free? You do that?" A spark of hope surfaced. "You bring me to family?"

"It's not my authority. But I will do all I can to see that you are freed. On that I give you my word."

"What about note?"

"You want me to get a message to your family? I will try, Alexis. I promise."

Once more he searched her face. "I think maybe you good person for him. Good woman. Good friend."

"Please," Allison whispered. "Help me. I don't know where else to turn."

Again his gaze returned to the scene outside his window. "Trucks."

"What? I don't—"

"Many, many trucks. Outside Aqaba. Is big market there for people on trucks. You know?"

"Yes," she said, fighting to hold herself down, seated, still. "The souk for the drivers. Of course."

"Was building on main road from trucks to port. Big building with apartments, highest I see. Near market. We stay in cellar many nights."

"The tallest apartment building on the main road running from the truck depot to the harbor," she repeated, struggling to find the breath to speak. "And not far from the souk. Is that right?"

"Yes. Except for first night here in Amman, we stay there whole time until Nuweibi."

"Amman? You spent a night in Amman? Can you tell me where?"

Alexis looked at her with naked appeal. "You not forget promise?"

15

"I fear I have no choice but to go with the major to Aqaba, and follow up this lead Alexis gave you," Cyril said distastefully. He clattered down the HQ stairs, accompanied by Allison and Judith Armstead. The army convoy stretching out before them was in the final throes of preparation. "We happen to be walking on very thin diplomatic ice just now. After all, it is their country."

"But to put all of your resources into searching one place?" Allison protested. "It just doesn't make sense."

"It does to our little Napoleon," Cyril replied. "And his commanding officer informed me in no uncertain terms that the major is responsible for our search."

"I understand," Allison said. "I just have this feeling that Wade is here in Amman."

"My dear, we have been through this twice already." Cyril raised a laconic hand toward where the officer strutted and shouted. "I concur one hundred percent. I have seen your so-called hunches pay off too often already to insist otherwise. But as I said, I must accompany the major to Aqaba, so I leave it to you and Miss Armstead to do what you can here in Amman. She is the best there is at this business."

"Second best," Allison countered.

"Yes, well, it is indeed kind of you to say so, considering our current state of affairs." He offered her his hand. "Now I really mustn't try the major's patience any further. Do take care, my dear. And may we meet again under far more joyful circumstances."

Amman was a sprawling, mostly modern metropolis with an overriding quality of sameness. Virtually all the buildings were constructed of concrete blocks, then finished in either white stucco or white-dressed stone. Larger dwellings had lawns and landscaping, but most others looked planted in unfinished construction sites.

Some of the structures were truly palatial, residences of wealthy Jordanians who had worked in the oil-rich southern lands. But the closer Allison and Judith Armstead came to the center of the city, the older and more cramped the quarters became.

And the more talkative their driver grew.

Judith Armstead had insisted they take a taxi for their search, in order to remain anonymous. The driver had started off in silent concentration, but the closer they drew to their destination, the harder he sought to keep hold of his Western clients.

"If you like," he offered, "I make special price."

"No thank you," Judith Armstead replied crisply.

"Why not, hey? How you know next driver not take you wrong way, maybe leave you far in desert?"

"Not likely."

"So is first time you are in Amman? You are welcome." He was a grizzled man in dirty robes and filthy headdress. "You come with group?"

"No."

"You come for business? You government officer from embassy?"

"Just drive the car, please."

"Is good to be government officer. They pay you and you pay me, yes?" He turned far enough around to see them both, then swung back when a horn warned him of impending doom. He swerved, braked, stuck his head out the window, and shouted oaths at the innocent driver. Then, "You must to hire other driver for returnings. You pay much more, maybe driver not so honest like me. I take you safe. Come, go, special price. Many accidents was happened on this road. But I am always safety."

"So happy to hear it."

"Yes. Am safety driver. So why you not let me take you come, go? I have all the good roads. Old roads. Special ways. Am born here, have all life in Amman. Know all good roads."

Allison leaned forward. "Do you know a road that climbs a hill behind the old Roman amphi-theater?"

"Is many hills in city. Amman built on hills. You like tour of Amman city?"

"Forget it."

"Wait, wait." His brow furrowed in concentration. "Hill from ampitheater? Old city?"

"We can find it just as easily on foot," Judith Armstead said.

"No, no, not easy. Old Amman very tricky place; roads all go in wrong direction, take you out, lose you in desert. Wait. Hill in old city. I thinking."

"We are looking for a pair of apartment buildings built side by side, and there is a view looking down across the rooftops and over the Roman amphitheater," Allison told him, relating all the information Alexis had given her. He had been granted one brief time out on the roof. The remainder of his stay, he had said, had been spent in the building's cellar. It had been dark and windowless and smelled of wet laundry. More he could not say. "He was looking out over the amphitheater to some old ruins."

"He?" the driver demanded. "Who is he?"

"None of your concern," Judith replied.

"The roofs were flat," Allison continued, "and both of the buildings were old. There were maybe five or six stories, but he was not sure."

"All roofs flat in Amman old city," the driver retorted. "All buildings old."

"But two buildings built together," Allison pressed. "So close that he could easily step from one roof to the other."

Again the brow furrowed. "I thinking. You pay good tip for help, yes? I wait, drive you come, go?"

"We pay a very good tip," Allison assured him.

"You've just designed an Amman taxi driver's dream day," Judith Armstead informed her. "Take two rich Westerners on a tour of the old town, look for something they're not too sure about, drive anywhere you like. This is going to cost us the moon."

"No, no, not moon," the driver protested. "I honest man. Do good safety driving."

He pulled up at the edge of a large parking area. In front of them stretched a white parade ground colonnaded along one side. To the right of that, the amphitheater climbed its way up a steep hillside.

The driver pointed to his right. "Jabal Al-Jawfa. Jabal mean hill. There Jabal Attaj. And there Jabal Al Qal'a. Where we go?"

Allison pointed toward the remains of what appeared to be an ancient Roman circus. "He said the ruins were behind the amphitheater. That means it would have to be the hill over there."

"Jabal Al Qal'a," the driver said. "I think maybe yes too." He ground the gears and raced the engine. "Now we start."

It was extremely hard to eat with his hands tied behind his back. Especially when the room was pitch black.

Wade had awakened to find himself crammed inside a jouncing coffin so small he could not

304

stretch out his legs. Then he had recognized the sound of a roaring motor and realized he was jammed into the trunk of a car.

The air was stuffy but breathable. His muscles ached, his head hammered, and the more awake he grew the more frightening his predicament became. So he did the only thing possible under the circumstances. He went back to sleep.

He awoke a second time to find a bright light being directed into his eyes. "Wakey, wakey, sport. Time to rise and shine."

"Why are you doing this?" he mumbled.

"If you hadn't slept the whole way you'd have figured that out for yourself already." Wade watched as the flashlight was handed to someone else standing beside Robards. Then strong hands pulled a black stocking down over his head and plucked him effortlessly from the trunk. "Stretch out your legs."

He did, and groaned as the circulation revived in areas long left dormant.

Robards showed no sympathy. "Okay, turn around." When Wade did not move fast enough for him, Rogue spun him about, leaned him roughly against the car, and tied his hands behind his back. "All right, let's move."

Wade started to tell him that he couldn't get away with it, then stopped. By the looks of things, he already had.

Robards led him up a set of crumbling steps, through a door, and down a flight of stairs. A key rustled and turned, a heavy door opened, and

Wade was shoved inside. He stumbled against the rough concrete floor and fell heavily, landing full force on one knee. He cried out sharply and rolled to his side.

"There'll be somebody outside this door all the time," Robards said. "Make any noise and you'll spend your days with a towel stuffed down your throat. Make any trouble and it's the last trouble you give anybody. That clear?"

"My leg," Wade groaned.

"Hey, I'd be a little more sorry if it wasn't for all that's gone down." He stepped into the room, ripped the stocking from Wade's head. "People don't find it profitable to get in my way, sport. For two cents I'd stomp your head in. So count your blessings and keep it quiet."

Robards returned only twice after that, both times in the quiet before the world awoke. Both times he jammed the stocking back down over Wade's head and led him limping down the corridor to a rudimentary toilet. Then he brought him back to the cellar room, retied his hands, and left him with two tin plates set on the bare floor. One held water, the other a portion of the poor man's food of the Middle East, a concoction of cold beans and onions and garlic called *foul*. The only way Wade could eat or drink was by kneeling and bending far over to lap it up like a dog. The pain in his swollen knee made doing so pure agony.

Wade counted the passage of hours by the sounds that echoed down from above him. Children crying, mothers yelling, dogs barking, a few cars passing, muzzeins' call to prayer, music being played from a dozen radios. Occasionally he thought of shouting, then recalled the cold detachment in Robards' voice and knew that if he did it would be the last sound he would ever make.

Allison knew from the first moment of their search that they faced an almost impossible task.

The hill called Jabal Al Qal'a was inundated with apartment houses, none of which were more than five or six stories high, and all of which were old. The roofs she could not tell much about, as the roads were winding and narrow and snaked back and forth in confusing, interlocking array. The taxi was airless and almost unbearably hot.

The only one pleased with their state of affairs was the driver. Every now and then he would break into a single-note warble, tapping time on the steering wheel as he ground slowly down one street after the other.

"I think we've already come this way," Judith Armstead announced. "Five or six times."

"No, no, lady. This new road. See? That house, you not see that house not ever before. And this one, maybe this the house, yes? Two up close, see how built?"

"No," Allison replied, marking a larger house looming up on the road's opposite side and blocking the view. "Definitely not this one."

"Okay, all what you say is okay. We take this road now, yes? You see, I good safety driver. Take all day and help what I can."

"They're all jammed so close together," Allison said, "I can't even tell if we're still above the amphitheater."

"Oh, yes, yes, you see, this why important you have honest driver. I know. Amphitheater just down there. We stay right where you want."

"Our driver," Judith Armstead murmured, "is going to be telling the story of this day to his great-grandchildren."

Allison pointed through her window. "Stop here."

"Sure, sure, anything you say. We stop here right now."

Judith climbed out beside her. "What is it?"

"See those two buildings? No, not these, up higher. The next road. See how they stick up over the tops of these others?"

"Maybe," Judith said doubtfully. "They all look the same to me."

"Me, too," Allison confessed. She sighed. "Maybe we should have gone with them to Aqaba."

Judith looked at her. "Is that the sound of defeat I hear?"

"Then if they hadn't found anything, we could have tried to convince them to come back this way."

"Come on," Judith said, climbing back in the car. "Let's go check it out."

"What are we supposed to do when we get there?" Allison asked, suddenly burdened by doubt. "Go up and knock on doors and ask if they've happened to see any kidnapped Americans lately?"

Judith Armstead was not the least concerned. "It's early hours yet. Ninety-nine percent of our work involves eliminating possibilities."

Allison pointed out her side window. "Can you take us to those buildings up there?"

"Sure, sure, no problem. I take you anywhere, you see."

Once they were again under way, Judith told Allison, "I met your father once, by the way."

"You did? When?"

"Oh, it was some time ago." For a moment her strong exterior softened. "I was just getting started. Your father had an almost mythical reputation in those days. He was giving a lecture, and afterward he took time to chat with me. I was young, a complete unknown, and yet John Taylor stops and chats, surrounded by all these officers and bigwigs, treating me like I was somebody important."

Allison felt a sudden kinship. "I never knew anything about that side of his work. I still don't, actually."

The taxi driver pulled over and stopped. "See? Just like you ask. I know all special roads."

"Wait here, please." Allison climbed from the taxi and surveyed the twin structures, asked, "What now?"

"Let's go see." Judith strode determinedly up to the first building, pushed at the door, found it unlocked. A moment's hesitation, then she walked inside. "The cellar, you say?"

"That's where Alexis was held." Allison answered breathlessly.

309

They walked down the stairs and entered a dank and moldy corridor with wires and cables strung overhead. Most of the rooms had no doors; the hallway opened directly onto fusty-smelling chambers full of refuse and old washing machines.

"At least he had the smell right," Allison murmured. She walked over to the one sealed door, hesitated, then knocked and whispered, "Wade?" She pressed her ear hard to the surface.

"Hear anything?"

"Nothing."

"They probably wouldn't leave him unguarded. Let's go try next door."

The cellar of the neighboring building was identical except for two women busy gossiping over a laboring washer. They looked up and gawked in utter astonishment as the two Westerners stepped into view. Their eyes opened even farther when Judith addressed them in Arabic. One of them answered her with a question. Judith replied at length, motioning around the chambers. The two women looked at each other and howled with laughter. Judith smiled in reply and waved a goodbye.

"What did you tell them?" Allison asked.

"The only thing I could think of. That the embassy was looking for downtown living space, and we needed a large basement for entertaining guests in safety." She pointed up the stairs. "Let's go take a look at what we can see from the roof."

At that height, there was at least a little wind. Laundry flapped in the sultry breeze. Allison gulped deep breaths and surveyed her surroundings. The taxi driver was correct; he had managed to bring them in a relatively straight line directly up from the amphitheater. Allison turned around, visually searching the other buildings. "We should have done this in the beginning."

"Everything is much clearer," Judith agreed.

"How about those two over there?"

Judith nodded, pointed to her left. "And those."

"And the two a couple streets higher. To my right."

"Try to fix them clearly in your mind. Things will look different from down below."

They returned to the taxi, pulled the driver from his car, pointed, and explained where they wanted to go. He agreed with the genuine willingness of one whose fortune was assured.

The next pair of buildings proved to have roofs separated by a high wire fence. Alexis had not mentioned anything of the sort, so they merely noted the location and left that building for later. The following pair of buildings had cellars as empty as the first ones. The next set were located on a street so narrow the taxi was twice forced to backpedal in order to permit through traffic. No sunlight filtered into the manmade chasm.

Allison climbed from the taxi and said, "I don't see how you can keep up your enthusiasm for a job like this."

"By having one in a thousand attempts pay off," Judith replied. "Don't give up hope."

The first cellar proved to be one vast chamber sectioned off by ankle-high concrete partitions.

The second building greeted them with a locked door.

Judith did not hesitate. She rang the top two bells, waited, and when nothing happened took the next two in line. This time the door-speaker squawked. Judith put her face close to the box and said in English, "We're the Avon ladies, come to see if you received your samples this week."

The box squawked and rattled and stuttered. "That's right," Judith agreed. "A free car."

Allison looked at her. "We're what?"

"These things don't work half the time," Judith explained. "And I doubt seriously that anybody on the other end speaks a word of English."

In reply, the buzzer sounded. Judith pushed her way inside, stuck her head up the stairway, and called, *"Shokran,"* thank you. She then guided Allison down the cellar stairs.

A leather-skinned Arab dressed in rumpled Western clothes and sporting a three-day growth rose from his chair as they stepped into view. He shouted vehemently at them and pointed back up the stairs. Judith started off in Arabic, but the man was having none of it. He started toward them, making sharp shoving motions at the air.

Allison took one step back onto the first stair and screamed at the top of her lungs, *"WADE!"*

It was impossible to find a comfortable position.

Standing was hard, with his knee complaining louder the longer he remained on his feet. Sitting up was best, with his back resting on the wall and his hands drawn up into the small of his back. But that eventually grew tiresome. Then he had a choice of either lying on one side or the other, with his head at a downward angle on the floor—and the floor was cool and mildly damp and extremely hard. Lying on his back meant crushing his hands, and they were already numb from restricted blood flow. Lying on his belly meant mashing his cheek into the moldy concrete.

And his knee thundered painfully with every heartbeat. Not to mention the agony he knew every time he knelt to drink.

The sound woke him from a fitful doze. For a moment he thought it had been part of a dream. He struggled upright, hoping against hope, opening his mouth to still the noise of his breathing.

There it was again. Shouting. Just outside his door. And then the shrill cry. It was her.

He stumbled to his feet, overturned his food, yelled, "I'm in here!"

"That's his voice!" Allison started forward, only to be slammed up against the wall as the Arab strong-armed her into the concrete. She felt the breath whoosh from her lungs by the force of his blow, and thought her legs would give way.

The Arab snarled and reached inside his coat, then froze. Judith Armstead had two-armed a small blue-steel pistol directly up his nose. Her voice was as cold as ice.

The Arab hesitated. She snapped out a second command in Arabic, and he stepped reluctantly back.

"Take his gun, Allison," she ordered.

With trembling hands Allison reached inside his coat, drew out the pistol stuck into his belt, held it aloft with two fingers.

"It's not a snake," Judith snapped. "Get a good grip on it."

The gun was surprisingly heavy. She pointed it at the Arab's face, found herself unable to hold it steady even with two hands.

"Go try the door."

Allison sidled over. She saw Judith take one step back and motion with her own gun for the Arab to move to the wall. He did not do so fast enough for her. Again the whipping sound of her voice, and with a snarl of his own the Arab complied.

Allison released one hand from the gun and knocked. "Wade?"

"Is that really you?" The voice was muffled but clear.

She caught the sob that rose in her throat and fought it back down. Allison glanced at the bolt set at chest level in the door. "It's padlocked shut."

"Tell him to back off and lie down. Then shoot

the hinge," Judith snapped. "And hurry. We're sitting ducks."

"I heard," came Wade's muffled reply.

"Here goes." Allison aimed the gun and fired. The recoil popped her hands up over her head, and the boom reverberated like a cannon in the enclosed surroundings. The smoke burned her eyes. As soon as the ringing diminished she heard screams and cries from throughout the building. The Arab snarled a curse and started to move, only to find Judith's gun jammed into the nape of his neck. She screamed a command in Arabic and then in English, *"Move!"*

Allison hit the stubborn bolt with the butt of her gun. Then she grasped the door handle and pulled with all her might. The door groaned, then gave.

Wade stumbled into her arms.

"Out of the way!" Judith hustled the Arab over and into the chamber, rammed the door back home. She whacked the broken hinge as much back into place as she could, then took the Arab's chair and slammed it up under the handle. She yelled, "Let's go!"

They raced up the stairs as fast as Wade's injured knee would allow. Allison supported him with one arm, the other still held the pistol. They saw fingers pointed at them from the floors above, then just as swiftly disappear with a chorus of screams.

Allison threw open the outside door and rammed straight into the arms of Rogue Robards.

It was the only thing that saved them.

Rogue's startled pause at having an unknown woman suddenly in his arms gave Wade just enough time to shout, "It's him!"

Judith Armstead rammed the gun into his throat. "Barton Robards, you are coming with us. The authorities wish to speak with you in regards to charges of kidnapping, extortion, and the smuggling of—"

"No!" Wade shouted, surprising them all, and jostled Judith from behind, surprising them even more. Judith stumbled and lowered her gun a fraction.

"Run!" Wade shouted at Robards.

Rogue did not need to be told twice. He leapt from the stairs and moved so fast that he left behind only empty space.

Judith searched the empty street. "What the—?"

"What have you done?" Allison cried.

"Let him go," Wade replied.

Further screams from inside the building sparked them into action. The Arab.

"Quick!" Judith cried, hustling them across the street toward the taxi.

Allison fell on Wade in the backseat. Judith clambered into the front and screamed, "Drive!"

"Wait, wait," the driver stammered. "I no drive for people in such dangers. We stop, you find new taxi, yes?"

Judith Armstead raised her gun. "Think again."

The driver moaned and ground his gears. The Arab slammed the apartment door opened and raced out, fists waving. "Quickly," Judith urged.

"Yes, yes, is speed now," the driver said, swerving to avoid the fast-approaching Arab. "All the day is slow and here and there and careful, and now is speeds and dangers. This not Gunsmoke. You no need for pistols."

"Can somebody untie my hands?" Wade asked.

"Lean over," Allison said. Then, "Why did you let Robards go?"

"My thoughts exactly," Judith Armstead added.

Wade winced as he rubbed the circulation back into his hands. "I owed him," he replied.

"He is a thief and a smuggler and a mercenary," Judith snapped. "Not to mention the fact that he kidnapped you."

"Not here," Wade said. "Before. Back in Russia."

"Didn't you tell me he stole a truckload of your pharmaceuticals?" Allison demanded.

Wade nodded, and glanced out the back window. "He also taught me courage."

The silence held for a moment. Then Allison ran a soft hand down one side of his face. "Are you all right?"

He captured her hand with his, and said, "Take me home."

Other titles by Thomas Locke:

The Delta Factor

Deborah Givens is a scientist with a mission. A victim of multiple sclerosis, she has dedicated herself to discovering a means of conquering viral disease. And it seems she and her research team have hit pay-dirt sooner than anyone expected.

Her employers, a second-tier pharmaceutical company in North Carolina, are anxious to reap the financial rewards of her work. They mistakenly expect Deborah's friendship with Cliff Devon, the Food and Drug Administration official responsible for new product approvals, to accelerate the release of this wonder-drug.

Then Deborah makes a discovery that undermines her scientific assumptions and suggests there is a risk of uncontrolled genetic mutation. But these grave doubts about the drug's safety go unheeded by the company executives, who are determined to bring the drug to market.

Confronted with a formidable conspiracy of commercial and political interests, the two friends are forced to make choices which threaten their lives, knowing that the lives of others may be at stake.

ISBN 0 7459 3177 4 (hardback)
ISBN 0 7459 3178 2 (paperback)

The Omega Network

Chase Bennett is a troubleshooter for the Chamber of Commerce on the Florida coast. Visiting an old friend, a woman detective, he unwittingly becomes the critical link in a chain of criminal evidence stretching from a narcotics raid in Washington to a telecommunications fraud in Miami.

Back home, a series of mysterious events unfolds. His boss threatens his job; a shady entrepreneur coerces him on a land deal; the detective disappears. When the beautiful but ambitious Sabine seeks to rekindle an old romance, Chase is haunted by the suspicion that he is being lured into a dangerous conspiracy.

As he struggles to untangle the web of intrigue, Chase discovers political corruption and money-laundering. Suspicion solidifies into fear for his life.

ISBN 0 7459 3181 2 (hardback)
ISBN 0 7459 3182 0 (paperback, available autumn 1996)

To the Ends of the Earth

The year is 338AD. The death of the Emperor
Constantine has left the far reaches of the Roman
Empire prey to chaos and corruption. At a Consul's
estate in North Africa, the rising tide of lawlessness
threatens a determined young man of Celtic
background. Kieran sets sail for Carthage and then
Constantinople, the glittering new capital of the
Empire, to uncover the mysterious plot against his
life and home.

Kieran's voyage confronts him with unprecedented
challenges: battles at sea, cults of sacrifice,
treachery within the family, unjust imprisonment.
His future becomes entwined with that of the
beautiful Lydia. Together they are drawn into events
which are shaping the Empire and conspiring to
keep them apart.

ISBN 0 7459 3651 2 (hardback)
ISBN 0 7459 3652 0 (paperback, available spring 1997)